WHAT DID THESE HUGE, WHITE, BATLIKE CREATURES EAT, ANYWAY?

"They're not herbivores," I said to the Dutchman, as something brushed against my helmet.
Suddenly the Dutchman smiled that smile that said he knew something I didn't. "Get your weapon free," he yelled.
Something hit me in the back. I turned. Something else thwocked off my helmet. Hands. My leg. My back again. And then my helmet.
The air was full of them. They boiled out of the nests, off the vines, down from the tree, and blew into the air like an explosion. My bubble helmet was laced with scratches.

Then they hit me, like a white-hot nail driven into my back, through the outer insulation, cooling/heating tubing, straight to the flesh. My gut clenched like a fist against sickness. Primal reflex: dump excess baggage and run. But letting go in a closed suit was not exactly survival-oriented behavior. . . .

Come Out of This World With SIGNET

(0451)

☐ **BLANK SLATE by Mark J. McGarry.** Would the people of Earth's long-lost colony Relayer welcome Brian Kuhl and the crew of the starship *Belfast* as saviors—or see them as a treacherous enemy to be quickly destroyed? (129210—$2.95)

☐ **BRIDGE OF ASHES by Hugo and Nebula Award-winner Roger Zelazny.** He was the "ultimate" man, the greatest telepath the world had ever known, and he was Earth's last hope against an enemy that had created the human race—and could also destroy it... (135504—$2.50)

☐ **THE HAND OF GANZ by Isidore Halibum.** When Earthmen Ross Block and Nick Siscoe accidentally discover an alien threat, it is the start of a planet-hopping adventure that will turn them into deadly star warriors— fighting to save their world from the evil telepath Ganz and his unstoppable Legions of the Dead... (133412—$2.75)

☐ **TIES OF BLOOD AND SILVER by Joel Rosenberg.** To David, stolen from Elweré as a baby and raised as a thief of the Lower City, it is a dream of paradise, a treasure trove to which he must find the key, no matter what the cost. That is, if Eschteef—twice the size of a human, with glowing eyes and rows of needle-sharp teeth—doesn't get to him first... (131673—$2.75)

Prices slightly higher in Canada

EMILE AND THE DUTCHMAN

JOEL ROSENBERG

A SIGNET BOOK

NEW AMERICAN LIBRARY

NAL BOOKS ARE AVAILABLE AT QUANTITY DISCOUNTS WHEN USED
TO PROMOTE PRODUCTS OR SERVICES. FOR INFORMATION PLEASE
WRITE TO PREMIUM MARKETING DIVISION, NEW AMERICAN LIBRARY,
1633 BROADWAY, NEW YORK, NEW YORK 10019.

"Like the Gentle Rains" and "In the Shadow of Heaven" appeared in
shorter and somewhat different form in, respectively, the February 15,
1982, and June 7, 1983, issues of *Isaac Asimov's Science Fiction Magazine*.

SIGNET TRADEMARK REG. U.S. PAT. OFF. AND FOREIGN COUNTRIES
REGISTERED TRADEMARK—MARCA REGISTRADA
HECHO EN CHICAGO, U.S.A.

SIGNET, SIGNET CLASSIC, MENTOR, PLUME, MERIDIAN AND NAL BOOKS
are published by New American Library,
1633 Broadway, New York, New York 10019

First Printing, January, 1986

1   2   3   4   5   6   7   8   9

PRINTED IN THE UNITED STATES OF AMERICA

Dedication

Everyone starts somewhere.

My first published science fiction began with the words, "I hated the Dutchman at first sight." Those particular words and a few thousand following them were bought by George Scithers, then of *Isaac Asimov's Science Fiction Magazine*, now of *Amazing Stories*. George has always been straightforward with me; his responses to my early efforts were harsh, stinging, eminently useful rejections, eventually followed by matter-of-fact rewrite requests and even more matter-of-fact acceptances.

Everything starts somewhere, too.

The schrift, whom some readers may have met in *Ties of Blood and Silver* and whom they will see another side of in the present work, began with "Forward Private Aaldz," a short-story situation in Barry B. Longyear's superb *Science Fiction Writer's Workshop I* (published by George Scithers' Owlswick Press; anyone who says he or she wants to write science fiction should either buy a copy or cop to not being serious), which Barry both challenged and invited me to finish. After much work, thought, and change, his lizards became my amphibians, his Aaldz became my Hischteeel, and his "Forward Private Aaldz" became my "Dutchman's Price."

All of which is why this one is
For Barry B. Longyear and George H. Scithers

Acknowledgments

When I was writing "Like the Gentle Rains" and "In the Shadow of Heaven," I received much sound advice from the members of Haven—Kevin O'Donnell, Jr., Mary Kittredge, Deborah Atherton Davis, and Mark J. McGarry. I even took some of it. The present version of "Dutchman's Mirror" is my rewriting of a collaboration between Mark and myself, which itself was a rewriting of a previous, less successful version.

For all the help, I am grateful.

I'd also like to thank my wife, Felicia Herman, who's been living with—and putting up with—Emile, the Dutchman, and me for longer than I like to think about; my agent, Richard Curtis; Art and Essie Swearsky, for the sunflower seeds; my editor, Sheila Gilbert, for sound advice and inhuman patience; all of the Boskone people, for the obvious; and, as usual, Harry F. Leonard, for the excessive quibbling.

Note to the Reader

You'll quickly notice that Major Alonzo Norfeldt is a drunkard, a smoker, a liar, a thief, a cheat, a braggart, and a bigot. He is also foulmouthed and arrogant.

Just for the record, while I do find some virtues in the man, those aren't them.

JOEL ROSENBERG

Prelude:
An Officer

All members of the Thousand Worlds Contact Service are officers. The great responsibilities conferred on each and every member of the Service are such that commissioning is requisite. Accordingly, all Contact Service officers shall conduct themselves appropriately. At all times they shall display conduct becoming an officer including, but not limited to, the following requirements:

*An officer is courteous at all times, in his encounters with subordinate and superior officers, as well as with the general public of the Thousand Worlds. He must remember that he embodies the Service; that the Service itself will be judged by his actions.

*An officer is competent, and responsible for maintaining his competence. Training at the Contact Service Academy at Alton is intended to assist an officer in instilling such competence; the failure of the Academy program, however, to include training in a particular field of knowledge or achievement does not excuse an officer from command of and/or competence in that field of knowledge and/or achievement, should the task at hand require it.

*An officer is fair and just. No deserved praise due a subordinate shall fail to be promptly voiced by an officer; conversely, no flaw in a subordinate shall escape his attention. While an officer shall exercise due process over fellow officers who have been duly placed under his command, such exercise shall be made totally with respect to the applicable regulations and facts; such exercise shall be made totally without respect to a subordinate's social status, sexual or associational preferences, rank, or ancestry.

*An officer is a willing servant of the human race, as embodied in its agent, the Council and Government of the Thousand Worlds. By accepting commission in the Contact Service, an officer has waived his rights under the Articles of Association of free speech, free association, free conscience, survival, and trial by jury.

*An officer shall always keep in mind that the universe is merciless; he shall always be aware that precedent is no excuse for failure.

*Above all, an officer shall always keep in mind the fact that the failure of the Contact Service or any officer of the Contact Service may endanger the survival of the human species.

Like the Gentle Rains

I

I hated the Dutchman at first sight.

"An officer is courteous at all times, in his encounters with subordinate and superior officers"—it says so, right on the very first page of *Contact Service Rules, Regulations, and Proprieties.*

"You the tin god Stan Morrissey sent me?"

Space aboard Major Alonzo Norfeldt's cabin was mainly lacking. The atmosphere wasn't improved by the stench of cheap wine mixed with the nauseating reek of stale tobacco. The fat man was no visual thrill as he lay back on the rumpled linen of his bunk, scratching at his hairy belly, just above the waistband of his shorts.

If he had bathed in the past week, there was no solid evidence.

I gave a mental shrug. *This* was the Dutchman? He didn't look like he was capable of much, unless you thought not bathing was a big trick.

Which I didn't.

"Sir. Second Lieutenant Emile von du Mark reporting to the Team Leader as per Regulation—"

"Shut the fuck up." He cut me off with a thump of his hand against the nearest bulkhead. "Listen real good, Mister; I'll only say this once: I don't *ever* want to hear you quoting regs at me. Ever. And regardless of how disreputable I look—or *am*—you just remember two things. If you can count that high."

He held up a stubby finger. It wasn't well manicured, but the nail wasn't bitten, either. The Dutchman wasn't the nailbiting type. "One, I'm a damn good Contact Team Leader. Matter of fact, I'm the best there is."

15

He tapped the finger against the diamond in his Team Leader's ring, his nail clicking. *Tick. Tick.*

"Two"—another finger—"I'm your superior officer. Understood?"

"Yes, sir."

"Good." He grunted as he sat up, rubbing his face in his hand. "Just siddown. Please." He gave a quick longing look at the corked bottle beside his bed before regretfully returning his attention to me. "What do they call you?"

"Emile, sir," I said. It's pronounced Eh-meal. Not *Ay*-muhl, not *Eh*mil, not anything else. I don't mind nicknames for other people, but any variation on my name grates.

"Oh." He gave an amused little half-smile at that. "You heard of me, Emilesir?" He reached a hand under his pillow and brought out a well-chewed cigar, then stuck the soggy end in his mouth while he fished around on the floor for his lighter.

"Yes, sir. I've heard of you." I wanted to leave it at that, but he pressed.

"And what have you heard, Herr Leftenant ffonn doo Mark?" A vague smile played across his lips; a childhood memory of my cat playing with a captured baby mole sprang up.

"That you are a competent—"

"None of that. I asked you what you heard."

I shrugged. To hell with him, too. "I have heard that you are a tyrannical, overbearing Team Leader, with a record of four good, solid Contacts—and two Drops—but an absurdly high fatality rate among your subordinate officers. I have heard that you are a drunkard, sir, and a smoker—both of which are manifestly obvious. I have heard that the Contact Service may have declared you an officer, but that you surely are no gentleman. Sir."

The Dutchman threw back his head and laughed. "You got guts, Mark."

I started to smile.

He stuck out his hand; I accepted it automatically. I returned his pressure quickly enough to prevent him from cracking my knuckles.

Barely.

"Me, I've always thought more highly of brains," he said, turning the pressure up.

While he attempted to grind my knuckles into sand, he took a moment to look me up and down. I squeezed back, remembering my Command & the Nature of Authority instructor explaining the importance to a commander of establishing, right up front, that he was in charge. But Captain Patel had also declared, in his musical Hindi singsong, that it was high art to do it without being a jerk.

The Dutchman didn't seem to care about high art.

"I guess I have to take what I can get," he said, releasing my hand. "Hot pilot?"

Supposedly, there used to be some sort of superstition among flyers against admitting that you were good. There isn't anymore, and even if there was, I wouldn't care.

"Yes, sir." I don't need to brag about it; it's just a fact.

"How'd you get stuck with me? Hang on a sec," he said, as he resumed his search for his lighter, finally locating it underneath a discarded sock.

He fired it up and brought his cigar to life, and blew a foul cloud of smoke in my direction.

"After Graduation, the commandant—"

"Stan Morrissey. Classmate of mine."

"So he told me. General Morrissey offered me a staff job, said he thought I was too inexperienced to go out on First Assignment just yet." Manny Curdova had taken the Personnel job that the general had offered him; as I stood there, looking down at Norfeldt, I wondered if I wouldn't have been much wiser to do the same thing.

Norfeldt shook his head, several of his chins waggling in syncopation. "You shoulda listened. Breaks old Stan's heart, sending out green kids every year, seeing what comes back. When it comes back." He gave me a sideways look. "You look a little like his son; maybe that's why he wanted to give you a break. Hmmm. Any idea why he didn't hold you back for another year at Alton?"

"I was third in my class. Sir. And number one in flying class, sir."

"Oh? Which ones?"

"Every one, sir."

I was proud of it, too. Maybe I should thank my ancestry for my ability in the air, but coming in third in my class hadn't come easily to me, not easily at all. I'd worked hard for four long years at the Contact Service Academy; aside from qualification courses, I'd been hard pressed to get in ten hours a month in the air.

And then, on Graduation Day, for the Commandant to call me into his office and suggest I take a staff post— temporarily, he said. Hah.

"Big deal." The Dutchman dismissed four years of backbreaking and mindbending work with an airy wave. "First Assignment is the real graduation, Emmy." He snickered at my wince.

"You psi-neg, kid?"

I started to bring a hand up to point at the See-No-Evil-Speak-No-Evil-Hear-No-Evil patch above my uniform blouse's left pocket, then caught myself. If he didn't want to see for himself . . .

"Yes, sir. And fully conditioned, sir." Not that I know a whole lot about how Gates work, but what little I do know can't be pried out of me by threat or bribe. Or psi, for that matter: to an esper with his eyes closed, I'm not even there.

"Yeah. I got the Three Monkeys myself."

Which was obvious. A Thousand Worlds Contact Service Contact Team Leader has to be psi-neg. The most common problem espers in the Service have is adopting the frame of reference of contactees—dangerous; we're supposed to protect humanity's interests. The human race doesn't need another Xeno War, and if we ever have one, it had *damn* well better be farther from a draw than the last one.

"Then I'd better tell you this before we go on down to the Rec to brief Buchholtz and McCaw: First Team did a pretty one-shot spectogram; the major continent on this dirtball planet we're going onto as Third Team has huge deposits of germanium. That mean anything to you?"

I wanted to answer, to say that I knew that germanium was the only metal that grabfields could get enough of a hold on to squeeze into a quantum black hole, the *sine qua non* of a Gate.

I *wanted* to, but I couldn't; the conditioning runs very deep—when you've cooperated with it, that happens. Supposedly, after a few years, it wears off enough to allow a reasonable amount of judgment.

But I was fresh out of the Academy, and this was a Navy ship, not a Contact Service scout; I didn't *know* that we couldn't be overheard. "Nothing in particular, Major."

He smiled and nodded. "Just checking. C'mon; you might as well meet the rest of the team."

II

Magellan was a *Cristoforo Colombo* class heavy cruiser, which was nice for us, not so nice for the Navy crew. Usually, the Navy prefers to stick Contact Service people on refurbished light cruisers, or heavily armed cruiser escorts, but maybe this assignment had come on unexpectedly, or maybe General Dupres' politicking for heavier escorts was having some effect on the Thousand Worlds Council.

Whatever the reason, I was grateful. Since Contact Service personnel are normally quarantined from the start of a mission—air, water, food, comp, and comm—*Magellan*'s size meant that we had to be given the whole second deck to ourselves. The elevator door was welded shut; the ladders to decks three and one were dogged from the other side.

Not a bad deal for us, but it must have been hell for the Navy crew; I'm sure they had to go to a full hot-bed system, including officers.

On the other hand, we had individual staterooms—suites, in fact; I even had a closet with a door—and the whole Rec Room to ourselves.

"Captain Aristotle McCaw, this is Emmy Mark, our new chauffeur." The Dutchman's voice echoed hollowly in the empty room.

The tall redhead turned from the chessboard, not noticing my wince at what was obviously to be the Dutchman's nickname for me.

"Lieutenant. Good to have you with us." McCaw nodded, his head bobbing on top of his long, skinny neck like an apple on a wire. He must have been a full two meters tall, weighing in at not much more than sixty kilos. I fancied I could see his ribs through his shirt.

Even sitting, his eyes were on the same level as the Dutchman's. "Briefing, Major?"

"In a minute, Ari." Norfeldt turned to me. "Ari's our comm officer; high psi rating. And he's good—when I can get him to pay attention to the real world. Which isn't often."

That may have been an exaggeration; on the other hand, the Dutchman may have been making the kind of allowances we all have to make for comm officers. Fewer than one man in ten million has a high enough psi rating to be useful as a Contact Service comm officer; we take what we can get.

Norfeldt pointed his uppermost chin at the captain sitting across the table from McCaw. The captain was waiting for the esper to move, like a leopard waiting for a gazelle to meander under its tree. "Kurt Buchholtz. Weapons and defense officer."

I wasn't exactly surprised. Buchholtz looked up at me, turning completely in his chair like a tank turret zeroing in on a target. There was a flash of discomfort in his face as he sized me up, then obviously decided that he could take me, if need be.

He was probably right; while I was a couple of centimeters taller, he outweighed me by a good ten kilos—not a gram of it fat.

"Never mess with Kurt, Emmy. He's not too bright, but he is good; did a bang-up job of covering my escape last time out—and even managed to get back aboard the scout before I hit the panic button, to take off to blow the Gate."

"A full ten seconds before, Al," Buchholtz said. "And I was hauling ass, at that—it didn't look like you were going to wait."

"You noticed? I'm pleasantly surprised." Norfeldt raised an eyebrow. "Any objections, shithead?"

"No." Buchholtz's placid expression didn't change. Names would never hurt him—I didn't want to try to find out if sticks and stones would really break his bones. "Not a one. It would have been called for. Tough assignment; solid Drop." He returned his attention to the board. I took a quick look. It looked to be the sort of complex jumble you get out a Bachiochi Sicilian, right before all hell breaks loose and the population of the board gets cut in half in twenty moves.

"Get some coffee, Emmy," the Dutchman said. "I take mine half cream and with four lumps." He sat down at the table and fired his cigar back up, taking a moment to pretend to check out the board.

There's nothing in *Contact Service Rules, Regulations, and Proprieties* that specifically says that junior officers have to fix coffee for the Team Leader, but this wasn't the time or the place to go into that.

I went over to the coffee setup in the corner—the pot

was an old NASAF model, the kind that would survive an explosion that would blow *Magellan* to bits—and poured the Dutchman a cup, conscious of how the combination of *Magellan*'s drive and spin made the hot black stream arc strangely. I dumped in some whitening powder—the label said "Dehydrated Stabilized Cream," but it didn't fool me—and enough sugar cubes to content the mounts of my father's entire polo club.

I poured a cup for myself, too. Black, of course.

I brought the coffee to the table, set the cups down, then sat down. The Dutchman took a swig of coffee and combined it with a mouthful of black cigar smoke. I guess he liked the taste; the smell had me wishing for a Paradram.

"Well, we've got another tough one coming," Norfeldt said.

Both men looked up, McCaw obviously irritated at being brought back to the real world, Bucholtz smiling evenly.

"I'll make it short," the Dutchman went on. "You can go over the reports later—I'll square it with the scout's computer—but leave the Pers records alone, Kurt; I'm tired of covering for you.

"In any case, scoop Theta Twelve, about a year ago, dropped a nucleus around an F9." Nerfeldt didn't tell us *what* F9 star it was; none of us needed to know. Maybe he didn't know, either. The acceleration algorithms for both our trip out and our return would be programmed into our scout's NAV computer; we didn't need to know them, either. There are lots more demanding tasks than going point-to-point in space. It's even easier than walking and chewing gum—it's like having someone else walk and chew gum.

"First Team went through via AlphaCee, built the Gate around the singularity on the other side, started the look, listen, and sniff.

"They found a live one, out at about two AUs— surface will be brighter than home; the dirtball's hotter, but tolerable. Atmosphere's decent—shirtsleeve temperatures over the northern continent."

"Damn." Buchholtz pursed his thin lips. "No armor?"

Norfeldt bit down hard on the end of his cigar, then spat a hunk of tobacco at the nearest bulkhead. It stuck.

"Am I telling this, or are you?" He didn't wait for an answer. "First did the pole-to-pole orbital sweep, got some good pictures. A lot of indigenous animal species; apparently one intelligent one. Erect, bipedal, vaguely amphibian. No abnormal neutrino emissions; no unusual synchrotron."

"Radio?" I asked.

He shrugged. "Not apparently. The star puts out a lot of RF and the dirtball's got a hot ionosphere; unlikely even the local equivalent of Marconi would think of RF as a good way to communicate. In any case, First didn't pick up on any radio. No promises, but the tech doesn't look too bad; maybe about middle, late Iron Age."

The Dutchman shrugged. Analogies between human history and any alien history were likely to be useless. "They've got small cities, but no evidence of warfare— any kind."

Buchholtz didn't look disappointed, which surprised me for just a moment. Then it occurred to me that he must have had faith in the Dutchman's description of the mission as a tough one.

Norfeldt puffed at his cigar. "So, Second Team went in. We know they made contact. There was no apparent trouble, no fatalities dirtside. The scout returned to AlphaCee intact, complete with crew—who were relatively intact."

"Relatively?" If I were an esper, I know that I would have heard Buchholtz inventorying the team's weapons.

The Dutchman shook his head. "That's the word. Don't know much more. Under psych testing on the AlphaCee side, three of the four Second Teamers turned up . . . changed."

"How?" I'm sure that McCaw didn't care; he was just asking out of a vague sense of obligation to participate.

"Don't know. As soon as their escort's computer latched onto the fact that the changes were beyond normal bounds—

except for the Team Leader's—the skipper of the escort opened fire. A bit too quick on the trigger; I would have liked to know more. One hell of a lot more."

I started to speak, then changed my mind.

"Well, Emmy? What is it?"

"I . . . don't understand. Wouldn't the records of the psych test still be in the escort's computer?"

"Good question." The Dutchman nodded as he rose and stretched. "Got another one?"

"Sure." Buchholtz snorted. "How about this: Where the fuck are the records?"

"I don't know. I wasn't given them, and I wasn't given an explanation, either. It could be that somebody's bullshitting around with classification games—they are classified high—or there's some sort of snafu. Central loses more records than they like to admit." He shrugged. "So we get to play it by ear. Fun, eh?"

Buchholtz spread his hands. "I don't see the problem. All we have to do is blow the Gate on the other side, no? Looks like a clear Drop."

Norfeldt pulled his chair out, swung it around, then sat down assbackward, resting his forearms on the back of the chair. "*No*, Kurt. We don't Drop this one, unless we absolutely have to. You don't have to know why."

Norfeldt gave me a meaningful sideways glance. It takes tonnes of germanium, squeezed by a grabfield into a quantum black hole, to make the nucleus of a Gate, and the germanium is *not* recoverable; it comes out of the evaporating nucleus as random quanta, some locally, some through other singularities. "You got that, too, Emmy?"

I didn't have any objection. I didn't want my First Assignment to end in a Drop. "Yes, sir. But, if we have to . . ."

"Then we have to. Don't bother me with the obvious." The Dutchman paused. "One more thing. The escort ship, the one that blew up Second Team's scout?"

Buchholtz nodded. "*Magellan?*"

"Right."

III

Even if I live to be a hundred—unlikely, given my line of work—I'll never get used to Gate travel. Back at the Academy, they used to explain that the nausea most people feel when they fly through a Gate is purely psychosomatic. They'll point to studies showing that blindfolded psi-negs can't even tell that they have gone through a Gate.

Which may be true, but it is nonsense. You can feed me chock-full, blindfold me and then put me in an absolute-direction trainer, then spin it like a top, and I won't even get queasy. But Gates are different. Humans weren't meant to be squeezed through to the other side of the singularity left behind when a quantum black hole evaporates.

It's just not natural.

Now, it's not that I'm afraid of collision. While it's theoretically possible that one ship entering the Gate could bump into another leaving it—the three-space projection of the singularity may be infinitely thin, but the ship isn't infinitely short and it is always traveling at finite speed—a simple protocol prevents that from actually happening. Outbound vessels—relative to either of the AlphaCee-Gates—use the Gates only during the first three-quarters of even-numbered hours; inbound vessels travel via Gate only during the first three-quarters of odd-numbered hours. That leaves fifteen minutes cushion, which is more than enough, by a factor of about a million to one.

So it isn't fear. Maybe there is something to the psycho-somatic argument, though. Knowing that an error of less than a thousandth of a degree in angle of insertion or a couple of centimeters per second too much or too little speed means that you'll end up coming out of some other singularity than the one you aimed for—probably one inside a stellar-mass black hole, almost certainly one at an energy level that'll fry you or freeze you—

Well, that isn't good for the digestion.

To make a long story short, I never looked at the screen as we approached AlphaCeeGate and *Magellan* released us, our scout's computer putting us into precisely the right insertion flight. It's just as well that the ship flies itself through the Gate: the Dutchman's the worst pilot I've ever seen wearing wings, and I was occupied.

"Occupied" is the nice way of putting it. The truth is that I had my eyes closed, vomiting up food that I must have swallowed in my childhood. My early childhood.

"You about done puking your guts out?" The Dutchman's hands were confident and sure as he ripped the sickbag's tapes from my cheeks, sealed the bag and pitched it into the open oubliette, then replaced the bag with a fresh one. "C'mon, Emmy—we're through already. Take a look at a new sky."

Cautiously, I pried an eye open, then looked at the screen in front of my couch. Stars, that was all.

I couldn't immediately make out any familiar constellations, but that wasn't unexpected. For one thing, the stars are a lot brighter when you're looking out of a scout's monitor than they are when you're looking out of a thick atmosphere; it sort of confuses the issue.

For another, in the two and a half centuries we've been sending point-five-one-cee ramscoops out to seed alien suns with the makings of Gates, some of the ships have gotten far from home. A lot of the familiar stars in our sky, the ones Papa used to point out to me at home in Graz or visiting cousins in Sao Paolo—Alpha Centauri B, Beta Hydri, Delta Pavonis, Epsilon Eridani—are just about as dinky as old Sol; they only look bright close up.

Hell, two of the three brightest, Sirius, and Arcturus, aren't all *that* far off. And in less than a hundred years, we'll have probes out past Canopus.

But the sky isn't just distorted; once you leave the filter

of Earth's atmosphere, better than ten times as many stars become visible.

Which is why it's easy to feel lost when you're looking out at an alien sky. A globe with a radius of just 125 or so light-years may only be an amazingly small speck of the galaxy, but that's the wrong way to look at it. Imagine a cube one light-year on each edge; you could fit more than eight million of them inside the rough globe of our ramscoop exploration, without one cube even coming close to touching another.

"What do you think, Emmy?" The Dutchman's wide face smiled knowingly. "Don't you feel somehow different, being under another sky, looking out at a view that no more than ten other humans have ever seen?"

I looked him in the eye and answered honestly: "Not really."

Norfeldt laughed, clapping a hand to my shoulder. "Like I said, krauthead, just maybe you got possibilities." He leaned over my panel and punched a strobing square button, then sat back in his couch, pulled a fresh cigar—well, a new one, anyway—out of his pocket, turned his ashtray up to a loud hiss, then lit the cigar.

He clasped his hands over his ample belly. At least he was wearing clothes that once could have been called a uniform. "Kurt, Ari—break out the poker table. We got two weeks till we hit dirt."

IV

"How's it look, Emmy?" The Dutchman belted himself into his couch.

I nodded. "Not bad, Major." I tapped at the screen. "That's the best landing zone, if you want to make contact at that village."

"Does mean a bit of a hike if we have to go out and meet the locals."

"Yes, sir, but it's flat enough to give me a bit of room to bring the shuttle down."

"Oh? You need a lot of room for error?" He flicked a finger against his own wings. "Back when I was using these for a living, I didn't."

I didn't answer that. For one thing, I didn't believe that the Dutchman had been all that hot a pilot in his youth; he didn't have the look. For another, anything I said to that effect was sure to get me gigged for insubordination.

I pointed at the monitor. "Maybe you want to pick another village, sir? The *nearest* flat ground to the village you picked out has no margin for error, not unless we blast something clear."

"Hmm." Norfeldt puffed on his cigar for a moment, then examined the stub and pitched it into the oubliette. "Shit. I guess I can use the exercise. We'll do it your way."

Trying to ignore the way the white-and-blue bulk of the planet overfilled the screens, I ran the ballistics program again, just to be sure.

"What *are* you doing, Emmy?"

"Everything's fine, sir. The comp knows where we are, and there's nothing else in this sky; I should be able to rendezvous by radar, if necessary."

He snorted. "Kid, if we have to depend on you to pantseat it back up here, we're in deep shit. Some problem with the computer?"

"No, sir. It's just stan—"

"Academy chickenshit, again. Emmy, if we ever lose the computer, we're dead. So don't waste your sweat taking precautions against it."

"But—"

"Shut up. How much margin do you figure to have? About a klick-second of delta-vee? At best?"

"Almost."

He pulled another cigar out of his pocket and stuck it in

his mouth, unlit. Even the Dutchman wasn't fool enough to smoke during a reentry; a bit of ash accidentally hitting me in the eye could mean me dumping the shuttle.

"Exactly," he said. "You're not good enough to pull a ground-to-orbit seat-of-the-pants rendezvous with just a klick-second margin. Nobody is. So don't worry about it, eh? That's why we have tell-me-a-hundred-times built into the astrogation module."

He turned to look at McCaw and Buchholtz, who were belted in their couches. McCaw sat back, his eyes half closed, while Buchholtz stropped his Fairbairn knife intently.

The Dutchman sighed. "Put the sticker away, Kurt; we're undocking."

Regretfully, Buchholtz gave the blade a quick buffing, then slipped it into its sheath.

"Quit stalling, Emmy," the Dutchman said. "According to the comp, we've got about three minutes to undock, or we have to wait an orbit." Norfeldt waved his cigar. "You're on. Let's see how hot a pilot you really are."

You don't use a joystick for point-to-point in space; I unshipped it, locking it into its socket with a solid *chick*, then cracked my knuckles as I settled myself into my couch. I thumbed for some wing just for practice, and then gave each of the pedals a trial push.

"Stand by," I said. I armed and pushed the UNDOCK button, and then pulled my harness just a bit tighter as the shuttle *thunk*ed itself loose from the orbiter.

I used the attitude jets to kick us gently away, and waited, watching the orbiter move away. You *don't* want to fry your orbiter with the exhaust of the shuttle's main engines.

Slowly, slowly, it receded.

Enough. I turned the shuttle until the belly cameras and computer agreed with me that we were flying tail-first. You have to do that, in order for the engines to slow you enough so that you hit atmosphere. Of course, if you and the computer forget to flip it back over after the burn, you're dead.

"Here we go." I punched PROGRAM and IGNITE.

It was magic time.

There are trickier propositions than dropping the shuttle portion of a Contact Service scout down to a planet's surface, but not many. Part of it is numbers—skin alloys can only go to a classified but finite temperature; braking spars and variwings can only take so much pressure—but a lot of it is feel.

Now, I'm not the greatest admirer of flight modules in copters and atmosphere-only fixed-wing craft—before the Academy, I spent a *lot* of time and money on bandit circuits—but for reentry variwings, they're an absolute necessity. At, say, Mach 25, just barely inside an atmosphere, an attitude change—usually adjustment of angle of attack—has to be done by attitude jet. The same change at Mach 2 is going to be a careful mixture of jet and elevon; at, say, four hundred klicks per hour it's going to be entirely elevon, and whatever it is will take much more elevon to do it.

Even a flier as good as I am can't make a smooth transition between using attitude jets and elevons the way the computer does. With fly-by-wire, any adjustment—say, bringing the nose down a couple of degrees while rolling to port to go into a bank—takes exactly the same movement of stick and pedals, and, with appropriate feedback, *feels the same*.

Which lets the pilot pay attention to flying. And there's plenty to do. The trick is to try to get both low enough and close enough to the landing zone so that on landing you don't have to burn the engines one second longer than necessary—the juice may come in handy for getting back up to the orbiter.

If you miss the orbiter, no matter by how little, there's no recall, no matter how many tonnes of fuel are waiting for you up there.

In any case, flying isn't something I have to think about. I just do it—and I'm damn good. In less than an hour, the shuttle was safely down.

V

The Dutchman had been lying back in his couch, deliberately irritating me by pretending to be asleep, his hands folded over his massive belly, the cigar clenched in his teeth.

The shuttle settled down on its landing pods. I went into the powerdown sequence while Buchholtz deployed the weapons turret and manned the foamer—after a quick trip through an atmosphere, the heat shield tends to start any vegetation around the LZ burning, which can make one unpopular with the locals. Norfeldt's eyes sagged slowly open, and he brought up his lighter and lit his cigar with one hand while he opened the biogel port with the other.

"Anything, Kurt?"

"Negative, Al." Buchholtz sounded disappointed as he eyed his screens, swinging the weapons turret radar and camera a full three-sixty before he set it on auto. "We've got a quiet plain. Want to go to Yellow, anyway?"

"Shit, no."

Planetside, we're always on alert, but doctrine allows for the Team Leader to take us to Condition Yellow—a state of high alert—pretty much at his own whim. The disadvantage of Yellow is that it gives the weapons officer more discretion to fire without consulting, and I can imagine that Norfeldt wasn't eager to take the safety off Buchholtz.

By the way, going to Condition Blue, "Attack Expected," allows the WO to assume anything is hostile without further evidence, and as far as Buchholtz was concerned, I had the feeling that there wasn't much difference between Blue and Black; Condition Black is "Attack Initiated."

"You getting anything, Ari?"

McCaw's eyes were dreamy and distant. "Just . . . a vagueness on a vagueness, sir." He shrugged, then resumed his reverie.

"Any feelings of hostility?"

"No."

I was waiting for McCaw to say more, but he didn't.

The Dutchman spat. "Okay. We're about five klicks from the village, and if they didn't hear us come in, they're deaf. So we're going to play it conservative, and let them come to us while we wait for the biogel to spoil.

"Buchholtz, you get the recoilless out of the skimmer and mount it topside.

"Emmy, you and Ari launch a comm balloon; swing-mount the III-b radar on the all-purpose flange. I'll sit with the panic button.

"Let's get to it, people."

Deciding what to wear outdoors on a new world is easy; until developments in the biogel have had a chance to show us whether there are local airborne bugs or toxins that like human flesh, we always have to go through the full decontam protocol.

When there's a significant overpressure outside, we either have to accept breathing thicker air or go with hard helmets. While hard helmets do have an advantage—they *are* tough—doctrine is to prefer membrane helmets, and run just a bit of overpressure inside, which keeps them inflated. The membrane helmets aren't exactly easy to puncture, and they do have one big advantage: they conduct sound better than air, which means we can rely on the natural acoustics of our own ears, rather than external mikes. Much better.

I tightened my helmet to the rubbery collar of my E-suit and immediately thumbed on my suit air to push the clinging plastic off my face. Then, as per doctrine, I checked McCaw's seal while he idly checked mine.

He looked like a frankfurter in foil in his silvery E-suit; despite everything, it was all I could do to keep myself from giggling while we both donned our olive-drab oversuits and stepped out into the lock, him with the balloon and gear tucked under an arm, me with a wiregun slung over my shoulder and some sampling gear in a beltpack.

Despite Buchholtz monitoring the situation, and able to fire the recoilless in support, if necessary, it's always a good idea to have a bit of personal weaponry. Others like slugthrowers; I prefer wireguns. Back when I was a boy, I used to skitter a ball around our patio with the garden hose. Using a wiregun is a lot like that.

The inner door *snick*ed shut behind us, and we stood in the airlock for a moment while the outer door wheezed itself open.

I put my hand on my belt and thumbed for the general freak. "Von du Mark here. Radio check. How—"

"Hey!" The Dutchman cut me off. "I've got a fucking *hangover*. Skip the tin-soldier stuff, Emmy, and just float the balloon, eh?"

McCaw followed me down the ladder onto the plain.

That's all it was, just a grassy plain. I felt vaguely disappointed, although I don't know what I'd expected. Some sort of eerie alienness, maybe. I probably shouldn't have expected anything. I'd been to Luna, of course, and had done practice landings on both Mars and Venus—the Mare Serentatis reminded me of the Schwarzwald; Mars was just a rocky field as far as the eye could see; Venus was like being inside a dirty cloud—but I guess I'd expected the first really alien world I landed on to look special.

It didn't.

While McCaw made ready to launch the balloon, I walked outside the broad black oval our belly jets had charred, took a sampler from my belt, then stooped to cut out and bag a piece of grassy turf. I stowed the bag in one

of the shuttle's outside lockers, just above the black slick-
ness of the heat shield.

There wasn't anything apparently special about the grass.
The leaves were more purplish than I was used to, thinner
and denser, but it was obviously just plain ordinary grass
on a plain ordinary plain.

Big deal.

Since McCaw was finished tethering the plastic line to
the shuttle, I opened the box containing the radar and took
the white plastic ball out, snapping it onto the gondola's
utility flange.

If there's anything simpler than flying point-to-point in
space, it's launching a Service comm balloon. You just
make sure that none of the lines leading to the electronics
package are tangled, and that the line is in a normal-
looking coil. Then you pull the ripcoard and stand back; it
inflates and launches itself.

It was a huge, inverted plastic teardrop, falling upside
down into the sky.

"Okay, radar's working, Emmy. You and McCaw get
back in."

We waited in the airlock while the blue biocides rose up
to our membrane helmets, eating away our olive-drab
oversuits, leaving both of us in shiny E-suits and bubbles.
The biocide fluid drained away, to be replaced by flicker-
ings of UV and IR, and by both rinsings of water.

Stomping our boots and slapping at ourselves to shake
off the last of the water, we went back into the shuttle and
removed our helmets.

My first time on a really alien world, and it had been . . .
. . . nothing special. Not really. Just like a drill.

The Dutchman was still puffing away at one of his
cigars. "The good news is that the biogel doesn't seem to
be changing."

McCaw stripped off his E-suit and settled himself into
his couch. He didn't take the bait; I guess anything going
on outside of his own skull was too dull to bother with.

"Well?" Buchholtz asked, both eyes on his screens. "What is the bad news? I don't see anything."

The Dutchman sighed. "Neither do I. That *was* the bad news. Okay, we go to single watches. Sundown is in . . . three hours; if we don't see anything in the night, first thing in the morning we take a hike." He sighed again. Sort of like a whale moaning. "Which means I'm on the wagon tonight. Shit. How much you want to bet nothing happens?"

I didn't say anything; I had a hunch that the Dutchman was right.

Sure enough, nothing much happened during the night. Buchholtz took first watch and spent the rest of the night sleeping in his couch, his headphones clamped on his head, the feedwire running into the radar alarm.

McCaw, being the comm officer, was exempt from being on watch; he spent the time in his cabin, no doubt communing with himself.

The Dutchman stood his watch without complaint, which surprised me. And apparently stayed sober, which surprised me more.

All that happened to me was that I got incredibly bored.

In the morning, we suited up.

VI

"Everybody got their bubbles on?" Another thing I hated about the Dutchman was his passionate need to ignore the obvious.

"I'd rather be wearing armor," Buchholtz said, giving a longing look at the armor locker as he tugged at the rubber seal that kept his inflated membrane helmet snug against the skin of his neck. "And taking the skimmer, for that matter."

I didn't blame him; I'd rather have been wearing full combat armor, too. But for different reasons: *I* would have wanted it for the added protection, not particularly for the extra weaponry. The wiregun pistol on my hip was enough for me. As far as the ground-effect skimmer went, the Dutchman had a point; if the shuttle had spooked the locals, the skimmer might, too.

The skimmer sat parked next to the shuttle, and each of us—except McCaw, of course—had a follow-me box that we could set off to call for the skimmer and its recoilless, as long as there was a cleared straight line between us and the skimmer.

"Don't worry about it." The Dutchman hitched at the Colt & Wesson point-forty-four Magnum revolver in his shoulder holster. Norfeldt turned up his nose at wireguns; he said he preferred the stopping power of an old-fashioned Glaser Safety Slug to the greater volume and rate of fire of a wiregun's two hundred silcohalcoid projectiles.

"I don't want to make us too hard to kill," he said. "That'd solve the problem, easy. No Fourth Team; *Magellan* would just fly through, drop the bomb, and fly back before it sealed the singularity."

Great.

"I'm ready, too, Major." If you exclude words like "check," "checkmate," "call," "raise," and "fold," that was a solid two percent of the words McCaw had spoken since I'd known him.

The Dutchman tapped at the hatch control panel. "Okay, children, it's show time."

In a few moments, we were all standing in the short purple grasses of the plain. My earphones hissed like a threatening rattlesnake. Sweating, I reached to the control box on my hip to turn up the squelch.

The air was hot, just not hot enough to require the more rigid suits, the ones with temperature control. Which made the job easier, at least in one sense. Unlikely as it was that any of the local bugs could bite us—and do us harm—

through standard E-suits, if they *could*, that would "solve the problem," too.

There are times when I wish I'd gone to work for my father.

As blasé as I was trying to be, there was a certain something about being on a new world. The bounce in my walk as we headed away from the scout couldn't be accounted for just by the planet's low gravity—it was low only relative to Earth, not to freefall. After more than two weeks in zero gee, I should have been dragging; in fact, even after the three klicks from the shuttle to where the forest broke on the plain, I was still ready to break into a happy lope.

But it bothered me that we hadn't seen any locals yet. Once we were into the forest, the skimmer wouldn't be able to come when called. Not that there was a problem with the radio, but the autopiloting wasn't nearly good enough to work its way through a maze of trees.

A few hundred meters from the edge of the forest, McCaw started muttering to himself.

"Here we go. Kurt." The Dutchman's voice seemed distant, even though he was only a couple of meters away.

"Peeling off, Major." Buchholtz jogged away to our left, his assault rifle in one hand, a Korriphila 10mm pistol in the other. He was moving quickly across the plain; even though he was moving diagonally to our path, it was likely he would reach the stand of trees before we would.

"Contact, Major." McCaw didn't sound bored, for once. "They are about a quarter klick ahead, concealed in those columnar vegetable growths."

"Trees, Ari, *trees*."

For once I sympathized with Norfeldt. What else do you call ten-meter-high, three-lobed plants, covered with what looked like purple moss?

"Major, I *like* them."

I shot a look at McCaw, then caught myself. No, he wasn't armed. Comm officers are *never* armed. You can't trust an esper who is supposed to open himself to telepathic—and telempathic—communication with aliens.

"So you like them. Big deal; let's go meet the natives. Emmy, keep your eyes open and your mouth shut. Kurt, you on station yet?"

My earphones hissed as Buchholtz thumbed his communicator. The damn F9s put out enough RF to interfere with FM.

"Got them in my sights, Major."

I could barely make out the words through the interference. But Buchholtz's eagerness came through loud and clear.

The Dutchman caught it too. "You fire on my order *only*—you got that, Kurt?" Norfeldt liked repeating himself; he'd only given that order to Buchholtz and me a couple dozen times already.

"Got it."

The Dutchman stopped the three of us about twenty meters from the sharp edge of the forest with a sudden, chopping gesture of his left hand.

"Ari, just translate what I say. No unnecessary interpretation."

Three aliens walked out of a dark gap in the wall of trees, then took up positions facing McCaw, as though Norfeldt and I simply weren't there.

They were erect, bipedal creatures, tall and almost comically thin. Their purplish skin looked slick, but not wet. I could understand how First Team had described them as looking like amphibians, but we humans resemble lemurs more than they resemble salamanders. The orange splotches on their naked skin *could* have been natural pigmentation, I suppose, but the stochastic quasi-regularity of the patterns seemed to suggest dyes.

"They are . . . powerful, Major." I could barely hear McCaw. While Norfeldt was closer, he must have been having trouble hearing him, too: the Dutchman reached over and flicked a switch on the tall captain's belt.

"Just translate, Ari—easy, now. Easy now, boy."

The fact that the Dutchman was treating him like a dog would have bothered me more if McCaw hadn't been trembling all over like he *was* a scared puppy.

"T-they say: 'Greetings. We are the . . .' Untranslatable, Major, but it's their species name. Overtones of justice, and power, such power. . . . 'What we have, do, or are, it is yours.' "

"Ritual greeting?"

McCaw brought his gloved hands up in front of his face, the fingers awkwardly writhing, as though he wasn't used to having fingers. "There's a trace of ritual, but no, Major—they mean it."

The Dutchman snorted cautiously. "Sounds good. We'll—"

"But just for me and Buchholtz. They're waiting for a response from one of us."

"Just you two?"

"Wait." McCaw's trembling worsened, then ceased entirely. "Wait. They don't see you and Mark as people, just objects. Wait. The leader is . . . expressing admiration at my species' ability to create complicated . . . toys."

"Don't clarify matters for them. Have they seen other toys like me and Emmy before?"

"Wait. 'Yes. We admired greatly the toy that your . . . associates brought before. This time you have brought two. Is one a gift?' "

"What if it isn't?"

"Confusion. Wait. They don't understand the concept of not giving someone what he wants. They keep asking me to explain it another way. Wait. Wait."

I flipped the slipguard off my holster and let my hand rest on the hilt of my wiregun. The Dutchman caught the motion out of the corner of his eye.

"At *ease*, Mister von du Mark. We're all expendable— you most of all."

Which was why I'd flipped the guard off in the first place. I don't like being expendable. "Yes, sir."

"Relax, Emmy—I don't think I'll have to—" Norfeldt

was cut off by the hissing of a wiregun, and then three quick gunshots. A muffled scream in our headphones was echoed off in the distance.

"*Aie*—Condition Red—" Buchholtz trailed off into a bubbling moan, then went silent.

McCaw crumpled to the ground; I drew my wiregun and thumbed the safety off.

Norfeldt drew his Magnum and fired off a shot into the air, but the aliens didn't make a move. Not at all. They just stood there, breathing slowly, watching us with their round, liquid eyes. The Dutchman squatted next to McCaw, keeping his eyes on the aliens.

"He's breathing," the Dutchman said. "Emmy, move. Condition Blue; fire if threatened. I'll stay here with Ari. Find him." He dropped a hand to the follow-me hanging from his belt.

A distant *whoop whoop whoop* sounded in my phones as the skimmer started toward the Dutchman.

"On my way." That last was unnecessary; I was already sprinting for the area where Buchholtz had entered the forest, several hundred meters to the west.

In five minutes, I was standing over what was left of Buchholtz, who lay in the middle of a horrid shambles that looked like something painted by Hieronymus Bosch.

I'd never actually seen a dead man before. Or a dead alien. It wasn't pretty. The claws that had ripped his outer suit and E-suit to ribbons hadn't stopped there; they had opened up his chest and belly like they thought he was a box of Cracker Jacks and they needed the prize right away. Pink viscera mingled with red blood and the brown pulp of half-digested food. Slick with blood, his ribs stuck out of what was left of his chest.

They'd ripped his left leg off; I could see the hip joint—

There was a strange calm in my head, although not in my stomach.

The night terrors would come later. I forced myself not

to vomit as I eyed the woods, and then sent a stream of wires hissing into the trees, just for good luck.

"Report, Mark. Dammit, *report*."

"Yelling won't help, Major." I leaned back against a tree, my eyes on the woods. "Buchholtz is dead. They . . . clawed him."

"Pictures."

"Yes, sir." Using my left hand, I took my holocam from my belt and started snapping, not using either my right hand or the viewfinder. Both my eyes and my right hand were occupied. "You see any weapons on your natives?"

"No."

"None on these, either. There's five—no, six—bodies scattered around the clearing." Buchholtz had given them a good fight. Trails of blood leading into the forest showed that it had taken more than these six filthy lizards to kill Kurt Buchholtz.

I stowed the camera, then stooped to check his weapons. "His rifle's empty." I slipped the magazine out of his automatic. "Major?"

"Yeah?"

"Did Buchholtz keep a round in the chamber?"

"Yeah. Five rounds left?"

"Yes, sir. Pistol's been fired three times." His Fairbairn knife was stained with dark-purple blood. "He made the bastards pay, Major." I cleaned his knife with a dirtclod, then raised it in a quick if sketchy salute. There wasn't anything else I could do for Kurt.

I wiped the rest of the blood off the knife and slipped it into my belt. Maybe I'd be having some use for it. I almost wished—

"Don't give with the bullshit bravado, kid. Just keep your head on. Maybe some injured ones around, some survivors. Lessee if we can't survive this one, which would be nice." The Dutchman just kept talking. I don't know whether it was to reassure himself or me. "C'mon back now; the skimmer'll be here in just a couple of minutes. And keep your eyes open, shithead. Take it easy, Emmy. Deep breaths. Get away from the—''

McCaw's voice cut in. He wasn't talking to me or Norfeldt, I'm sure. "Thank you. Please. If you could . . .''

"What the fuck? Ah, no—*Ari*, Ari. *Shit*.'' Norfeldt's voice was suddenly calm, even. "Not back here, Emmy. Meet me at the skimmer.''

"But—''

"Take off in twenty minutes, if I don't meet you. I want the skimmer back at the shuttle ay-sap, fuckhead. If I don't make it, you're going to have to Drop this one, all by yourself. That's an order. Acknowledge.''

I swallowed. "Aye aye, sir.''

"One more thing before you go. Take a look at Kurt's face.''

"Sir?'' It was hidden by his bloody, deflated helmet.

"Shut up and look, Mister. Is he smiling?''

Using Buchholtz's Fairbairn knife, I cut the rest of the helmet away. It was hard work; membrane helmets are tough.

"So? Is he smiling, Emmy?''

It was hidden by the blood, but he was. I couldn't understand it. "Yeah.''

"So's McCaw. And he's dead, too.''

VII

"Lesson time, Emmy.'' Norfeldt's hands were again folded over his ample belly, as he sat—well, floated, really—in his couch, puffing clouds of smoke toward the ashtray.

I'm not criticizing. There wasn't a damn thing to do until we reached the Gate.

But it still didn't seem right. "None of that crap, Major. We blew it. It's going to be a Drop."

The Dutchman shrugged and blew a cloud of smoke at the exhaust over his head. "You're right—but why?"

"Because they *kill* people—espers in particular. I mean, they had to claw Buchholtz to death, but they didn't even have to touch McCaw to kill him. Both of them were psi-positive. Both died. We didn't."

"Don't be stupid. Think about it. Second Team didn't die, and all of them except the Team leader were highly positive—more than Kurt. Well," he said, waving his chins at the screen, "at least they didn't die here—they died back on our side. How much do you want to bet that the only First Team member who didn't change his psych profile was the TL?"

"I don't understand."

"Figures. Try thinking about it."

"Wait! They . . . didn't think of you and me as people."

"You're beginning to get it, Emmy." The Dutchman chuckled. "We learned enough down there, just enough to work it out. Remember the greeting that the leader of the aliens gave McCaw?"

"Something like 'We'll give you what you want,' no?"

"Close enough. Hey, Emmy," he said, like an idea had just struck him, "you want a beer?"

It's strictly against regs to drink on duty. And since there were two of us in the scout, one of us had to be on duty.

"Sure." But a spaceside watch isn't something that you really need to be completely sober for, and a beer was going to do me good. Besides, the Dutchman had told me not to quote regs at him.

He leaned over toward the server and punched up a couple of frosty bulbs, tossing the yellowy one to me, saving the purplish one for himself.

I opened mine and took a deep drink, careful of the way it tended to bubble out of my mouth. Usually, I don't like drinking anything bubbly in low-gee, not even out of a bulb—it feels as if I get more in my nose than in my mouth.

"Tell me, Emmy—what do you think Buchholtz wanted, more than anything else in the world?"

I sat back and thought on it for a while. No rush, no rush at all, dammit. Nothing I could say or could think of would bring either of them back. "Maybe . . . maybe he really wanted to die in combat."

"Bingo. That was Kurt. I knew that from the moment I met him, way back when. He was more of a kraut than you are, kid; wanted to die gloriously, in battle final. Kurt Buchholtz was always a *Götterdämmerung*, looking for a place to happen. The natives gave him that place—just like he wanted."

"And McCaw?"

"C'mon, kid, it's even more obvious about Ari McCaw. He was always bored with the real world. They gave him that way out." Norfeldt rubbed a hand across his face. "Somehow or other, they've developed an esper society based on giving everyone what he wants. And if you've got a strong enough stomach, you'd have to admit that they gave Kurt and Ari what they wanted. A kind of justice, really." He shrugged. "That's the way it goes."

"But that means we don't have to Drop! We don't have to blow up the Gate."

The Dutchman didn't like wireguns; he usually carried an old-fashioned Colt & Wesson point-forty-four Magnum. The "forty-four" comes from the old-fashioned measurements of the diameter of the cartridge; it comes to just a bit more than a centimeter across.

It looks larger when a fat man is holding it in his hand, not—quite—pointed in my direction.

It looked like a cannon, is what it looked like.

"Yes, Emmy, we do have to Drop it. And we will, understood? Any further discussion on the matter is going to get you gigged for insubordination, *if* I don't shoot you down where you stand. You got me, shithead?"

"Yes, sir."

"Granted, it's not the way I'd like to do it—if I had my way, we'd bring *Magellan* back through the Gate, unleash a worldwrecker, and blow that dirtball to bits. But there's no way I can count on that, so we're going to take the sure way."

"I . . . don't understand."

"That's because you're still green, Emmy. If you started giving everybody what they want, too damn many millions of them would end up like Kurt and Ari—or worse. *Justice*." He snorted as he shook his head sadly. "Ever ask anyone, back at the Academy, why all Contact Service people are officers? No enlisted. Why?"

I quoted from memory. " 'The responsibilities of each and every member of the Contact Service are—' "

"No. It's because we're not really military, Emmy. We're cops.

"Go ask a cop sometime, kid. Ask him whether he thinks people need justice. Or mercy."

Interlude

Destination: Second no First Lieutenant Manuel
Curdova, Tee Double-you TWCS,
CENSORED
    Contact Service Administrative Bureau
    Building 5, Level Sub-two
    Very New York

Routing: I8OORQW5R43EE83 change those Os to
           zeros
Origin: Second Lieutenant Emile von du Mark,
           TWCS Aboard TWS MAGELLAN (#LC2-
           559)
Subject: Personnel no eye said _personal,_ you
           CENSORED
File
Created: 3 September 2241

if this machine doesn't start listening better it's
going to take me more time to clean up this let-
ter than it should to write it in the first CEN-
SORED place and the CENSORED pause button
only works when you're pushing down on it?
and what is this censored CENSORED question
mark
Ridiculous besides this censorship program is a
CENSORED piece of
CENSORED—this is private mail, not

start again and I've _got_ to check out whether
or not this thing is hooked into _Magellan_'s main
computer mmm appears not which is typical
service nonsense they're more concerned about
me saying CENSORED than they are about me
talking about how you build a
grmpmhl
can't even say it

46

at least eye can talk honestly though with nobody listening

Manny,
CENSORED but eye hate this typewriter—why
are all military models half deaf? I would have
brought my own, but I've spent most of my life
being being hassled for being a rich kid; eye
figured I'd try and avoid it here. Not that it matters. The Dutchman gives everyone trouble, regardless of race, creed, or what-CENSORED-ever.
Paragraph. CENSORED you I <u>hit</u> the bloody
punctuation button. CENSORED thing must have
been stuck—try again.

Better. Hmm, can eye say bloody question
mark.

Start again.

Many

har rumph!!!

Manny,

It took me more than three hours to drag the
routing code out of the ship's computer. Me-
thinks that <u>Magellan</u>'s skipper takes this isola-
tion bit too far. It would be nice if he'd just let
us access the damn user's manuals, for God's
sake!

Norfeldt and I have just finished the en route
portion of our psych testing, and have been
cleared by the computers. Seems that I still hate
stewed carrots and love parboiled spinach,
so I must be sane—well, crazy in the way that
the service likes, anyway.

Yes, I've met the Dutchman. I don't know why,
but I'd always had an image of the famed,
feared, CENSORED Major Alonzo Norfeldt as being
somewhat taller—he's actually an average-
height fat man. Although he's not necessarily

quite as soft as he appears; if a weak man were to actually fire that point-forty-four Magnum of his, it'd him knock head over heels.

Like eye did to that bastard Brubaker, or that blond hooker with the uneven CENSORED did to you ellipsis

CENSORED— ...

Sorry. The punctuation button seems to be sticking, although the <u>inflection</u> routines are working awfully well for a military model. Doesn't matter—I'll clean this up later, you'll never see it. But you're going to see some expletives in here that you'll think a bit too mild for your old buddy Emile, since I'm not going to have half my favorite adjectives be CENSORED censored. Trust me, and substitute appropriately.

In any case, the Dutchman is an interesting person, for an CENSORED. I'm not sure that I don't believe that he <u>really</u> believes that human-ity'd be better off if we just blew away every sen-tient species we ran into, instead of trying to Contact them.

But he may. Me, I'm still conservative old Emile, who accepts the Contact Service philosophy that we'll have enough to answer for, whenever we bump into a really advanced civilization.

Enough of that. I'm getting philosophical in my dotage, of all things. Ridiculous.

We just had a delivery, and we're still docked with the mailboat, so I'm going to have to hurry this. I may not have time enough to com-pletely clean it up.

In any case, the new ALSERV was on the mail-boat. Congratulations, First Lieutenant. As soon as I hit Vee en why cee—VNYC, we're going to drink up a good quarter of my trust's interest and celebrate—matter of fact, if you can ac-

cess Magellan's TOA, feel free to make some
appropriate reservation's at Virgin Mary's, and
we'll get ourselves properly swived.

Hey! That worked. Wheee!

In any case, don't worry about allowing me time
for rest. Rest is all I'm getting—sometimes (like
about twenty times an hour close parenthesis I
wish that the Contact Service allowed woman
officers. Either that, or we'd stayed in the Navy.
Remember Ella what ever her name was from
New Haven? I swear she could

Mmmmm, never mind.

If this wasn't going on flimsey, eye wouldn't say
this, but I'm working on getting a look at the
rating Norfeldt gave me, but so far I haven't been
able to crack the codes. Again, if I had my own
machine with me, I'd probably be able to—the service can't use the heavy-duty codes for personnel
records, can they?

I know. You can't answer that, and won't.

You're going to find this hard to believe, but
I'm actually losing at poker. Yes, me. The Dutch
man plays five-card stud better than even that
kid who dropped out in our second year—what
was his name?

Nevermind.

In any case, let us coupling get down to the
main body of the message, which is that eye
have gone through FIRST no first no First CEN-
SORED Assignment and have come out okay, although Captains McCaw and Buchholtz did not,
either of them. Requiescat in pochem. Open parenthesis Got the air of a female dog. I know I
pronounced the latin correctly, but it didn't
spell it right. I'm going to take along my own

machine on the next job and to CENSORED with
this machine.)

As I was saying, I've gotten through First
Assignment intact. There are times when I
almost wish I was a bit less hot with the stick
and pedals, though; the weak pilots get the
nice, safe, First Team photo surveys, where the
worst that'll happen to you is a case of low-gee
acne.

I said almost, Manual

That's not right, either. Manny, when we're
both wearing stars, we've got to see if we can
arrange to have whoever ordered these writers
shot. In the kneecap, to start with.

Speaking of First, we've gotten orders for a quick
orbital survey of an M-zero, which promises to
be dull. I suppose there'll be some leave sometime after that; although there's going to be a
thousand cheapjack stars Gated this year, until we get a comm officer and a weapons officer
assigned, I doubt that we'll get any Second or
Third jobs.

Yeah. Third. I don't know what it is, but there's
something about being Third Team that I like.

Maybe because it's important, dammit. At least,
it damn well had better be.

In any case, congratulations again. I'll write
again soon, honest.
One question, though—why didn't we take the
court-martial?
All they could have done was shoot us.
Well

Hey the mailboat's leaving in three minutes
minus a scant Emmy you might think about mov-

ing your CENSORED and get your CENSORED let-
ter on it thanks major I should
print out and
I mean
File Transmitted: 3 September 2241

Training Ground

I

Puffing on another of his cigars, the Dutchman waddled into *Magellan*'s Rec Room, a compboard under one arm, a bottle of some possibly nontoxic Chianti under another. He was clean, for once—directly out of the shower, wrapped in four of the seemingly endless supply of huge, fluffy Navy-issue towels that came with *Magellan*'s Rec level.

"How they hangin', Emmy?" he said, as he seated himself across from me at the table and popped the cork. He took a quick swig and smacked his lips, then flicked cigar ash on the floor and stuck the moist end back in his mouth.

I was tempted to ask if he'd ever made a mistake and stuck the lit end between his lips, but he might have figured that for a wish—which it was—and gigged me for insubordination.

"I'm fine, sir," I said. I shut down my compboard and rubbed at my tired eyes. I had been busy working on a Qualification Course—Logistics; if there's anything duller, I don't want to have to study it—and any excuse to take a break was welcome.

Well, almost welcome; the Dutchman was barely an exception.

"Entirely a matter of opinion." He puffed another cloud of foul smoke in my direction. "That all depends on this—I've been working on your Quarterly, and amusing myself with your Pers file."

That last is nonreg: accessing a Personnel file without proper need is, technically, a court-martial offense. On the other hand, a commanding officer presumably has the need to know anything and everything on record about his subordinates. On another hand, the purpose is supposed to be to help him do his job better; strolling through Personnel records isn't supposed to be a hobby.

I've run out of hands, but I wasn't about to try and do anything about it: tattling on senior officers about trivial offenses isn't known to do a lot of good for junior officers' careers.

Besides, everybody I know in the Service seems to spend inordinate amounts of time cracking, or trying to crack, computer security systems. I'm not sure where it comes from, but it is traditional.

He furrowed his brow for a moment. "Trouble is, I can't seem to find any paper on you before you showed up at Alton—either the data ain't onboard or I can't access it. You were a transfer from New Haven?"

"That's right." In a manner of speaking. . . .

"Asshole." Norfeldt smiled. "I thought you were a dumbass kraut, but now I know it."

"Sir, I am *not* German. My family has been Austrian for more than two hundred years, sir."

"And the transfer? To the CS? If that doesn't make you a dumb shit, what does?"

I snorted. "I had a hell of a choice, Major. Either transfer or sit down at a Naval court-martial. I didn't think I'd like ten years at hard labor on Thellonee . . . so I picked the CS transfer."

One moment of letting my anger loose . . .

"Oh? Tell me about it."

"I'd rather not."

The Dutchman raised an eyebrow. "I'm sorry, Emmy. I guess I must be hearing things—*you disobeying a direct order, shithead?*" He jerked his head at my coffee cup. "Take a swig and start spewing it out. From the beginning, Mister."

An order is an order.

Of course, there are usually more ways than one to obey an order, unless the giver is very careful. "Yes, sir. To begin: my Grosspapa was born in Vienna—"

"Shut up, Mister. A touch of white mutiny, eh?" He downed some more Chianti. "I wouldn't, Emmy, I really wouldn't. Start again, and take it from where you arrived at the Naval Academy."

I thought it over for a moment. I could go into such detail that I'd never get past the first day, or . . .

Oh, to hell with it. Why not? "Sure, Major. I arrived by copter . . ."

II

A klick below, the grounds of the Thousand Worlds Naval Academy were white, green, and gold, clusters of low granite buildings spread out over the grass, cupping the sandy beach of New Haven harbor.

I eased over the cyclic and gave it a bit more throttle as I banked the Hummingbird for a better look.

And instantly caught a buzz on the comset.

NEW HAVEN CONTROL flashed on the heads-up display.

"VNYC 401, we show you as deviating from your logged flightpath. Is it a wind gust, or are you having, ahem, 'autopilot difficulty'?" the firm contralto said, the voice carefully larded with just the slightest bit of sympathy, as well as the sarcasm.

"Negative, Long Wharf. No problem."

I switched off my throat mike and allowed myself a light chuckle. She must have been a pilot, too, and understood that I wasn't having any kind of difficulty at all. One minute after I'd taken off from Koch, the moment that radar showed that I was safely outside the cluttered VNYC approaches, I'd set the deadman on the yoke, then toed the bandit switch and put the copter on full manual, not the so-called "computer-assisted" version that only lets you think you're flying.

I like fly-by-wire—as long as there's sufficient feedback to the stick—but copters don't need all that computerized stabilization gunk the way frontswept airframes or variwings do.

Even if real flight was illegal, it wasn't really unsafe, no matter what the regs said. If, say, I suffered a stroke or heart attack—and never mind how an eighteen-year-old in perfect health is going to suffer a stroke or a heart attack—my hand would slip off the yoke, popping the deadman and bringing the Hummingbird's flight computer back fully online.

In any case, as long as I didn't deviate too much from the flight path or exceed speed limits by too much, I'd be unlikely to be called on it. Even if I was, so what? I was reporting as a cadet candidate at the CS Naval Academy, and from the moment I'd left Graz I had been officially under TW military discipline; I wasn't subject to the laws of the North America Federation, and neither the NAFAA, the NAFBI, nor the local police could touch me; all they could do would be report me. The Navy would be unlikely to want to punish a pilot for insisting on really flying.

Hmm . . . the ATC sounded nice; if she was as pretty as she sounded, it might be worthwhile to get her phone code.

I turned the mike back on. "I repeat, negative, no problem. Just a wind gust," I said, damning myself as my voice cracked, and dropping the idea of asking for her code. I was eighteen, dammit—that was supposed to have stopped.

I toed the bandit switch off, then thumbed the GCA on. I don't have anything against computers—for one thing, they handle final approaches in traffic much more safely than humans can.

I thumbed the mike again. "Request landing vector."

As I let my hand come off the deadman, both the cyclic and collective went dead on me while the pedals retracted.

The Hummingbird took a slight lurch to starboard, away from the field; I dropped my hands and looked out the window.

A thousand meters away, the regular VNYC noon copter was already down, its front-and-back rotors grinding down into visibility. I gave the von du Mark eagle on its broad side a halfhearted salute. I have never liked Sikorsky Whales, but then I've never had the chance to really fly one—inspections for larger craft are both more frequent and more severe than for small ones, and being a biological backup for a computer has never excited me.

Besides, you can't do a really hot landing with a twinrotor job; they're not built for it.

My Hummingbird passed over the outer marker and plodded its way, fifty meters above the tarmac, to its berth, descending, hovering, roller-coasting a few meters above the ground, going up, then down.

The Haswell flight module is terrible at feeling when you pass from a hover to ground effect, when you transfer from actually flying to riding the cushion of air your rotor is pushing against the ground.

The technical term is transitional lift; whatever you call it, it's the source of a lot of accidents among beginners. If you slip out of transitional lift, fall off that cushion of air, you've got to adjust both cyclic and collective quickly and correctly, or you're going to go somewhere you didn't intend—usually down. The accidents tend—repeat: *tend*—to be minor, because ground-effect mishaps start from less than three meters up. But there's a lot of energy in fast-moving rotors; if you crash, you'd better pancake.

The Haswell kept missing the landing; I decided I'd had enough nonsense. So I clamped down on the deadman, the controls coming half-alive, then toed the bandit switch and landed it myself.

There are better modules than the Haswell, but who needs them? If you can't land a copter, fly an airframe.

I let the computer do the final check and powerdown, then put itself on standby; I was already in a half-crouch in the rear cabin, gathering my suitcases together and throwing them in the tagalong together with my trunk. I debated a moment whether or not to leave the tagalong behind and have a parcel service pick up the gear, but then I shrugged. It didn't matter; if I was going to be unpopular with the peasants for being the scion of Mark Airways, then I was.

I tried to look on the bright side. It had to be better than the hell I'd gone through at Auckland Prep. I hoped.

Clipping the follow-me onto my belt, I opened the door and stepped out onto the tarmac, the tagalong lowering itself after.

I sniffed happily. There was a trace of fuel in the air; there always is. *You* may think av-fuel stinks; to a pilot, it means he's home.

My phone chimed; I dug a hand into my flight suit and pulled it out. "Yes?"

"Emile," Papa's gentle voice said, "your mother just interrupted a staff meeting to . . . remind me that you promised to call as soon as you arrived in New Haven."

"I just got in, Papa," I said, as I walked quickly toward the registration building, the tagalong rattling behind. "And I will call you and Mama just as soon as I get settled in. Meaning no offense, Papa, I do have to get the Hummingbird tied down, the berth paid for, and myself checked in at the Academy before one o'clock."

The orders said to report by public transportation by 1:00 P.M. on September 4, 2237, and the Navy was sure to be picky about the time.

Although . . . I glanced down at my thumbnail; it was already a quarter past noon. "And I'm almost late now." Damn. If I'd been able either to bring one of the servants or to fly in the Northeast corridor at anything near the Hummingbird's top cruising speed, I wouldn't have had to rush.

"Well . . ." He paused. "I just wanted to remind you that as long as you are in New Haven . . ."

"I know. If things don't work out, there's always Yale."
Wrong, Papa.

I'd followed the family tradition as far as Auckland went, but that was where it stopped. New Haven, yes; Yale, no. Not with the Naval Academy's buildings beckoning at me in the distance.

Now, there's nothing wrong with Yale—at least you don't have to play idiot games with swords the way they pressure you to at Heidelberg—but what would they teach me to do there? Manage Mark Airways as Papa was doing and Grosspapa had done before him?

Ridiculous. Do you know how rarely the CEO of a major airways can actually get his hands on controls? Papa was lucky to get a hundred hours annually, and he'd *earned* his way onto the flight-test team for the first Hummingbirds, back in the nineties, before he'd let Grosspapa sidetrack him into management at Airways.

None of that for little Emile. No, sir. I'd go through the Academy, become a flying officer, then get myself a berth as a piloting officer on a cruiser—or maybe a destroyer; destroyers have nice thrust-to-mass ratios—then maybe first officer and finally a captaincy, once my reflexes were too far gone to actually hold live controls in my hands.

But Papa had to give it another try. "Emile. I could talk to Dean O'Donnell and have you admitted today—"

"*No*, Papa."

"Boy, you have your mother's stubbornness." I could almost hear Papa cringe at what he'd just said. Mother tyrannizes everyone else by remote control, but Papa has to sleep in the next room. "Don't tell her I said that."

"Of course not, Papa."

He sighed. "Very well. Just remember, you are a von du Mark—"

"Yes, Papa. I've got to go. I'll call you tonight. Goodbye."

"*Aufwiedersehen*, Emile."

I hung the phone back on my belt as I entered the registration building. The terminals were near the door; I stuck my left thumb in the slot of the nearest one and tapped on the keyboard with my right hand as the menu came up. I made arrangements to have the Hummingbird hangared and fueled, its engines and drive train serviced, and its avionics package tested remotely, only—when the bandit's off, it's transparent to remote testing.

Someone cleared his throat behind me.

"I'll be done in a minute," I said, "just finishing—"

He cleared his throat again.

"—or you could just use another terminal."

He tapped me on the shoulder.

Now I was starting to get angry. "Do that again, and you'll eat that finger." I asked the machine to repeat the price list for various tiedown and hangaring services. If he was going to be annoying, I'd take more time.

"If you are Cadet Candidate Emile von du Mark, *Mister*, you have exactly three seconds to turn around and come to attention, or you will be *former* Cadet Candidate Emile von du Mark."

I pulled my thumb from the slot and turned around.

"You call that attention?" he asked. Rhetorically, I assumed. He was a tall, raw-boned man in his early twenties, dressed in Academy White informals, his cap firmly on his head. I couldn't—then—read the short row of cadet ribbons over his heart, but I did see the two broken silver stripes on each sleeve.

Goddam. He was a cadet lieutenant—not just a j.g. The ident bar on the right side of his uniform blouse said *BRUBAKER*. I pulled my shoulders back.

"Never mind." Smiling sadly, he shook his head slowly. "Slouch. It comes much more naturally to you. I am Cadet Lieutenant Ernest Brubaker."

"Pleased to—"

"*You don't speak out when you're slouching at attention.* Are you Cadet Candidate Emile von du Mark?"

"Yes, I—"

"First lesson, Cadet Candidate Emile von du Mark. When you speak to an upperclassman, the first word out of your mouth will be 'sir.' The last word out of your mouth will be 'sir.' Both the words are the same; I hope they won't strain your puerile little memory." He looked at me, a corner of his mouth twisted up.

"Sir. Yes—"

"Second lesson, Cadet Candidate von du Mark. Except when answering a question, you do not address an upper-classman without asking permission."

Pray tell, how do I ask permission to talk to you? Would you like me to stick a love note in your shorts?

I thought it, but I didn't say that—this fellow had me fully intimidated.

"Very good. You have your orders with you?"

"Y-sir. Yes, sir." I don't know what it was, but this Brubaker person actually had me stuttering as I reached for my hip pocket.

"I didn't ask to see them," he said.

As I let my hand drop to my side, he sneered again. "They read in part, and I quote, '. . . inasmuch as you have accepted Cadet Candidate status, you are required to report, utilizing public transportation, to the Thousand Worlds Naval Academy at New Haven NAF on 4 September 2247.' Correct?"

"Yes."

He pretended not to hear me.

"Sir. Yes, sir."

"Very well. Now, for your information, Mister von du Mark, the Whale that just landed is the last regularly scheduled public carrier due into New Haven before the reporting deadline, and of all the six hundred-odd cadet candidates, all but one had either previously reported or were on that shuttle.

"Further—and again for your information—there are thirty-four cadet candidates sitting aboard a non-air-conditioned bus that is *supposed* to carry them immediately to the Academy, and I suspect that these, your future classmates, are none too pleased with you for blithely choosing to disobey the orders that said you were to report by public, and not private, transportation, and—yes, what is it?"

"Sir. The Hummingbird, sir, that I came in on, sir?"

"You didn't ask permission. But never mind—speak up, Cadet Candidate, speak up."

"Sir, it's owned and operated by the Public Transport division of the company that owns the Whale, sir. I believe that means that it is public transportation, sir."

"Huh?"

"Sir, my . . . father is von du Mark of Mark Airways, sir."

"Nicely put." Brubaker's smile grew broader; I had the feeling that he already knew that.

"Very, *very* good, Cadet Candidate von du Mark. Let me give you some more information. There are two things in the universe that I absolutely despise: rich boys, and barracks lawyers. Despite that, despite the fact that you are both of the things that I most despise, you might notice that I'm smiling. Have you noticed that, Cadet Candidate von du Mark?"

"Sir. Yes, sir."

"Doesn't it impress you as strange that I'd be smiling, given the situation?"

"Sir. Yes, sir."

"Oh? You think I'm strange, do you? Never mind, Mister, we can discuss your lack of respect for an upperclassman later. The reason that I'm smiling, Mark, is that it is going to be my great personal pleasure to run your rich barracks lawyer's ass out of the Academy. Now, about that landing of yours—did you override the autopilot?"

As I opened my mouth to deny the accusation, he raised a warning finger. "Say whatever you want now, Cadet Candidate von du Mark. Right now, you're a cadet candidate—but if you pass your physical and take the oath, you will be a cadet—of sorts—and cadets don't lie, cheat, steal, or tolerate others who do. Understood?"

"Sir. Yes, sir."

"Now, was that a legal landing?"

I didn't say anything. He probably couldn't kick me out for it, but he might try.

"Very good, Cadet Candidate von du Mark, very good. There's nothing in the honor code that forbids a cadet from standing mute." He held out a palm. "Oh, and I'll have your phone—we don't need you crying on your mommy's shoulder. *Now*."

Reluctantly, I handed it over. He set it gently on the floor and then ground it under his heel.

"Get on the bus."

The Dutchman chuckled. "Damn, but this Brubaker sounds like my kind of person. He rode you hard, I take it?"

I nodded. "Fair to medium. Not just me, but all three of my roommates. Drove Gardner right out of the Navy—"

"Right out? I thought the deal is that if you drop out of the Naval Academy, the sailorboys can still hold you to two years enlisted service."

"If they want to; in practice, they only do if you don't have any pull. But he really *broke* Gardner; the poor bastard was carried off on a stretcher." *He spent four years in an asylum, Major,* I thought. *It isn't funny.*

"Maybe he wasn't the Navy type after all."

"Permission to speak bluntly, sir?"

"Sure." The Dutchman nodded. "I take it you don't agree."

"I've heard that bullshit ever since my first day as a plebe. I didn't believe it then, and I don't believe it now, Major. *Anybody* can be broken by the right kind of pressure—maybe, with a bit of time and patience, Gardner could have been one hell of a good officer, maybe even a fine captain."

The Dutchman snorted. "You don't think command is all that big a deal, do you?"

"Not necessarily." I shrugged. "And I don't think that riding someone until he breaks will ever help him exercise it."

The Dutchman didn't answer. "Go on."

"It went on for what felt like forever. There was the nonsense about the cow and leather and the Contact Service, and what a plebe was. Now, that was the normal sort of hazing that goes on at the Naval Academy. But Brubaker had some extras in mind for me. . . ."

III

I was in full uniform, book bag tucked under my left arm to keep my right arm free for saluting, heading down the quad to class. My uniform was absolutely immaculate, a spare pair of heavily shined shoes tucked into my book bag because earlier there had been a light rain and the water on the walk was certain to spot the shoes I was wearing.

I was taking special precautions to be spotless for this class: Lieutenant Commander Farrell was a stickler for clean uniforms.

I smiled inside. You have to keep the smile inside: an upperclassman might—*will*—notice a plebe with a grin on his face. And you don't want the upperclassmen to notice you; the idea is to try to get through the first year doing a Claude Rains imitation.

But I was excited about the class: Rotary Wing Familiarization. With a bit of luck, Farrell would let me have a turn at the controls; at the very least, I'd get in some time off the ground.

My feet flew out from underneath me, and I landed flat on my back in a puddle.

"Good afternoon, scumsucker," Brubaker said, smiling down at me. "And be more careful next time."

I leaped to my feet. The filthy water had soaked me from the back of my neck to my ankles.

"Go ahead, plebe. Please. Assaulting an upperclassman?"

*   *   *

"Chickenshit." The Dutchman smirked. "What's the penalty for assault? A couple of weeks in jail?"

I shook my head. "Military discipline, remember—court-martial."

"You could have run into him off grounds."

"I might have, if I'd ever been *allowed* off grounds. But even so, I wouldn't have. Try that and the upperclassmen'll run you right out of the Academy. At least with Brubaker bullying me I had a bit of sympathy coming from some quarters."

The Dutchman snorted. "Yeah. Sympathy."

"Such as it was."

"You were saying that he was riding all three of your roommates. One of the others was this asshole buddy of yours?"

I gave the Dutchman a long, hard look. It was intended to say, *There are some lines you had better not cross, Major. It's been tried before*.

Norfeldt shook his head. "Not really, Emmy. How about the fourth roommate?"

"Ortega took an upperclassman's suggestion and transferred out. Of the room, that is."

IV

Phil Ortega spread his hands. "I am very sorry, my friends. And if you ask me to change my mind . . ."

Manny Curdova shook his head as he sprawled back on his bed, smoothing his uniform blouse underneath him to avoid leaving wrinkles. Technically, lying on the bed between 0600 and 2200 was a violation, but Phil wouldn't tell—an officer and a gentleman doesn't go out of his way to squeal on his comrades.

Besides, if Brubaker wanted to find something to punish Manny or me for, he would, regardless of whether or not we had violated a rule.

"Maybe there's an easier solution. Hey, Manny," I said idly. "How good are you with a knife? Think you could put a blade in the bugger's ten-ring?"

He chuckled thinly. "Actually, I can hit a flying sherry cork at twenty paces."

"Serious?"

"Close. But, as I understand it, the Navy would be likely to . . . frown on our killing the pig."

True. Our actual policy was to keep our noses clean enough to avoid trouble from Tac officers and benign upperclassmen, but not to bother doing anything to avoid the attentions of Brubaker and the few other uppers who made a hobby of finding new and interesting ways to harass plebes in general and us in particular.

Ortega frowned. "I repeat: I will stay, if you ask me."

"No need," Manny said, slipping back into his thick Castilian accent. "I get the feeling that it isn't you that Brubaker wants." He shrugged. "You're not a *ricon*, after all."

"Or a smartass," I put in, taking out my ruler and measuring the placement of my compboard. Its edge was precisely six centimeters from the edge of another one of the Navy's contradictions; the high-tech compboard and a battered but decent voicewriter sat on an unpowered wooden desk.

Ortega finished rolling up and tying his mattress, then hoisted it to his shoulder with one hand and picked up one of his Val-paks with the other. Manny and I each grabbed one with our left hands, leaving our right hands free for saluting.

I swung the door open and stepped out into the hall. It was 2030 or so, well into the study hour. Down the immaculate white hall, each door was ajar at precisely forty-five degrees, plebes all sitting at their desks and studying, their commitment aided by the two guards, one at each end of the hall.

The walls were whitewashed wood: I'd whitewashed them myself, once each weekend in place of Sunday liberty. Even the cracks between the floor panels were clean—that was Brubaker's usual assignment to Manny and his toothbrush. Nice fellow, Brubaker.

We walked down the hall three abreast, pausing at the guard table to drop our burdens to the floor, come to attention, and salute.

The guard was a senior cadet sergeant named Morphy. Not quite as much of a jerk as the rest, but not a prince among men, either. He had a certain affection for a phrase that I don't particularly enjoy hearing:

"Puke it out, lady," he said, clearly bored.

I was senior, for the moment; my most recent full demerit was three days old. That's sort of like being senior by being the one busted first—it doesn't exactly get you the red-carpet treatment.

"Sir. Plebes von du Mark, Curdova, and Ortega requesting permission to leave the floor. Purpose: to move Plebe Ortega's belongings down to his new billet on the fifth floor. Sir."

"The cow, Mister—" He caught himself. "Never mind, Mark. Leave it be. Sure, sure, permission granted." He scribbled out a pass. "Take a couple of hours—that might keep you out of Brubaker's way for a while. Asshole," he snorted.

While Brubaker's rank was higher than Morphy's, Morphy was a senior, which put him beyond Brubaker's authority in all but strictly line-of-duty situations.

Morphy shook his head. "Transferred in with soph status last year. No fucking plebe year for him, but he's got to—never mind. Tell me, any idea why he's got it in for you in particular?"

"Sir, no, sir. Unless it's because I'm a rich sonofabitch

and a know-everything smartass and barracks lawyer to boot, sir.''

Morphy's eyes twinkled. ''I guess that could be it. Oh—and you can forget about your usual way of spending Sunday leave this weekend. On your way back, you might want to check out the posting for the next survival drop.''

I didn't say anything.

He sighed again. ''Okay, you've probably got a question—puke it out, puke it out.''

''Sir, any particular reason, sir?''

''Yeah. It's on for the weekend—you and Curdova, and guess who your upperclassman instructor is.''

I shuddered. ''No. Please. Not Cadet Lieutenant Brubaker, sir?''

''Right on the money, plebe. And the first word out your mouth is *sir*, scumbag. Give me thirty, then grab your bags and doubletime your ass down the stairs. *Now*, plebe.''

The Dutchman raised an eyebrow. ''Survival drop, *singular*?''

''It's the Navy, Major—and it was just more bullshit.''

''Oh. You think that survival training isn't relevant to Navy officers?''

''*Sure* it is, Major. Really important. Just like it is to be able to spurt out a memorized definition of leather. Makes as much sense as an officer being really good at whitewashing walls. Makes every bit as much goddam sense as making a man with an Expert Pilot's license—with prop, rotary, jet, *and* transsonic validations, sir, even then—go through familiarization training on a Piper.''

''Well . . .''

''Survival training doesn't make sense, Major. Not for a Navy officer; they're not Contact Service. What are the chances of a Navy man—flier or not—ever having to live off the land?''

He snickered at that. ''You got a point, Emmy. They actually made you take beginning flying?''

"Yeah."

He looked down at his compboard. "I see you got extra credit for teaching flying at Alton."

"After they had a senior IP check me out—thoroughly—I was detailed as a student instructor in airframe, rotary-wing, and advance RW—everything offered except combat tactics, transsonic, and skipshuttle. The Service occasionally isn't totally fucked up."

The Dutchman snickered again. "Ah. The soul of reason and grace, that we are. This survival drop where everything hit the fan?"

"Yeah."

"Go on."

V

Now, as I understand it, parachuting in has been obsolete for a couple of centuries, even for the military. Not that they call it parachuting in. "Vertical envelopment" is the technical term for jumping in.

That's what they call it. I call it stupid. Anywhere you can parachute in, a copter can get you in just as fast or faster, and bring you down with more equipment.

Maybe I shouldn't complain. After all, vertical envelopment has been obsolete for only a couple of centuries; the reason that we're taught close-order drill is that the Greeks and Romans found a phalanx a handy thing to have around, and—never mind that there hasn't been any use for it since pikemen were put up against horse-borne cavalry—it might come in handy again.

All of which may be just a rationalization for the fact that from the moment I set foot on the Zeus I was slightly nauseous. My stomach really started heaving when Manny

Curdova finished checking the straps that held my chute to my back and my pack to my front.

Brubaker was grinning, of course, which didn't make things any better. I would have loved to get the bastard in the right-hand seat of a trainer—if you know what you're doing, you can make anyone vomit.

Finally, we were over the drop zone. The red light over the door went yellow, and we checked our altimeters and oxygen masks. And then the jumpmaster clipped the releases to the line, and we waited for the green light.

All too soon, it flashed.

Manny went first. His face a bit pale inside his faceplate, he braced himself for a moment in the open door and then kicked out, his static line paying out for a long moment before going slack, whipping in the wind.

Me next. At the door, I looked down at about twelve klicks of air, and decided to quit. There's a difference between looking at that much air through a windscreen and a faceplate, honest.

"Whatsa matter, rich boy?" Brubaker's voice whispered in my ear, "Chickening out?"

To hell with it. "Sir, yes, *sir*. As a matter of fact—"

"Shut up. Be ready for a full inspection by the time I'm down."

Something connected with my butt, booting me out into nowhere.

I turned and reached, but all I caught was air.

It was a long way to the desert sands. I vomited all the way down.

"Barfing seems to be a way of life for you, Emmy."

'I've got a sensitive stomach. You want me to go on, or not?"

"Go on."

VI

By the time Brubaker had made it down, both Manny and I had our gear neatly arranged on our clear plastic tarpaulins, as the bastard had ordered. Each of us had:

One parachute, together with rigging and quick-release straps
A first-aid kit, complete with drugs
One plastic-handled survival knife
Five one-liter plastic water containers
Eighteen wooden matches, their heads covered with paraffin
One fire kit
Two two-meter lengths of clear plastic tubing
One mylar tarp
One clear plastic tarp
Eight mealbricks, each fully dehydrated and sealed in plastic
One plastic cup
One instruction manual, sealed in plastic

Everything was sealed in plastic. Plastic is the Navy's unofficial mascot, sort of like the way the Service has olive drab.

I didn't know why they kept the instruction manual sealed for a desert drop—it's supposed to be for jungle environments, where the main problem is to delay everything rotting.

Brubaker smiled as he swaggered over, his own kit properly slung, his chute tucked under his arm.

"First thing, rich boys, is to make sure that things don't go too easy for you." Over our cut-off protests, he scooped up both of our chutes and instruction manuals and piled them on top of his chute, several meters away on the hot sands.

Digging into his pack, he came out with a small plastic vial, lit its fuse, and tossed it onto the pile.

The chutes and packs burned with a thick black smoke; Manny and I worked our way around so that the wind was at our backs.

"Good. Now, you two have a problem," Brubaker said. "We're not due for pickup for three days. You need, in this heat, at least a liter of water per day."

And we each had five liters. Did he really think we were going to let him take the water away from us?

I looked at Manny. He gave an expansive Latin shrug, as though to say, *I'd rather get a million demerits than die of thirst.*

Good man. I walked over to my gear and began to pack it, Manny following me.

"Easy, there, Mark."

I stood up straight, gesturing at Manny to keep packing. "*Sir.* Plebe von du Mark requests permission to speak informally, *sir.*"

"Granted."

"You're not confiscating our water. No way."

Brubaker smiled. "Agreed."

I'd never seen anyone move so quickly. One moment, he stood there empty-handed; the next he had a wiregun in his hands, and had drilled through all our water bottles.

As we stood there, shocked, our water drained out into the sand. I leaped over to the containers and tried to hold the holes shut with my fingers, but there were just too many of the fine holes; all I got was fingers full of wet sand.

I drew my knife and stood.

"Don't even think about it, rich boy." Brubaker smiled at me. "In the field, assaulting a superior officer doesn't buy you a court-martial, not when the officer in question has a sidearm. It buys you about two centimeters of wire in the head.''

I didn't think that he'd actually shoot us out of malice, but he might in self-defense. I clipped the knife to my belt.

"It's really simple, rich boys. Between your belt canteens and what you have there, you can improvise a water source." He snickered. "Matter of fact, I order you to do so."

Neither holstering his pistol nor taking his eyes off us, he reached over his shoulder and pulled a tube out of his pack. He sipped on it as he seated himself on the ground.

"Don't worry about me," he said around the tube, patting his pack. "I've got a nice ten-liter jug in here. I'll be curious to see if you can do it. Or if you die of thirst."

The Dutchman snickered. "That's an easy one—improvising a water source from what you had there? A baby could do it."

"Right. *If* he knew the trick. Which we didn't. Either of us."

He nodded. "I take it you hadn't read the manual."

"We hadn't had our *hands* on the manual until we were handed our kits upon boarding the damn plane, and we hadn't been briefed, other than that we were due for a survival drop. I'd heard about some of the others—they were no big deal, nothing like the Spring Break in Swaziland they put us through at Alton, just a few days of minimalistic camping. Hell, Rivers and Edwards and their instructor ended up on some Polynesian island, complete with coconuts and a freshwater spring."

"Then again, they didn't have Brubaker as their upperclassman instructor."

"True."

"So, what did you do?"

"The obvious. We used our clear plastic tarps as groundcloths, and pitched our mylar ones as lean-tos to keep the heat off. I remembered reading somewhere about how the desert sand cooled off a few inches down, so we tried digging a bit. Basically, we just sat there for twenty-four hours."

"And the water?"

VII

There really isn't much that's worse than thirst, particularly when you have a little bit of water. You always have to decide: do I drink it now, or do I wait a minute? An hour?

Please don't tell me about how necessity is the mother of invention—I couldn't think clearly; the only thing running through my mind was how good the hot water in my canteen would taste.

Our canteens contained about a liter each—maybe enough for two days—and that wasn't going to make it.

But moving around would make us sweat more, and that would be the end. We just sat there, talking with each other, trying to figure out how we could get our hands on Brubaker's water.

And we just got thirstier, the words bouncing around in my head.

—improvise a source of water—improvise a source of water—improvise a source of water—improvise a source of water—improvise a source of water—improvise a source of water—improvise a source of water—

For a whole day.

The Dutchman went over to the server and punched me a beer, without having been asked. I popped the top and drained it. Reliving it was thirsty-making.

"Sounds pretty tough, Emmy."

"Emile. And yes, sir, it was. What would you have done, if you were in that kind of spot?"

"And didn't know the right way?"

"Yes, sir."

"I would have walked up to Brubaker, tried to get him to drop his guard for a second, and then I would have snapped my instep into his crotch, hoping to give him a new necktie. That what you did?"

"Not quite. I was a bit more creative."

It hit me like a thunderbolt. I'd been thinking of it the wrong way, putting the emphasis on the wrong word. No, no, not "We didn't know *how* to improvise a source of water," but "*We* didn't know how to improvise a source of water."

Got it. I'll show you an improvised water source. I turned to Manny. "You any good with a survival knife?"

He smiled at me out of cracked lips. "Champagne . . . cork."

I passed him my knife. "Manuel," I whispered, "I want you to get his water. Use this one as a spare."

"I can't get it—"

"No, not take it. Two throws: open up his jug."

I didn't wait for an answer. I forced myself to my feet and walked out into the hot sun.

"Hey, *Brubaker*."

Brubaker poked his head out of his lean-to. "Give me fifty, plebe. The first word out of your mouth had better be—"

"Stuff it, scumbag."

That got him angry—he lunged out into the daylight, his pack firmly on his back.

Manny's knife *thwock*ed firmly into his pack. For a moment, I thought he had missed the water container and had stuck the knife in something else. But then the knife fell to the sand, a stream of water following it.

Brubaker's first reaction was the natural one: he quickly

shrugged out of his pack and pulled the jug out, obviously intending to improvise a patch.

That's when I moved: I tackled the bastard, pulling his wiregun out of his belt as I rolled clear.

I snapped the safety off and caught Brubaker in the sights for a moment before I settled for his leaking waterjug.

"Stand back, Brubaker."

I emptied the damn thing into his waterjug, then ejected the clip, thought about it for a moment, and stuck the empty wiregun into my belt.

Manny stood beside me, the spare knife in one hand, his canteen in the other. "We understand it is possible to improvise a water source, Señor Brubaker," he said. "We strongly suggest that you go ahead." He gave what he always called—I don't know why—his Frito Bandito smile. "Or you can try to take this away from me."

I sat back and drained the last of my coffee. "Of course, the method was easy, once he showed it to us. You dig a round, shallow pit, about two meters across, and put your cup with one end of the tubing stuck in it into the center, then cover it with a clear piece of plastic, and weight down the edges. Then—"

"Then the sun shines through the plastic and bakes traces of water out of even the driest sands, and the water condenses on the plastic, runs down into the cup, and you use the tube like a straw to sip it. And you make a point of urinating right near the water trap, or cutting down cacti, chopping them up, and throwing the pieces under the plastic—I know all this stuff, Emmy. I take it you survived the rest of the drop."

"Sure. We made it to the end, and were picked up by chopper. And were immediately placed under arrest. . . ."

VIII

The commandant's voice was gentle, almost affectionate. "At ease, Mister von du Mark, Mister Curdova. Please, be seated." He gestured at the guards. "You can wait outside." He waited until they had left before offering us coffee.

We both accepted. Our short time in the guardhouse had persuaded us that this was likely to be the last time either of us would get filtercone coffee in a long while. Although maybe Papa or Manny's father could get us a hotshot civilian lawyer—

No. We were going to face a court-martial, not a civilian court. The Navy officers would want us to be guilty, and that would be that.

"You know," Admiral Braithwaite said, "there's a purpose to everything we do here. Mmm, but maybe you didn't know that, Mister von du Mark?"

"Sir?"

"Mister Curdova?"

"Sir, I don't understand. You were saying that Brubaker was right to try to kill us, sir?"

"I doubt that the court will think he was really trying to kill you, Mister Curdova. A ship, gentlemen, is a machine, and so, to a certain extent, is its crew. We can't have officers or men who choose to disobey lawful orders of their superiors—or who attack them." He sipped his coffee. "That kind of mentality is one that admissions testing is supposed to weed out, before even a provisional appointment is made. Although . . ." He let his voice trail off into a deep sigh. "Sometimes we do end up with disappointments like the two of you."

Manny started to speak up, but I motioned him to silence. My Uncle Horst is a criminal lawyer, and he's often said that many of his clients have made it worse on themselves by opening up their mouths, but that he's never heard of anyone making it worse by keeping quiet.

"Very good." Braithwaite eyed me levelly, a trace of amusement around the corners of his eyes. "Now, I've spoken with Cadet Brubaker, and made a suggestion to him. One of which he seems to approve."

He waited for us to respond, and when we sat there silently, went on, "I've suggested that you plead guilty to refusing to obey lawful orders and take two years' hard labor, and a BCD. Either that, or . . ."

"Or, sir?"

"I have your attention, do I, Mister von du Mark? Good. Frankly, I don't like any of this. I don't like it *at all*; it's a blot on the Academy for this to have happened in the first place. And, just between the three of us, I think Cadet Brubaker probably pushed you to the breaking point."

"But—"

"But that doesn't excuse assaulting a superior officer, Mister von du Mark. Not at all. That *A* was guilty of inciting to riot isn't a defense for *B* to the charge of rioting. Check your codes, gentlemen.

"I can't just ignore it and keep you two around, not after what you've done. And if I just let you resign, the next time some plebe is unhappy about being harassed by an upperclassman, he's going to say, 'To hell with it, resigning wouldn't be so bad,' and take a poke at him. On the other hand . . ."

"Yes, sir?"

"If you were to transfer to the Contact Service Academy, it's entirely possible that all of your records would be lost in transit. Think about it."

"How long do we have?"

"Thirty seconds." He tapped a fingernail on two flimsies. "Sign those, or I'll call the guards and have you hauled away."

* * *

Fifteen hours later, we were checking in at Alton. The duty officer had told us to go right to our room and settle in, and we would handle the details in the morning.

Our billet was in the old wing of Wingate Hall. As we were walking up the stone steps an empty beer bulb flew out of the door and hit me square in the chest.

It was quickly followed by a cadet captain in an immaculately pressed set of ODs.

I looked at Manny, and he looked at me; he gave the kind of expansive shrug that you're not allowed to use unless you've got sufficient Latin blood.

Here we go again, I thought, nodding. We dropped our bags and came to attention.

The cadet captain wrinkled up his smooth face. "What the—you the two pieces of new meat?" He shook his head, slowly.

"Sir. Yes, sir."

"My name is Jim Moriarty, not sir—outside of duty hours. And before you ask, yes, they call me Professor—outside of duty hours," he said, stooping to pick up my bag. "*Hey, Julio*—the new suckers are here. Get your ass out here and lend a hand."

"Right away," sounded from inside the building.

He looked from me to Manny, and then back to me. "And bring two beers. These poor bastards look like they can use them."

I almost cried.

IX

"I don't need to hear about Alton. I graduated from Hell High, remember? I know all about shovel-the-shit on duty, have-a-beer off."

"Right." I shrugged. "Well, in any case, that's how it happened."

The Dutchman snickered. "That's not quite the way it happened." He nodded smugly. "I didn't think I could see you enlisting voluntarily in the Service. . . ."

It was my turn to snicker. "Major, I don't know if you've noticed, but Naval officers live a nice, clean life. They don't—"

"Shuddup. More specifically, Naval cadets—even ones that psych testing has indicated *might* make decent Contact Service officers—don't volunteer for transfer to the Service—"

"Damn straight."

"—unless they get a bit of persuasion." Norfeldt took the compboard off his lap and handed it to me. My eye quickly scanned down to the bottom.

. . . despite more difficulty than this officer had expected, with the assistance of Admiral Braith-waite, said officer was able to secure voluntary transfers from Cadets von du Mark and Curdova.

At present, there are no further cadets at the Naval Academy whose psych profiles sug-gest that they would be more appropriate to the Service; accordingly, this officer hereby suggests and requests that he be relieved of his recruitment duties and detailed back to a Contact Team.

Respectfully submitted,

Ernest Brubaker,
First Lieutenant TWCS
(detailed RECRUITMENT)

"Son of a *bitch*!"

The Dutchman just chuckled. "Welcome to the real world, Emmy."

Interlude

carpetbombs were particularly destructive of soft targets—humans, livestock, wood-framed houses—while the blastbombs burrowed their way into the ground, and then threw vast chunks of earth into the air. It is entirely possible that blastbombs were originally intended for nonmilitary use of some sort.

Europe was the least hard-hit. Paris, Berlin, Bonn, Düsseldorf and Ploiesti were damaged, but not destroyed; a chain of burrowing blastbombs chewing northward from Trieste almost to Graz killed less than a hundred thousand, as Austria obtained a seashore and a deepwater harbor for the first time in its history.

Perhaps the Xenos had some way of scanning for population density; the Chinese coast and the Indian subcontinent were among the hardest-hit. While one series hit People's China from Shenyang south to Phnom Penh, ten clusters smashed the Ganges plain; separate carpetbombs hit Nagpur, Poona, Hyderabad, Sholapur, and Bangalore. While large numbers were indeed killed by the bombs themselves, the vast majority died with the destruction of the fragile economic superstructure of that polyglot nation.

No continent was left untouched. One small carpetbomb impacted on New Mecca, just south

von du Mark/Origin of the Contact Service/Twelve

of David's Gift; in Africa, fifty-seven were scattered across the continent, from the most northward, which spent itself uselessly in the Erg Iguidi, south to where the destruction of Port Elizabeth put a final exclamation point on the Greater Zimbabwe Race War.

In South America, a burrowing chain turned the Panama Canal into the Panama Straits; other bombs missed the major cities, with the single exception of Rio de Janeiro.

In North America, Mehico DF and Great Los Angeles were targeted squarely, while New York's bomb merely completed the long-pending destruction of the South Bronx. What was almost certainly intended to be the Philadelphia bomb hit nearby Harrisburg, putting an end to that city's long history of near disasters. Quebec was almost blown off the map.

Although there is still much speculation as to why the Xenos attacked at all, it is interesting to note that the <u>how</u> isn't as yet settled, either. Careful examination of the remains of most sites left it beyond doubt that the Xeno bombs, both blast and carpet, used neither atomic fusion nor fission. Early testing might have been able to determine whether the weapons were based on some powerful chemical explosive, or—perhaps more

von du Mark/Origin of the Contact
Service/Thirteen

likely—employed subatomic fission or fusion as
their powering principle. There is no evidence
that the boron-11 propulsion system known to
power the Xenos' battleships was in any way involved in their bombs.

Everyone was too busy to conduct research. A
high priority among the newly formed World Government Council was the location and execution
of the incompetent leaders and representatives of
the former "United Nations" regime. Interestingly,
much of the move was led by the Chiefs of the
"United Nations" Navy, perhaps in an attempt to
divert attention from their own guilt.

After the destruction of the original SolGate,
the priorities were as executed: the reconstruc-
tion of the planetwide economy, the building of
the lower-level SolGate and the five Mercurian
"trapGates," and the substitution of the twin
AlphaGates as the gateway to the Solar System.

What surprised many contemporary observers
was to what a great extent life went on as before.

During the early years following the Xeno
War, there were suggestions that the proper
policy was to continue the exploration
program, but simply to exterminate any possibly intelligent species we might find. But
wiser heads prevailed, and the present policy of

Communication

I

I wasn't surprised when the Dutchman slouched back in his chair as the ambassador and his aide walked into the briefing room, although the other two were. Three, if you include Ambassador Vitelli.

Maybe four, although I couldn't tell anything about the aide; she kept her smooth face impassive. Without a word, she crossed her long legs as she seated herself at the table at the front of the room, then opened her briefcase, removing a multisteno; she shrugged her shoulders to clear the hair away from her ears as she plugged in the earpiece, and then turned, either to face the ambassador or to give us the benefit of her profile.

Or both. It was a spectacular profile, at that—then again, I've always had a weakness for well-built redheads.

"Good afternoon, gentlemen," Vitelli said. "I am Ambassador Dominic Vitelli. This is Consul Janine Urdway, my secretary and aide."

I was on my feet, of course, and so were the new weapons and comm officers of our Team.

Vitelli looked at me. "You are?"

"First Lieutenant Emile von du Mark, pilot."

"You?"

"Second Lieutenant Akiva Bar-El," the huge, ugly man said. "Weapons officer." There was no particular expression on the flat face that sat above his bull neck. He was just answering a question, neither taking offense at Vitelli's brusque tones nor caring if Vitelli took offense.

Bar-El's voice was moderate and airy; there was nothing overt in his manner to offer a threat. In itself, that was almost threatening. He wasn't like Kurt Buchholtz—when he looked at someone, Akiva Bar-El wasn't deciding whether or not he could take them; he was deciding how.

"And you?"

"Second Lieutenant Donald Kiri N'Damo," the dark little man said. Donny was just a bit overweight, delicate, and nervous. "Comm officer." His fingers fluttered up to touch the tip of the psi symbol on his uniform blouse.

"And you are Major Alonzo Norfeldt?"

"Kinda," the Dutchman said. He puffed on his cigar thoughtfully. "But what I really am, right now, is bored stiff of chickenshit."

Vitelli raised an eyebrow as he glared at the Dutchman. "Your general ordered only you and Lieutenant von du Mark to report to me here."

"So?" Making no effort to get to his feet, the Dutchman eyed him coldly, blowing a foul cloud of smoke Vitelli's way. He settled farther back in his chair and propped his feet up on the desk. That he'd managed to get and keep mud on them on such a bright, clean day amazed me.

"You are AWOL, Major."

"Oh?" The Dutchman raised an eyebrow. "You mean I'm not here?"

"AWOL is defined, Major Norfeldt, as not being at the proper place, at the proper time, *in the proper uniform.* For one of you people, that means a full Class A uniform, complete with pistol and knife, both properly holstered—"

"Scabbarded."

"Excuse me?"

"Scabbarded, for the knife," the Dutchman said. "It isn't holstered, it's scabbarded. Or sheathed. You ex-Navy, Vitelli?"

"Ambassador Vitelli. And yes, I used to be a Naval officer, although I can't see as that's any of your concern, Major."

"Figures. Navy always bathes in chickenshit. You can fuck off, sailor boy."

*   *   *

It was interesting to watch Vitelli get himself under control; for a moment, I thought the little man was going to burst a blood vessel in his neck.

Finally, he shook his head slowly. "You'd like me to throw you in the brig, wouldn't you, Major?"

The Dutchman just shrugged.

"Why did you bring the other two without orders?"

Bar-El's brow wrinkled. "No orders?" The big Metzadan turned toward the Dutchman. Akiva Bar-El was probably the ugliest man I'd ever met; even at twenty-three, his ruddy face was deeply lined, his nose a broken fleshy lump, his scraggly blond hair thinning.

"Relax, jewboy, you had orders. From me. Okay?"

Bar-El thought about it for a long moment. "Yes, sir," he decided.

Donny just smiled, his bright white teeth standing out against his coffee-colored face. Donny was a full head shorter than me, and light-boned, almost like a bird. Where Bar-El was a big mass of flesh, Donny N'Damo was a little man with delicate features, almost effeminate in his movements.

"In any case, I thought . . . but it may be my eyes." Norfeldt furrowed his brow and dug two grimy fingers into his shirt pocket, pulling out a flimsy and handing it me. "Yours any better, Emmy?"

HEADQUARTERS
Thousand Worlds Contact Service
New Berne, Suisse

SPECIAL ORDERS NUMBER 11938   DATED:04/23/43

E X T R A C T

****

19. MAJOR ALONZO NORFELDT TWCS 298373 Tm Ldr Con Tm
377 and FIRST LIEUTENANT (brvt fr 2LT; prmnt stat pndng)
EMILE VON DU MARK TWCS 687657 plt & exec dsgnte Tm 377
are rcl CS Off Schl (PG) and detached Con Tm 377. NORFELDT
dtld TDY Tm Ldr Spec Con Tm 377(a). VON DU MARK confirmed 1LT and dtld TDY plt & exec Spec Con Tm 377(a).
SECOND LIEUTENANT DONALD N'DAMO TWCS 949873 Comm Off
Tm 377 and SECOND LIEUTENANT AKIVA BAR-EL TWCS (prov.)
973267(M) Weap Off Tm 377 auth ninety days UNSUPERVISED
TRAINING STATUS, not chg as lve.

Spec Con Tm 377(a) will rpt soonest repeat SOONEST by avlble
trans Rm 2119 DFR Building New Anna purp brfing in re
ASSIGNMENT 7983, to which Spec Con Tm 377(a) herewith
assgned. After compltn brfing, Spec Con Tm 377(a) will rpt via
Mil TP abd TWS Magellan and place selves under orders AM-
BASSADOR DOMINIC VITELLI TWDFR as per Section 23 CONSERV-
RULREGPROP.

By order Cmdnt, with the concurrence of Chf Nav Ops, all
CONSERVRULREGPROP and NAVREG requiring nonintercourse
suspended duration of ASSIGNMENT 7983.

Spec Con Tm 377(a) auth TPV, TPubV, Mil TP. Offs not auth
civ clthing en route. Delay-en-route leave not repeat NOT auth.
When tvling by Mil TP, Spec Con Tm 377(a) priority status
AAB1, upgradeable to AAA1 upon dmnd.

Copy of this extract is to become permanent part of all
mentioned offs Pers files.

****

BY COMMAND OF GENERAL DUPRES
Anthony Snow, Major General, TWCS
Adjutant

I hadn't seen the orders before. When the messenger had brought the four of us out of a practice survival drop—an easy one; just Thule—the Dutchman had grabbed and pocketed all the copies. Under normal circumstances, he didn't exactly encourage his subordinates to question him, but for the last few days he'd been even more close-mouthed than usual.

I nodded; it figured. "So this is why you had me fly us over."

Normal procedure would have been to voucher two seats on some airways, but the Dutchman had flashed the orders and our priority at a TP clerk and gotten us use of a Falcon, one of my favorite long-range birds.

"I thought you'd enjoy the hop." He shrugged, then blew a particularly foul cloud of smoke my way.

Right. I'd enjoyed flying the Falcon, of course, but that wasn't why the Dutchman had ordered it out at Alton. With our priority, we could have bumped almost anyone off a liner, but, even at AAA1, our orders would have gotten us only *two* tickets. He wanted N'Damo and Bar-El in on this, despite the fact that they weren't supposed to be.

But why did he want them in on it? And *what* did he want them in on? In between the refresher classes at Alton, Norfeldt had spent little time in his quarters—but he'd been spending a lot of time on secure phones. Maybe he'd heard something in the wind?

"See, Dom," the Dutchman said, tapping the flimsy with a dirty fingernail. "After completion of barfing—"

"Briefing," I put in. "Briefing."

"Shuddup, Emmy, I can read good, good as you. —After we finish upchucking, Dom baby, Emmy and I have to report to you aboard the *Maggie*. Then we're under your orders. Not now. So start the fucking briefing, okay?"

"I see." Vitelli stood silently for a moment, controlling himself with increasing ease. He had decided that the Dutchman wanted to have him lose his temper, although I didn't know if he'd figured out why. "You can include Bar-El on your special team. Not N'Damo. You won't need an esper officer for this assignment."

"Damn." The Dutchman looked disappointed.

"Well?"

"Deal, Dom." The Dutchman dug out his wallet and handed Donny a card after scribbling a phone code on it. "N'Damo, you go on back to Alton, VOCO. You with the chest—yeah, you; Urdway, isn't it?—you go with him to Receiving and get his ticket punched."

"But, Major—" Donny looked disappointed, the damn fool.

"You're out of this one. Be grateful for small favors." Norfeldt jerked his thumb toward the door. "Enjoy the vacation. See you in a few months, peeper."

At Vitelli's nod, Janine Urdway rose and preceded Donny through the door.

The Dutchman waited until the door had closed behind Donny and the girl. "Nice stuff, Dom. You tapping it on a regular basis, or is it an only-when-you've-been-a-good-boy kind of thing?"

Vitelli ignored him. "If you'll shut your filthy mouth, we can begin the briefing.

"No need."

"You're refusing duty?"

"No." Norfeldt ground his cigar out on the seat of the chair next to him, then unwrapped and lit another cigar. "Not at all. Instead of telling me, let me tell you." The Dutchman leaned back in his chair. "As I understand it, a couple of months ago, a ramscoop dropped a new Gate around a star. . . ."

*   *   *

There is no such thing as a perfect vacuum. Which is both a problem and an advantage.

The advantage is that it makes ramscoops possible.

If a ramscoop could think, it would think of the one atom of hydrogen per cubic centimeter it finds in interstellar space as fuel. As the robot probe cruises between stars, its grabfield scoops up the thin traces of hydrogen.

Granted, a grabfield has trouble getting hold of hydrogen; at the ramscoop's top speed of just better than half the speed of light, it's lucky to pick up ten percent of the atoms that enter the mouth of the scoop.

Which is why the mouth of a ramscoop's grabfield is more than five thousand klicks across, dwarfing the small center that is solid matter. Deceptively huge, the probe travels so quickly that enough free hydrogen is scooped up by the grabfield, gathered together to be fused, to power both the probe's transitional fusion engines and the Level 2 grabfield generators that scoop up more hydrogen, to power . . .

But there is no such thing as a perfect vacuum.

As the probe crashes through empty space, it's bombarded by the hydrogen nuclei that the grabfield has missed. In another context, we call being bombarded by hydrogen nuclei— protons—radiation.

Very hard radiation.

Which is why no humans ride ramscoops.

Which is why we wait for the robot probe's limited, redundant mechanical mind to steer it toward an interesting star, one that just might have a planet that just might be habitable. It drops off one of its Gateseeds, quantum black holes, prevented from evaporating by a Level 3 grabfield. With its limited supplies of hydrogen, the Gateseed brakes, steering itself toward the star, then eases itself gently into orbit where the gravity gradient is exactly as far away from flat space as Outbound AlphaCeeGate's is from Alpha Centauri A.

And then the Gateseed shuts itself off. With the grabfield

dead, the quantum black hole inside evaporates, destroying the Gateseed, but leaving behind a naked singularity, a hole in space.

Or, to be more accurate, a two-dimensional projection on three dimensions of a five-dimensional hole in the hypersurface of four-space:

The core of a Gate.

". . . a First Team went through, via Outbound Alpha-CeeGate . . ."

Forget for a moment the fact that all Contact Service Teams consist of highly trained, extremely dedicated professionals. Forget that they fly an unusually heavily fueled scout, with an extra deetee tank. Forget all the technology that goes into keeping air in, the vacuum out, and the scout moving.

Forget all that. Just think of a First Team—either a Contact Service First Team, or an old United Nations Exploration Group, which was part of the UN Navy—as a pair of hands, linked to a set of ears, eyes, and a nose. They fly through, and then the hands proceed to build a Gate on the other side of the hole. They do that very carefully, because if the Gate doesn't work, nobody is going home. Ever.

Then the ears listen. They listen for any regular or quasiregular sound on the twenty-one-centimeter band. They listen for any regular or irregular emissions of neutrons or neutrinos, protons or positrons—anything.

And the eyes look. They take constant parallax shots of the sky around them, looking for planets. If there are any that might be habitable, they take up an orbit around them and take pictures.

And the nose sniffs. Space isn't a vacuum, after all. It isn't done with a nose, after all, but it's still sniffing. The Team shuts off its scout's drive and waits for its ever-so-light effluvium to be washed away by light pressure. And then it extends sensitive probes into the vacuum and . . . smells. Usually, there's only the heavy background of hydrogen with the light trace of helium and the almost imperceptible background of heavier elements that mark an active star. There's almost never anything else to smell, not in quantity.

More than one hundred and fifty years ago, before there was a separate Contact Service, a UNEG Team smelled something else: boron.

Which they shouldn't have. Not in free space, not in any quantity. Boron, after all, while a light element, is by no means as common as hydrogen or helium.

What they did smell was a warning; a hint that someone had taken the idea of a boron fusion-fission drive, and made it work.

You take an atom of boron-11—the isotope of boron with the extra neutron—and plop a proton squarely in its nucleus. It goes into a long series of changes—no Krebs cycle or Stellar Phoenix, granted, but long enough, long enough—that ends up in four helium-4 atoms.

Now, while all the protons and neutrons add up to the same total before and after, there is some extra energy left over—five and a third million electron volts per atom of helium—which comes out as heat, giving you very hot helium; hot fast-moving, *not* hot radioactive.

That's theory. Now, in practice, if you actually took a few pounds of boron and bathed it in a stream of protons, you wouldn't hit every atom of boron; most of matter is space, and the nucleus of an atom is an awfully small target.

What you would get is a very hot mixture of very hot helium and very hot gaseous boron.

Hot gases. Very hot gases. And very hot gases are handy things to be pushing out the rear end of a rocket engine. In fact, *all* rocket designs—solid-fuel chemical, liquid chemical, NERVA, DUMBO, ion, fission bottle, transitional fission—are designed to do just that: produce some very hot gas.

At least in theory, a boron drive could do that very well.

And in practice, it seemed to work just fine, for the Xenos. Which bespoke a dangerously high level of technology, maybe even higher than ours. Possibly, whoever was using a boron drive hadn't worked out some of the tricks that we had—Gates, for example—but certainly they had made practicable one trick that we hadn't: boron drive.

The UNEG team should have Dropped it. They should have flown back through the Gate, leaving a small fusion bomb behind to destroy the Gate and seal the singularity. They *should* have. . . .

They didn't. Instead, they found a habitable planet and put the scout into orbit around it, then began hailing by radio and laser, trying to make contact.

Three years later, ten percent of the human race was dead. Just a tenth.

That wasn't much, of course.

Only two billion people.

". . . Now, as I understand it, Murphy's First Team picked up traces of boron. Which means either that this particular star is putting out weird quantities of the stuff, or—vastly more likely, given that a dogshit-simple spectrograph would pick up on that, in which case the word would go out to send for the astronomers, not the Service, and in which case nobody would be getting their peckers out of joint—"

"All that's classified information, Major."

"—there are Xenos in the system, or, last possibility, which would be too much to expect, there's someone else using a boron drive." The Dutchman smiled. "Questions, class?"

Vitelli nodded his head. "I see that you've been nosing around."

The Dutchman snickered. "I don't like to be kept in the dark, and after you've spent a couple of decades in the

Service, you do tend to have some connections. When I tried to get in touch with my old buddy Rafe Murphy and found that some brainless security feeb had slapped a TOP SECRET over his assignment on the WHERE board, I got suspicious, and went on the earie. I do have connections; it didn't take all that long. The only thing I can't figure out is why *you*.''

"Eh?"

"Why an ambassador? Why just the *Maggie?* Why not just call out the whole fucking fleet, and then blow the whole fucking Xeno homeworld into microscopic traces? That's why we have a fleet, after all—it's not *just* to put down local insurrections and give you Navy faggots a place to play drop-the-soap.''

Visibly ignoring that last, Vitelli shook his head. "How do you know it's the Xeno homeworld, Major? It isn't the same system, after all. And how do you know the aliens are even Xenos—*the* Xenos? Remember, we never captured any of them in the Xeno War. Other than the fact that they're psi-neg, all we know about them is how their attack ships performed more than a hundred years ago.''

"We took them then. Not easily. But we took the bastards. We can do it again.''

"Only if necessary, Major.''

There is and was a school of thought that says that all we ought to do, as we expand the globe of human habitation, is blow sapients into very small bits.

Retail killing is one thing; a lot of Contacts involve some of that. Doing a bit of slightly wholesale killing might be another, if we ever run into the Xenos again. But doing it on a grand wholesale really wouldn't put us in a good position, once we run into a really powerful alien race. They might think of it as a precedent we'd established.

Norfeldt blew smoke into the air. "So we open contact?"

"We try, Major. More precisely, you try.''

* * *

Norfeldt looked over at me. "Well, Emmy?"

"You asking my opinion, or are you telling me?"

"I'm asking."

"Lieutenants don't have opinions."

"Then I'm telling you—cut out the bullshit." Norfeldt smiled. "Seriously, what do you think? Maybe we ought to take our chances with a court-martial instead?"

"Nah." Look, there's no point in failing to give out with a bit of bravado when it doesn't make any difference. The Dutchman wasn't seriously asking my opinion; that wasn't the way Norfeldt operated.

"Bar-El?"

"As long as I have written orders, Major," he said carefully.

"You know what the chances are, don't you?"

Bar-El nodded. "Yes, sir."

"And you don't give a rat's ass, do you?"

"With all due respect, that's not properly your concern, sir."

"Fuck you very much, jewboy." The Dutchman chuckled. "I can't remember being told to go to hell so nicely—two hours' fatigue, shithead. Okay, Emmy, what is it?"

I drew myself up straight and looked Vitelli in the eye. *"Ave, Imperator, nos—"*

"Can the German—"

"That's Latin, Major."

"Shut up. Bar-El, you—"

"Wait." Vitelli spoke up.

"Shuddup, Dom. Do it my way, or forget it." The Dutchman got to his feet. "You and Emmy can finish up the barfing. C'mon, you ugly Jewish ape, we're gonna report to the provost. Call ahead, Dom: either they can slap the cuffs on me, or they can have orders for the Hebe cut by the time we get there. Emmy, if the little dago decides to go for the orders, we'll meet at the shuttle up to the *Maggie* in, say, two hours. If not, see if you can hire me a good civvie lawyer."

He beckoned Bar-El to his feet. "Your play, Dom. Oh,

and make sure you bring that cute little . . . aide of yours aboard the *Maggie*. Gotta make sure there's something to distract me on the trip.''

The two of them walked out of the room, Bar-El gently closing the door behind them.

Vitelli turned to me, his thin, dark face displaying the expression that I've always thought of as Chief Executive Officer Basic; Father always used it when he was negotiating with someone outside Mark Airways. It's every bit as stylized as a kabuki mask, sort of halfway between a deadpan stare and a lifted-eyebrow show of interest.

"You know this better than I do, Lieutenant von du Mark—"

"Emile, please." I smiled. Someone had to establish some sort of communication with the ambassador; once through the Gate, Norfeldt—and by concatenation, Bar-El and I—were going to be under his orders.

"Emile." He nodded. "You know this better than I do, Emile, but that man is . . . slime."

"You're too kind to him."

"Possibly, possibly." He returned my smile. "Would you like a cup of coffee?"

Someday, I may meet a pilot who doesn't drink coffee, but it won't be when I look in a mirror.

"Definitely," I said.

"Even if Janine wasn't as good an aide as she is, I'd keep her around just for her coffee." He reached over and pushed a button. "Two cups, Janine—make it three, if you care to join us."

"I just finished making it, Dominic," the slightly metallic voice answered from his desk. She was at the door in just a few seconds, a coffee tray easily balanced overhead on the palm of her right hand.

"Nicely done," I said as she smoothly set the heavily laden tray on the desk and then poured and handed the ambassador and me each a cup. I took a sip, then added cream and sugar until it looked like tan milk.

Way back when, I used to drink it black, being a purist at heart. Purity doesn't last around the Dutchman.

"Thank you," she said, smiling. "I put myself through college waiting tables at the Playboy Club, if you can believe that."

"I've swallowed larger improbabilities. Like the sun rising in the east."

"Mmm. Nice man."

"Business, Janine. You can seduce Lieutenant von du Mark some other time." His brow furrowed for a moment, and he gave the slightest of shrugs.

"En route?"

"No. You're not going."

She looked me straight in the eye. "Pity."

The tone of their exchange made me suspect that the Dutchman's loudly voiced suspicions were wrong; if the two of them were carrying on in private, they'd be more careful in public.

(Not that it makes any difference, but I later found out both that I was right and that Ambassador Vitelli's own preferences made Janine's prettiness irrelevant to him, except abstractly.)

"Tell me, how did that . . . ." Vitelli's voice trailed off.

"Bastard? Son of a bitch?" I supplied. "Poor excuse for a human being?"

". . . *ever* become an officer?" With long, aristocratic fingers, he smoothed down the front of his tunic, his hand pausing at the gold-and-green medallion resting against the center of his chest.

"Damned if I know." Once I'd figured out how to work the CS system without leaving an obvious audit trail, I'd tried to break into the Dutchman's Personnel records, but without any luck. Pers records are tough. "But I do know how he gets away with it, Ambassador."

"Oh?"

"There's an unwritten law in the Contact Service, Ambassador. It goes like this: 'if you're good enough, you can get away with anything.' The Dutchman thinks he's the best officer that the Service has ever had, and that he can, therefore, get away with anything. The minor reason he puts on the show is to prove that to himself. And to everyone else, maybe.''

I wasn't sure about the last. I don't think the Dutchman ever gave a damn about what anyone else thought.

Janine raised an eyebrow. "*Minor* reason? What's the major reason?"

I smiled at her, making a mental note to have some flowers sent to her. Red roses might be a bit much— orchids, perhaps? I've always liked beautiful women, and I've a particular affection for anyone who will throw me that kind of straight line.

"Because he *is* a bastard, of course."

"Of course."

II

I caught up with Bar-El and the Dutchman at the New Anna shuttle pad.

A quick glance at the lift board showed me that it was another two hours until the next personnel shuttle up to *Magellan*, although there was a cargo shuttle taking off in a few minutes.

Norfeldt waved me to a seat. "Take a load off, Emmy. Bet five quid you didn't get her phone code."

"Done. But that was a sucker bet, Major." I pulled the slip of paper out of my pocket and waved it, just out of reach. "If I didn't have her number, I wouldn't have bet."

The Dutchman nodded as he reached for his wallet. "Good point. I'll take it off you later, at poker."

I ignored the attempted distraction. "What are you really up to, Major?"

The Dutchman eyed me slyly. *"Moi?* Nothing in particular, Emmy. Just getting ready to be the sacrificial lamb." He took a deep breath. "I'm going to get myself and my special team the hell on *Magellan*, and we're going to take a ride out via SolGate to AlphaCeeGate and then the new Gate—for once not being locked up as though we're contagious—after which, you, the big Hebe, and I are going to climb into our scout, and peacefully go out to meet the Xenos, and then get our asses fried to a crisp, which will prove to the TW Council and the Navy beyond a doubt that there's no way to open communication with the Xenos, which will trigger a second Xeno War that humanity just might win, and will at least attempt to cover humanity's collective butt when we *do* run into some superior civilization." He leaned back against the wall. "Why do you ask?"

"Just curious." I looked over at Bar-El. "You're going along with this?"

"I . . . don't make those kinds of decisions, Lieutenant." Bar-El shook his head. "Not my department, sir."

"Second lieutenants don't sir first johns, jewboy." The Dutchman spat. "And you don't try to mess with Bar-El's head, Emmy. He's only provisional—his oath is to Metzada, not the Thousand Worlds. As long as he obeys orders and doesn't make any trouble, his paychecks and/or his Service life insurance goes to paying Metzada's trade deficit."

"Correct, Lieutenant." Bar-El nodded slowly. "I wouldn't want there to be any misunderstanding."

"Understood."

"Two hours to liftoff." The Dutchman stood, pulling a deck of cards out of his tunic pocket. "Let's get aboard, see if there's some money around. At least we don't get isolated on this one, thank God."

"Huh?"

The Dutchman handed the flimsy back to me. "Reread the orders, Emmy. Looks like Dom didn't want to either leave us alone for the voyage out or get locked in with us—suspending of nonintercourse rules doesn't mean you get to bed the girl. All it means is that we're human, for once."

III

There may be places where a Service officer is made to feel less at home than in a Navy battlecruiser's wardroom, but, if so, I don't want to know about them.

Part of it is prejudice. Perhaps on both sides: we tend to think of the Navy as a bunch of pasty-faced, soft-bellied, effete automatons; they think we're crude and rude past understanding or forgiveness.

Mmm . . . maybe that isn't prejudice, after all.

I think, though, that we put each other on, at least a bit. Sitting at the first officer's table, I decided that under normal circumstances, this assortment of ensigns, j.g.s, and full lieutenants wouldn't wear *that* much cologne; after just a couple of weeks, it'd surely foul *Magellan*'s air conditioning.

But I did say it goes both ways.

"More roast?" Ferret-faced Lieutenant Hardesty smiled with patently false geniality, dabbing at the corners of his mouth with his napkin. "You seem to be dreadfully hungry, Lieutenant von du Mark, almost to the point of . . . oh, never mind." Since Commander Bender was on watch, the head of the table had gone to Hardesty, along with the obligation to try to make me uncomfortable under the guise of being a good host.

There really isn't a lot of precedent for social protocol between Navy and CS people aboard a Navy ship, but we were improvising just fine, thank you, to the credit of both services.

"Why, thank you, my dear Hardesty," I said, lifting my plate to accept his unintended offer to carve. "If you

would, a bit of well-done? Blood-rare beef is so . . .
dreadfully, dreadfully barbaric. Wouldn't you say?'' Since
the Navy was going to treat me like something that crawled
out from the gutter, I had two options: either be sloppy
enough to nauseate them, or even more after-*you*-my-
dear-Alphonse than they were.

Now, while I can be messy, the Dutchman was holding
up the Service's dignity from that end: over at the captain's table—as senior CS officer present, his status was
with-but-after Captain Arnheim and the ambassador—
puffing on a cigar, the Dutchman was hacking away a
piece of roast with one of the spare Fairbairn knives. Not
his own knife; you use your own assault knife *only* on
something living you want to make dead in a hurry.

With a shadow of a scowl, Hardesty took up the carving
knife and started slicing.

I guess I just could have let it all slide. Akiva Bar-El
didn't care. He just eyed me soberly, with perhaps a hint
of amusement, while he continued putting away enough
calories to power a small city. Occasionally he'd let himself go enough to shake his head and mutter something
suspiciously like *goyisher kopf*, but nobody chose to acknowledge that. Safer? Not really; the big man wasn't in the
service to take offense at a few words and end up cashiered for fighting. But he didn't find it necessary to
advertise that fact, and I didn't see any need to point it out
to the Navy folks.

Hardesty finished slicing, and stacked enough beef on
my plate to feed two Akiva Bar-Els.

I wielded my silverware deftly enough to make Mother
proud, and nibbled at a forkful. ''I say, Hardesty, that's
most generous of you. Allow me to return the favor.'' I
picked up the platter of lyonnaise potatoes that Hardesty
had been glancing at—apparently he liked lyonnaise potatoes, but was exercising admirable restraint. I stopped
myself. ''No, no, I'm dreadfully sorry. My apologies,'' I
said, helping myself to a heap.

Sitting next to me, Ensign Rodriguez' plate contained

only a politeness helping, which he'd barely touched. "Oh, I see you've finished yours, Ensign. Please," I said, plopping some onto his plate.

I took a mouthful and washed it down with a long drink of water. "When one leads such a . . . sedentary life, it must be difficult to keep in shape." I eyed Rodriguez' waistline, which, to be fair, sported only a tiny potbelly. "Very difficult."

Physical fitness is another bone of contention between Service and Navy personnel, as though we need one. Now, the Navy folks do try to stay in reasonable physical condition—TLGA, transient low-gee aesthenia, is a chronic danger—but they don't have to stay in top shape the way Service people do. Nor are they encouraged to display the kind of arrogant cockiness that comes with CS khakis.

Out of the corner of my eye, I caught Captain Arnheim repressing a grin, and then giving out the tiniest of sighs. I've always found Navy ship commanders to be a different sort than regular officers and files. I guess it's that they have to exercise a bit of independent judgment, be able to think for themselves. That's the way ship command had worked for millennia; by the time you can send home for orders, you'd better have made the right decision anyway.

Although I do have to wonder how four stripes can turn a humorless automaton like Lieutenant Commander Bender into someone like Captain Arnheim. What do they do to them? Drugs? Electric shock? Tell them they don't have to play drop-the-soap anymore? I guess that makes ship commanders sort of kindred spirits to CS men, although I'm sure they'd deny it and I'd definitely rather not be quoted as admitting that.

But I think it's true. "Precedent is no excuse for failure" is something I would have expected Captain Arnheim to understand.

In any case, it was easy to figure why none of the officers at my table was choosing to take overt offense at my occasional veiled insults: they were under orders to avoid incidents, and you don't take offense at what a dead man says. The assumption they were making was that the Dutchman and I, once we hit the new system, were going to button ourselves into our scout and go out and get blown away by the locals, which would allow *Magellan* to Gate back and pick up the rest of the Fleet—in effect, using the Dutchman and me as a tripwire.

I sipped more of the water, wondering if Janine had known that that was the plan, or if Vitelli had kept her in the dark. Perhaps even the light bit of flirting was intended to distract me from thinking things through; you don't want the Judas goat chewing through the rope.

No complaints, mind; the universe is a nasty place.

My head said there wasn't anything to worry about, not more than usual. The Dutchman wasn't worried; his consumption of booze was up—which, by the way, is the difference between a heavy drinker like Norfeldt and an alcoholic like my Aunt Gertel.

There had to be some sort of fix in, but what? There was always one possibility: there wasn't any trick to it at all, and this was going to be both Norfeldt's and my last assignment.

One of the reasons they teach you martial arts at the Academy is for the mental discipline. Now, I was no expert, but I could reach in and find the quiet center, just abaft of my solar plexus.

Unfortunately, my quiet center was just as fucking scared as the rest of me.

But damned if I'd let the Navy know that. "Allow me to pour you some more water, Lieutenant Chang," I said, picking up the water pitcher and pouring slowly, careful of the Coriolis effect. My hand was steady as a rock.

Not my gut; just my hand.

Enough of this, I decided. It was about time that Norfeldt and I had a face-to-face. Right after supper.

But first, a bit of diversion. "Hardesty, Hardesty . . . damn me, but that name does sound familiar. We used to have a gardener named Hardesty, but he was arrested for molesting little girls. I'm *sure* you're not related. . . ."

I found the Dutchman in the armory. He had kicked the Marine armorer out, and was busy checking the action on a Korriphila 10mm pistol, of all things. I could have understood it if it was the forty-four Magnum—that was part security blanket for the fat man—but the Dutchman's often gone on about how if you put decent loads in an automatic, it's more likely to jam than fire right. .

I disagree—for my taste, the Korriphila Ten Thousand is the best conventional pistol made, a hair better than the Ruger Ultra Blackhawk II, which is a revolver, not an automatic—but my preference is just a lay opinion; I don't have the Dutchman's knowledge of or interest in single-shot slugthrowers. I prefer automatic weapons—wireguns, miniguns, whatever—anything where you hose instead of aim. Aiming means you can miss; hosing is a lot more accurate, in the long run.

Norfeldt opened a box of 10mm Glaser Safety Slugs and began to thumb them into a clip.

"Why the Glasers?"

He pretended not to hear the question.

Again: I'm no armorer. One thing I *do* know, though, is that loading an automatic with the old-fashioned Glaser Safety Slugs that the Dutchman prefers for revolvers isn't a good idea—while Glasers have great stopping power and create enough *Sturm and Drang* to scare to death whoever they don't hit, the oversized charges can jam up the action after only three, maybe four rounds.

If your preference is for semiexotic ammunition, much better to use Geco-BATs or Expandos—or Penetrators, if you're either planning on shooting through walls or more concerned with the size of the hole you blast through the target than with stopping power.

"Major . . ." I didn't bother trying to keep the reproach out of my voice. "What are you doing? If I'm not being nosy, sir."

"You're being nosy." He set the clip down on the table in front of him, then picked up the empty pistol, working the slide. "But pull up a chair, kid. I'm checking out some weaponry—what does it look like?" He followed his own advice, lowering his bulk into a too-small chair.

"Weaponry? You think we're going to get in close enough so that a pistol is going to do any good?" A pistol isn't a silly weapon for intership warfare—it's not that *good*.

I shook my head. "Now, if you want to talk about jury-rigging something on the scout so we can get some decent free-space use out of the weapons turret—"

He snorted. "There are three very large marines on watch on either side of the launching-bay lock. The orders are that everyone except the guards—particularly CS personnel—stays on this side."

He slammed the clip into the pistol's butt with a solid *chunk.* One of the Korriphila's flaws is that the cartridges are held slantwise in the clip—it can only hold seven of the oversize rounds, giving you a maximum of eight if you carry one chambered.

"You seem to be forgetting that this isn't a regular contact, Major. We're not supposed to decide whether or not it's safe to open contact with the Xenos—we open contact with them, period."

Norfeldt shook his head, several of his chins waggling in syncopation. "You'll grow up someday, Emmy—if you're lucky. There's lots of ways to communicate. Think about it for a moment. Way back when the original UNEG team tried to open contact with the Xenos, what did they do?"

"Any reason to believe that they got creative?"

"No."

"Then it'd be like our own First Team operations; doctrine hasn't changed." I shrugged. "Standard doctrine is to take up an orbit and signal. Radio, message laser, blinking lights."

"Right. And what happened next?"

* * *

I tried to visualize it. Back then, there had been only one level of Gate, all deep in their gravity wells like Old SolGate. That was before we destroyed Old SolGate and put the present SolGate high in the gravity well, leaving the only path from Outside to Earth via the high-and-low AlphaCeeGates.

Well, that isn't strictly true. It is, at least theoretically, possible to travel from any Gradient One Gate to where new SolGate swings in orbit, somewhere—never mind exactly where—about halfway between the orbits of Jupiter and Saturn. You'd have to hit the alien Gate just at the right angle, at just the right speed, of course.

But, even so, you can't repeal the law of conservation of energy—it's not safe to travel through shortspace from a Gradient One Gate to a Gradient Two gate. Moving suddenly from deep in a gravity well to high up in another gravity well would cause you to lose energy; the Gradient Two Gates—new SolGate and Inbound AlphaCeeGate—are both high in their respective star's gravity wells. There's no effective direct route from any star to Sol except via Alpha.

Transfer from, say, Ophiucus A's tightly orbiting Gradient One Gate to New SolGate and it'll loose energy, freezing the vessel and all its occupants solid. Make the mistake of transferring from OphiGate to one of the even more tightly orbiting trapGates inside the orbit of Mercury, and the reappearing energy will fry you in microseconds, long before Sol does.

It had been simpler back then. The UNEG team had just cruised through Old SolGate to the new Gate, not needing to transfer via the fraternal-twin AlphaCeeGates.

They had looked at the new system, and listened and sniffed . . . and found something.

And then they had signaled. Peaceably—it would be impossible for a culture sufficiently advanced to be a danger to see a small scout as a threat. Stripped of its deetee tanks, the scout wasn't much larger than the first space shuttle—which wasn't the *Columbia*, by the way: it was the *Enterprise*; look it up—and couldn't have been mistaken for a warship.

So why had the Xenos attacked?

I looked over at the Dutchman. "I don't know, dammit."

"You're right."

"Huh?"

"You *don't* know," Norfeldt said. "And neither do I. But my guess is that they did something a lot like what that Vitelli is going to order the two or three of us to do."

"I think—"

"*Shut up*." I'd seen the Dutchman hostile before, but it was always . . . casual. Until now: now, his nostrils flared and his face grew beet-red.

"*I'll do the thinking around here, shithead*. You just obey orders like the good little boche you are, and keep your fucking mouth shut. We've got another two weeks until we hit the Xeno system—homeworld or not—and I want you in shape by then. You've been on vacation for too long. From now on, it's one full shift of workouts with Bar-El, every day—half in the low-gee gym, half in the skin gym. I've given him your training schedule. Just do it, don't think about it—that's an order, Lieutenant."

He looked at me. "I can't hear you, Mister."

"Aye, aye, sir. One question, though?"

"Yes?"

"How about Bar-El? If you're expecting some hand-to-hand, well—"

The Dutchman shook his head. "The Hebe is not trustworthy—you heard him: he serves Metzada, not the Thousand Worlds. So you keep your mouth shut around him—if he asks you what time it is, you don't know and you don't want to know. Understood?"

I quelled the vague glimmering. I didn't want to know what was going on. The Dutchman had just told me that, in so many words.

"Aye aye, sir."

IV

Low-to-no-gee hand-to-hand combat is a little like something out of a classic comic book, like Sharkman, Captain America, or American Flagg! or whatever. In all those comics—still one of my secret vices—the heroes leap around, jumping their own height in the air or higher, somersaulting into a fight.

Low-to-no-gee combat is something like that. Unless you're as good as Akiva Bar-El.

I kicked hard off the padding—think of it as a wall, ceiling, or floor; it's all a matter of taste—and spun half over, lunging feet first at where he hung in midair, floating just about a meter from the curved wall.

He seemed to shift microscopically to one side, then, as I went by, he tapped me lightly on the calf, groin, solar plexus, throat, wrist, and forehead. There was no doubt in my mind that any of the blows could have hurt me badly, if this had been for real.

I let my knees give as I hit the opposite wall.

"Even allowing for skill differences, you still have to consider the mass, Lieutenant," he said. "You have to strike a vulnerable point as you pass by me, or my greater mass will tell."

He untied the towel from around his waist and mopped at his forehead. In low to no gravity like that in the tubular gym at the center of rotation of the *Magellan*, surface tension tends to keep sweat on and around the body, unless you turn up the longitudinal fans high enough to blow you against the outflow, which would defeat the purpose of a freefall gym.

So, you sweat, and if you don't mop down frequently, you suffer.

Stripped to the waist, Akiva Bar-El was even uglier than he had been clothed; the coiled muscles under his mottled skin were powerful, certainly, but hadn't been developed with looks in mind. His hairy chest was dotted with a greater variety of scars than I'd ever seen on a human being. He didn't talk about it, but it couldn't have been from Metzada Mercenary corps work—he had arrived at Alton at eighteen.

He beckoned me over. "Alternately, think about this," he said, taking up a zero-gee parody of a karate stance. His back was straight, and his knobby left fist extended at the end of an arm, his right fist at his side—but his feet were curled up underneath him, like a perching bird.

"Conservation of angular momentum." Slowly, he mimed a punch, pulling his left arm back as he thrust his right arm forward.

That was the only movement. "Now, if you don't compensate with the other side," he said, demonstrating, "you spin opposite to the direction of force. Try again."

I measured the distance by eye and tried again, kicking off the padded walls, trying to time my spin so that I could catch him off-guard with a backfist.

"Very nice," he said, easily catching my wrist with a monkey-block. "Again, sir. If you please."

V

I was in the middle of a nice dream. I didn't know it was a dream, and later it turned out that Janine really did enjoy—

"*Three hours to AlphaCeeGate,*" the speaker blared metallically, then shut off. Some idiot had apparently put my cabin speaker on the distribution list for the ETA announcements.

"Wonderful," I said, and then rolled over and tried to get back to sleep. We wouldn't be on for days after *Magellan* went through to the new Gate, and maybe if I could sleep through transfer I could avoid the nausea.

Just as I was dozing off again, the speaker chimed again. And again. And again.

I slammed the heel of my hand against the stop button. "Shut the—"

"*What?*" The Dutchman sounded more amused than angry.

"Hmm, nothing, sir."

"*Lieutenant,*" the Dutchman's voice rasped, "*you're on. I want to see you on the bridge one half hour before transfer. Full uniform. Repeat: full uniform. Understood?*"

"Yes, sir. Bar-El?"

"*Negative. I've ordered him to check out our scout—got both the ambassador's and Captain Arnheim's permission. Repeat: full uniform.*"

That was ridiculous. A weapons officer doesn't check out the scout—the pilot does.

"Major, what's up?"

Strangely enough, the Dutchman didn't bite my head off for asking. Unusual for him.

"Vitelli has been assuming that there's not going to be a bunch of Xeno ships around the new Gate. I'm willing to bet that the skipper won't count on it. I'm not."

"Why should there be?" It was possible that the Xenos had a system-wide skywatch that could spot a distant Gate being built, but I doubted it.

And, if so, what could we do? Either the Xenos would give us a chance to make contact *very* quickly, or it would be up to the Navy crew to use the *Magellan*'s armaments well enough to give us a chance to escape back through the Gate.

I didn't like it at all. If the Xenos knew where the Gate was, they could blow it. Granted, the destroyer on watch around Outbound AlphaCeeGate had been sending robot probes through, and none of them had failed to return, but it was still possible that the Xenos would blow the Gate in the time between when the last probe went through and when *Magellan* would go through.

If that happened, we wouldn't come out in the system we were supposed to. We'd come out of another singularity, most likely one inside a stellar-mass hole.

I shrugged. No need to worry about that. It would be over before we'd feel it.

"Why should there be?" I repeated.

"Honestly, I don't know," the Dutchman said. *"But I'm hoping that there are. I'll see you on the bridge."*

"But—"

"Shut up and get dressed. Norfeldt out."

There wasn't much sense in talking when nobody was even pretending to listen. I shut up and got dressed. In full uniform. Which, in my case, meant both Fairbairn and wiregun.

VI

During my short period in New Haven, I'd gotten in a few hours on the TWS *Immovable*, the constantly upgraded mockup of a Thousand Worlds battlecruiser's bridge that, together with its supporting facilities, occupies a good portion of Rickover Hall.

But most of that time was spent as the bridge talker, which is probably the least skilled job in the Navy and certainly was the lowest-status job aboard the *Immovable*; perfectly suitable for a shitlisted plebe. My real experience in out-atmosphere flying was in a Contact Service scout, a vessel a four-hundredth the mass.

Add to that the curious stares and the frankly hostile ones that I was getting from the bridge crew, and you'll understand why I was about as comfortable on the bridge of the *Magellan* as the Dutchman would have been at a meeting of the Thin Man Society.

Well, actually there was a difference. The Dutchman wouldn't have cared.

There was another difference, actually. I had no doubt I could handle the helm of the *Magellan*—if it flies, I fly it. Period.

"Lieutenant von du Mark." Captain Arnheim's voice was brisk, deep, and businesslike as he spun around in his chair. I quickly swallowed my third Paradram.

"Sir." The skipper of the *Magellan* had no real authority over me, except for the fact that he was the skipper of the *Magellan*.

He seemed to figure that that was enough. "Contact Service officers are not normally found on the bridge, and particularly not during transition," he said. Someday, I'm going to learn that tone; sort of a cross between a question and a bland but accusatory statement.

"Yes, sir. Major Norfeldt told me to meet him here during the second shift. Something about Ambassador Vitelli . . . but if you're ordering me off the bridge, I'm not going to put up a fuss, Captain. I try to get along, sir."

One thing I don't envy about regular Navy people is that they have to keep DP people happy; I was hoping that the half-lie—yes, half; I didn't finish it, after all—would keep him from pressing the matter.

"I've noticed that last, Lieutenant." Arnheim rubbed at his chin with a beefy hand. His nails were neatly trimmed, and his fingers scrubbed almost pink—one of the badges of upper-ranks Navy. He pursed his lips together for a moment, then let himself notice that I was wearing khaki and leather, not zero-gee fatigues. He didn't notice the Fairbairn or the wiregun; those were just part of the uniform.

I could almost hear him thinking that there was no point in giving a dead man a hard time.

"Well, just keep out of the way, Mister. I don't antici-pate any serious course change, but when the horn blares, you strap yourself to that wall. I'm not having you bounc-ing around in freefall. Understood?"

"Yes, sir." Not aye-aye, just a simple yes.

"Very well." He turned back to his panel, which gave me a chance to look at the main screen. I'd seen Gates before, of course, but this was different. Normally, a Navy escort releases the scout a few tens of thousands of klicks away—and scouts are tiny little ships, with small view-screens, not like this one, that was easily eight meters by five.

On the screen, Outbound AlphaCeeGate grew slowly. It looked like a huge metal flower, aluminum foil cupping a node of black.

Superimposed on the bottom part of the screen were the numerical and flightpath displays. Momentarily, a red flash of a deflection vector appeared, then vanished. It must have been a tiny one; I couldn't feel any sudden boost change at all, just the slowly diminishing gravity as the ship's main-axis flywheels were spun up to take the spin off.

The direction of the pseudo-gravity changed too; the boost wasn't being cut back.

It didn't make any difference to the bridge crew; their panels were swing-mounted to their couches.

I kept an eye on the helmsman, the closest thing to a pilot that a Navy ship has. Most of the time a ship is flown by numbers—nav data extracted from the computers, decisions fed back in by typing numbers into a keyboard. Sort of like making love wearing an overcoat; no real flying, no magic time.

But *Magellan* was a battlecruiser, and there are times when a battlecruiser really has to be flown. There was a sure-enough joystick clipped to the side of the helmsman's panel, and steering yokes over at the fire control panel.

"Okay, Stan," Arnheim said to the commander strapped in the couch off the internal panel, "I want the rest of the spin off, pronto, then get the shields up."

Commander Bender turned to the talker. "Sound ack stations; spin off minus two minutes; time to impact by the minute, now."

"*Acceleration stations,*" the speaker near my ear blared as the talker mouthed the words into his microphone. "*Spin off warning. Spin off warning. Two minutes to spin off . . . impact minus eleven minutes.*"

Bender punched some numbers on his panel as the elevator door hissed open, and the Dutchman stood there in his poorly cut khakis and leathers, his automatic in a shoulder holster, Vitelli at his elbow.

While Vitelli made his way over to Arnheim's command chair, Norfeldt blew a cloud of smoke onto the bridge ahead of him as he floated his way in and grabbed a handle next to me.

"How they hanging, Emmy?" Norfeldt muttered.

I looked over at him. As the steering jets came on, I

went dizzy for a moment. Mind you, I can snap a bird into a barrel roll blindfolded, but I always have a bit of dizziness trouble when I'm not the one flying.

"Impact minus nine minutes. Shields up."

A battlecruiser's ablative outer skin is always brightly polished, then sprayed with some reflective compound—the highly reflective shields that are extended from the hull are just another attempt to give the ship a few more moments of life if it finds itself in a laser's path; the shields can't stop a fist, much less a projectile.

"Impact minus eight minutes."

"Where's Bar-El?" I whispered.

The Dutchman shook his head. "I still don't trust the big Hebe. He's not an obedient little kraut, not like some people I could name."

"Maj—"

"Shut up." The Dutchman quirked a smile. "Just curious—could you fly this thing?"

I didn't let myself think why he was asking that. "Yes, sir." *And a fine time to be asking, Major,* I added silently. What if my oft-repeated claim that I could fly anything had been nonsense?

The elevator hissed again, and two of *Magellan*'s marines made their way out of the shaft. Standard procedure aboard a Navy vessel—I guess it gives them something to do during transition.

"We're on the money, Skipper," Bender called out. "Computer will be cutting drive in ten seconds . . . mark."

Ten seconds later, *Magellan*'s drive cut out, and we floated rapidly toward the Gate that was growing ever larger in the forward screen. The silvery sheen was picked up and reflected on the sweaty faces of the bridge crew as we approached the singularity.

The last minutes are always the worst. Just a few scant thousandths of a degree off and . . .

I took my tube of Paradrams out of my pocket and brought it to my mouth, tonguing another one.

The Dutchman produced a gas hypo. "This is actually more useful," he said.

"I'm fine, Major. Just fine."

"*Thirty seconds to impact.*"

"Not for *you.*" He jerked his head toward the two bored marines, who floated near the bridge elevator. "It might help them."

"*Twenty seconds to impact.*

"*Ten seconds to impact . . . seven, six, five, four, three, two, im—*"

"*—pact.*"

We were through, and the main screen went wild.

Among the stars, three points of light blinked on and off like a dancer's strobe.

The captain must have ordered sensor ports opened and chemical sensors set for boron; ugly red letters flashed on the screen, superimposed over the field of stars:

BORON DETECTED

I swallowed. Three lights.

"Holy Mother of *Christ*—we got three bandits, Skipper." Numbers flashed so fast I couldn't follow them. "Two of them mass half a million tonnes each, the other's not much smaller than we are—"

"I don't want your goddam opinion, I want—"

"—eleven hundred thousand tonnes, sir."

I didn't know Norfeldt could move so quickly. One moment he was floating next to me, the next he had kicked off the wall and bounced off the two marines, flipping end over end toward the captain's couch as he left the marines and the two now-empty hypos floating in the air.

"Get the talker's microphone, Mark!"

I kicked myself toward the bridge talker and jerked his microphone rig off his neck as I hooked one leg around the back of his couch. He clawed at me, but I slapped him across the throat, hard, and he lolled back in his couch.

At the fire control panel, Hardesty had already un-hooked himself from his seat and was floating toward me; I ducked under and slammed a bottom-fist into his groin as he passed overhead.

"Everybody, freeze!" His plump thighs locked around the back of Arnheim's couch, the Dutchman had the cap-tain's hands handcuffed in front of him and his Korriphila pressed against Arnheim's head, the safety off, the ham-mer back.

Arnheim smiled thinly. "I don't know what you're trying, but it won't work, Major. —Rush him!"

Bender dove through the air toward the Dutchman, but Norfeldt slugged him with the gun butt, then braced him-self against Arnheim's couch and fired a round into the comm panel.

The explosion of the Glaser was incredibly bright, and incredibly loud in the tight confines of the bridge.

"I don't fire two warning shots," the Dutchman said.

Sparks danced behind my eyes. Nobody moved while the air conditioner swept the acrid smell of powder away.

"Emmy?"

"Yes, Major."

"Order battle stations, please—and take over the fire control panel."

Not the helm? Bizarre. I shrugged. In for a penny, in for a pound.

Vitelli started to speak up, but the Dutchman gestured him to silence. A 10mm automatic's good for that; while the Korriphila is reasonably compact, when it's pointing at you, it looks like it has a maw instead of a barrel.

I donned the talker's rig and thumbed the mike. *"Battle stations, battle stations,"* I said, hearing my voice echoed back as the klaxon started to bark. *"All hands to battle stations."*

"Bring the ship about, Mister," the Dutchman ordered the helmsman.

* * *

The fire control officer was a young lieutenant I'd met only casually. He was just about my age, I guess, but Navy people look a lot younger than Contact Service folks do.

He drew himself up straight in his couch. "No, *sir.*" *You're not moving me out of this chair while I'm alive*, he meant. The pride of the Navy.

I drew my wiregun and thumbed it to single fire. I probably wouldn't have to shoot him, but I wouldn't miss him by much.

"Belay that, Mark," Arnheim snapped. "Bolanger, get out of the couch."

"Everybody over by the racks," the Dutchman said as I strapped myself in. He floated over to where I had belted myself in the couch and quickly exchanged his Korrophila for my wiregun before it could occur to anyone else that he didn't dare fire his weapon while unanchored.

"Set the lasers for one one-ten-thousandth full," he said, "then get the fuck over to the helm and strap yourself in."

"Yessir." I did. One-ten-thousandth power wasn't enough to fry a healthy fly. If the Dutchman didn't want to sucker the Navy into fighting this battle for us, what the hell was he doing?

I unshipped the stick and clicked it into place, then closed my eyes for a brief prayer while the roll pedals rose out of their places in the couch. This was a battlecruiser, massy, not a light scout—I'd have to remember about all that inertia.

"Bring her about, Mister von du Mark. Vector in on the largest of those babies—evasive."

"Aye-aye, Major." I thumbed the mike—"*Boost warning, boost warning*"—punched for a variable acceleration centering on a half-gee, and heeled hard over on the stick.

The universe spun as *Magellan* waddled around.

Magic time. It doesn't matter how, when, or what. I fly.

"Gimme a hand, here," the Dutchman said, beckoning

to Bolanger, the helmsman. "Center that fucker on the crosshairs for me, then—

"Captain?"

Later on, at the disciplinary hearing, they played the bridge tape. Frankly, I didn't believe a lot of what I heard. For one thing, my voice came out a lot smoother and calmer than I remember it.

For another, I *know* it took forever for Arnheim to decide, not the scant two seconds the tape shows. It wasn't a difficult decision for him, although it was a hard one.

But the Dutchman had been counting on the captain's understanding something about command: that the only thing worse than a successful mutiny was a mutiny in progress. In one case, the wrong decisions are likely to be made; in the other case, there can only be stasis until the mutiny is settled one way or the other.

Condition Blue is not a situation where you want arguments over who is in command.

Better to have the wrong person in charge.

"Do it." Arnheim nodded slowly.

Vitelli finally spoke up. "Captain, this is—"

"Mutiny, and a successful one so far. Now shut your mouth and let the mutineers do their job, Ambassador." He gave me a thorough glance as though to say, *We'll discuss this later, Mister. At your court-martial.*

At that moment, I sincerely hoped so.

"Fire!"

You never actually see the laser beam, not in a vacuum— there's not enough dust to reflect it. But sensors can pick up the ever-so-faint glow of the hydrogen ionized by the beam, and display it on the screen.

The phony blast caught the main battleship squarely, and played across its hull for a few seconds before it skittered out of the beam.

"Now, full power—and get those crosshairs as close to

the ship as you can, *without* touching. I don't want you to singe the buggers, just let them know you could.''

"Captain . . . ?''

"Do what he says, man, and snap to it.''

"Fire!''

This time, a real blast barely missed the Xeno battle-cruiser.

"And again.'' This time, the Dutchman dialed for one-hundredth power. With a gigawatt-plus laser, that was enough for a sliding blast to score the bright surface of the battlecruiser, but not enough to burrow into the hull.

"Cross your fingers, Emmy, and get ready to roll us the hell out of the way.''

A light lanced out from the Xeno battlecruiser; alarms clanged as it played across our hull, then died as I rolled the *Magellan* into a long turn.

"Damage report, dammit,'' Arnheim barked out.

An ensign looked up from his panel, astonishment written all over his white face. "None, sir. Absolutely none.''

"What's our speed relative to the big boy?''

"We're separating at . . . a bit more than a klick-second, Captain.''

"Mark, bring it down to zero.—If you don't mind, Major.''

"Listen to the nice man, Emmy.''

"You got it, Major.''

That was a job more properly belonging to the computer, but I didn't know how to set up the program. It took me five minutes to wrestle the ship around and kill the relative speed between us and the cruiser.

And all the time, the Xeno ships lay still, in a loose formation around the Gate.

"Start the signal laser blinking, Emmy—and you can turn the helm over to Captain Arnheim.''

The Dutchman slid the clip out of the wiregun, signaling to me to do the same with the Korriphila. Which I did, careful to work the slide and pump the round out of the chamber. Mimicking the Dutchman, I unclipped my

Fairbairn's sheath and pushed it slowly toward the floor, along with the now-empty automatic.

"Raise 'em, Emmy." Norfeldt held his hands over his head. Absurd, in the low gravity.

"Captain," the Dutchman said, "we surrender."

It was more than a week later that Vitelli came down to visit the three of us in the brig, causing me to miss a flush.

Yes—*three*. While Bar-El wasn't implicated in the mutiny, Captain Arnheim had ordered him jugged as a material witness, just to be on the safe side. I don't think Akiva particularly minded; he was up a bit in our ongoing poker game, although Norfeldt was the big winner.

As usual.

At the moment Vitelli tapped against the bars, I was looking down at a pair of red aces and three little hearts, debating whether to draw to my two aces or go for the flush. It's not one of my favorite decisions to make under the gun.

Norfeldt had raised before the draw. The Dutchman bluffed a lot; it could have meant anything from a five-card Yarborough up.

I'd just decided to go for the good hand when Vitelli's tapping interrupted.

"Good afternoon, gentleman." Vitelli's eyes were so shadowed that he looked like a racoon; the armpits of his zero-gee coverall were stained with sweat and white with salt. "I see you're adjusting nicely."

"Vacationing," the Dutchman said. "Now, what's your draw, Emmy?"

"Emile," I said, reflexively throwing away the three little hearts. It's hard to split aces; goes against the grain. "Three."

"Vacationing?" The ambassador raised an eyebrow.

"Vacationing. I take it things went well with the Xenos."

The ambassador started to open his mouth, and then closed it. I later found out that he knew then that these weren't exactly our Xenos—same species, different subspecies, different culture—but that the Sesss could be just as dangerous if handled wrongly. Think of them as Nungs, rather than Rhades—the differences may be important to them, but not to outsiders. To us, the main importance is that the Sesss *can* be reasoned with, from a position of reasonable power.

But he didn't say that.

What he said was: "I'm going to see if I can get you shot."

The Dutchman snorted. "I don't think it's going to work, but you're welcome to try."

I'd wanted to go over defensive strategy, but the Dutchman insisted that it wasn't necessary. Strategy is for the chickenshit at heart, he'd explained.

Norfeldt dealt me three cards. A jack, a ten, and a three—and the jack was the jack of hearts; if I'd gone for the flush, I would have gotten it.

"What do you mean?"

"We're fucking *heroes*, Dom baby—the kraut and I are going to get DSDs to go along with, mebbe, a slight reprimand. I'm going to see if I can get a DSD for the Hebe, too, but I doubt if—"

"Meaning no offense, Major," Akiva said, "but I'm not interested in a Distinguished Service Device. I don't need your medals, sir."

The Dutchman looked him over. "I could do with a bit less polite disdain, hear?" He turned back to Vitelli. "In any case, you don't shoot heroes."

"You—"

"It's a rule; look it up. The Thousand Worlds is going to be too busy putting us through tickertape parades to—"

"You're mutineers!" Vitelli hissed. "And cowards."

"We're Servicemen." The Dutchman smiled. "And what we did is we fucking made it possible for you to open contact with these semi-Xenos."

"You tried to bring *Magellan* into combat with their battlecruiser! All so that Captain Arnheim would have to retreat back through the Gate." Unspoken: *All to save your miserable lives.*

The Dutchman shrugged.

"Major? Can I?"

"Go ahead, Emmy. But he won't understand. It took you a while, and you're not a piece of chickenshit Navy crud."

I turned to Vitelli. "Mr. Ambassador, we could have actually fired to damage the cruiser. But we didn't. That'll show up on the bridge tapes. Instead of going out and trying to get ourselves blasted, we announced to the Xenos or whatever they are that we could hurt them, but didn't.

"Different signals apply to different cultures, Ambassador. You should know that."

"They could easily have taken it as a call to combat!"

"Possible. They *did* take it as a warning shot, no? It said: we can hurt you, and we will if we decide to, but we choose not to, for now. That's how they took it, right?"

Vitelli pursed his lips. "Correct."

"And because they did, you were able to open communications with them."

Low-powered comm laser flickering from ship to ship, pulsing with the on-off beginnings of understanding between two very different species, each able to do immense damage to the other; each terrified of the damage; neither willing to accept the damage that the other could surely do . . .

"But how did you know that would work?"

The Dutchman could have said that our last contact with this species hadn't worked out the way it should have, and that the refreshing honesty of a battlecruiser firing what was clearly a series of warning shots would tend to suggest to any rational species that the owners of such power concealed even more.

Or he could have said that since what had been tried the last time we met the Xenos clearly hadn't worked, it was best to try *something* different.

But he didn't. All he said was: "Just a guess, Dom."

A few minutes later, the Dutchman reeled in the pot with two small pair.

A couple of months later, both of us picked up our DSDs.

And reprimands, of course. No big deal; the CS is always much more impressed with results than with ruffled Navy and ambassadorial feathers.

But as General Dupres was pinning Norfeldt's medal to what passed for the Dutchman's chest, I saw the two of them grinning at each other. Over the clangor of the band, I tried to listen to what the general was saying to Norfeldt. It sounded like: "This is the first time I've given an award to a major for being gutsy enough and dumb enough to stare down a whole alien species."

No. It couldn't have been that, it couldn't have been—I *know* that I heard the Dutchman's answer:

"Yes sir. The last time, I was a captain."

I didn't wait around to ask. The Dutchman wouldn't have answered.

Besides, I had a date.

Janine.

Interlude

Destination: Captain Manuel Curdova, TWCS
Contact Service Administration
Bureau
Building 5, Level O
VNYC

Routing: I8OORQW5R43EE83

Origin: First Lieutenant Emile von du Mark,
TWCS Aboard TWS DA GAMA
(#LC2562)

Subject: Personal

File Created: 21 October 2244

Dear Manny,

An advance wish of <u>Felice Navidad</u>, to you and
your family, from an envious friend.

Please convey my love to Veronica—and would
you do me a favor? I have no idea whatsoever
of what kind of present would appeal to Emilita—
my experience with women doesn't extend to two-
year-olds—but <u>damned</u> if my namesake is going
to suffer for my ignorance. I've sent instructions to my family's lawyers; they'll process any
voucher you send them.

And don't repeat <u>don't</u> repeat <u>DON'T</u> you dare
spend less than a hundred quid on her; you're
not the only <u>ricon</u> in the Service. If the girl does
not grow up spoiled, it won't be because <u>I</u> haven't
done my best.

Really, were something to happen to you and
Veronica, I hope that I'd take my responsibilities seriously enough to apply discipline when
necessary. But as things stand, I'm perfectly
happy to continue to be soft-in-the-heart-and-
softer-in-the-head Tio Emile and come bearing
presents. Since I won't be there this Christmas,
please do it for me.

*   *   *

I'm glad you liked Janine, by the way. In answer to your unvoiced question as to how serious it is, the answer is that I—we—don't know, and it's probably going to take a while for us to figure it all out, what with me being offplanet so much of the time. Things seem to mesh, granted—and you should try a bit of offplanet work yourself, my friend; everything they say about Homecoming Syndrome is true—but she's the out-of-sight-out-of-mind type, and I have no illusions about that. I'm always very careful to let her know when I'm going to be Earthside, and let her call me. Not that I particularly give a damn, but I don't want my nose rubbed in it again.

Yes, again.

We had a little mixup late last year, and I walked in at the wrong time; she and some brainless bodybuilder were—never mind. In any case, he decided to take umbrage, and after the ambulance left, we talked it out. Janine was appropriately apologetic, I was appropriately apologetic, and we both decided that me having key privileges was perhaps not the best idea that either of us had ever come up with.

I don't believe in one-way faithfulness, though; the next time I'm on leave, I think I'll check into Virgin Mary's for the first couple of days.

Yes, it could fall apart. Easily. I wasn't really seriously suggesting that you spend a lot of time offplanet, Manuel—look at what it does to marriages. Which I guess is the answer to my own situation. I don't know if Janine and I will ever make it official, but it can't make sense doing that until I take a desk assignment or hit retirement age.

Frankly, I can't imagine that she'll wait that

long; and I'm <u>not</u> hot to give up having live controls in my hands.

Hmmm ... her new boss has her shuffling
around almost as much as I am, which could work
either way.

I almost envy Akiva Bar-El; it must be nice
knowing that your wives are always going to
be waiting at home.

As to how I spend my shipboard time, well, I
blush to admit it, but I've been letting my Qualification Courses slip of late. There's a rhythm to
a Team's shipboard life—both on the transport
and in the scout—and I've fallen into it.

My alarm is set for at 0845—not exactly like
0500 at Alton, eh?—in order to let me get first
crack at the head, after which I eat a very light
breakfast and go through my aerobic exercises
while the others are washing up.

After that, I take a break until 0930, when
Akiva Bar-El is through with his warm-up, and
then he and I get a half hour of hand-to-hand, if
we're aboard our transport—the inside of a scout
is no place for even mock combat. A half hour of
hand-to-hand is plenty with Bar-El, and at that
it's really more like ten one-minute sparring
rounds, each with two minutes breather between
them. I wouldn't want to go more.

At 1100, I exercise my limited seniority by getting the first shower, in order to be first at table for the complete breakfast, which is finished
by noon, at about which time the Dutchman
stumbles out of his quarters.

After which, we put the greene baize slipcover
over the table, and get to the main business of
the day:

Poker.

*　　*　　*

Speaking of which, the evening session is about to start, and I've got a lot of catching up to do. It isn't losing the money I mind as much as it is the Dutchman winning.

Got to do something about that.

Best wishes,

Emile

File Transmitted: 26 October 2241

Dutchman's Mirror

I

The four of us were playing poker in our quarters when the subject of cheating came up. The stakes were high: one quid ante, ten quid limit before the draw, twenty-five after.

Personally, I would have preferred to play for less, but that's another tradition: Contact Service officers *always* play for high stakes.

When the shit hit the fan, I was down about three months' pay.

The other two weren't so badly off. Donny N'Damo, the little comm officer, was about even, and Akiva Bar-El was up a trifle. The big winner, of course, was the Dutchman. Sitting across the table from me, he grinned at me as he held the deck of cards in his left hand, the fat index finger of his right hand making little circles near the pot.

He let out a cloud of cigar smoke in my direction, but the table sucked it up before it could get to me. One nice thing about playing poker in low-gee is that the table is connected to the outflow, which not only sucks the cards and chips down to its surface, but prevents poker smog from forming in the room.

"You're stalling, Emmy," the Dutchman said. "Bar-El checked. The bet's up to you."

I looked at my hand. Three kings. Not exactly a bad hand to be dealt; the trick was how to maximize the win.

Best to try a little bit of a sandbag. "I'll open for a tenth."

To my left, Donny N'Damo tossed his hand face down to the surface of the table. "Too much for me. I can't even beat Akiva."

Bar-El shook his head slowly. "You will *not* peep me, little man. Not again."

"*Shut the fuck up, the both of you.*" While I wished he'd use his toothbrush as often as he used profanity, the Dutchman rarely yelled; he saved it for special occasions.

Like this one.

I studied the robin's-egg-blue paint on the low ceiling. I didn't really want to be here.

The Dutchman started by letting his breath out in a low sigh. "N'Damo, you do not use your psychic abilities," he said, slamming his palm down, his Team Leader's ring hitting the table like a gunshot, "*which the goddam service trained you in*, to cheat other members of your Contact Team. You're a fucking valuable little spade, but you're *not* valuable enough to get away with that. Understood, shithead?"

Donny looked shocked. "I was just kidding, Major. Honest. I wouldn't, really—"

"Sure." Norfeldt snorted. "Sure."

I knew that Donny had been joking, but the Dutchman never gave anyone the benefit of the doubt. Ever.

"And you, Lieutenant Bar-El—"

"*Sir.*"

"*Shuddup when I'm talking to you, jewboy.* You don't bully your teammates, you don't threaten your teammates. All of our lives can depend on how well N'Damo does his job. I don't repeat DON'T want him spooked."

"Yes, Major." Bar-El's ugly face was as impassive as ever, but his jaw twitched.

"Now." The Dutchman said, still white-lipped. "It's up to me. I'll see your tenth and make it a quid."

It took me a moment to realize that he was dropping the subject and getting back to the game.

Bar-El looked at him for a long moment. "I fold," he said, dropping his cards face down on the hissing table.

"I don't," I said. "Reraise ten."

"Ten?"

"Ten." I pushed the chips into the pot, one by one.

"Call," The Dutchman said. "Cards?"

Time for a little cleverness. "I'll play these," I said. The chances of improving trips are poor; I had a better chance of the Dutchman thinking I was bluffing.

"Shit." The Dutchman snatched up the deck and dealt himself a card. Then he picked up his own hand and threw a card away before slipping the drawn card on top of the other four. Theoretically, you're supposed to discard before you draw, but the purpose of that is to make you decide before you see your new card or cards; it's not just ritual. Since the Dutchman had made his decision before picking up his new cards, I didn't complain, although I was wondering why he wasn't looking at his new hand.

Probably just a little ploy to rattle me.

"Your bet, Emmy," he said.

"Two quid." Never mind what you hear about not betting into a one-card draw—just don't bet heavily, most of the time.

Norfeldt pushed a stack of chips into the pot. "I'll raise twenty-five."

"Without looking?"

He smiled at me. "I kinda liked my hand before. Emmy. Hope it's still okay."

It was up to me.

I thought about it for a while. Norfeldt *hadn't* looked before betting into my allegedly pat hand. But he'd been bluffing me all night.

Damn.

I thought it out. Clearly, unless he was bluffing again, he'd started with two pair, or four of a kind—or the Dutchman was holding a kicker with trips. Dishonest plays would vary from absolute garbage, to a pair of aces and trash, to some sort of open-ended straight or four-flush, hoping I'd jump the wrong way.

I could forget about four of a kind. The Dutchman would have sandbagged with fours. Besides, you can waste a lot of mental sweat and lose a lot of folding money worrying about low-probability disasters.

Well . . . my trip kings left him with only two honest winning possibilities: three aces, or some sort of back-in hand, both unlikely.

I didn't like it, but I wasn't going to be bluffed this time. Not with better than fifty quid in the pot; the odds said call.

"Call," I said, flipping my hand over. "With three kings."

Norfeldt scowled at me as he flipped over the card that he had just drawn. The scowl vanished; he smiled down at the queen of hearts.

Then he flipped over his other four cards, one by one. All hearts.

"Well, well." He smiled. "A nice semibluff, Emmy. If you dropped, I got the pot. And if you called, I still had one chance in—"

"Enough, Major." The light on the wall over the door turned amber. There were shouts in the corridor outside, the rustling sounds a crew of sailors pulling themselves along in low-gee make, like bugs in a pipe. Down in the hold, they'd be swarming frantically over our scout—as though they'd just gotten the word about an assignment that we'd been on for hundreds of hours.

I assembled the deck and handed it to the Dutchman. "Are you going to brief us on this one, Major, or do we play it by ear?"

I almost smiled. I sounded like Buchholtz, way back when.

The Dutchman eyed me momentarily. He wouldn't have taken that from N'Damo on Bar-El; I was more than a little curious about whether or not he'd take it from me.

"Fair enough." He stored the cards in their box and stashed his chips in their bag before shutting off the table. He settled back in his chair, folding his fingers over his ample belly.

"Actually," he said, "it looks like an easy one."

I snorted, and he pinned me with a glare.

Easy one? We were Third Team, this time. As usual. A

Third Team goes into a stellar system only after a First Team reports a promising planet, but a Second Team hasn't resolved the question of whether or not it's safe.

The question isn't whether or not it's deadly to Servicemen; we're expendable. A permanent colony of thousands of men and women, billions of quid of equipment, and a lot of promise is somewhat less expendable.

The human race is *not* expendable.

Norfeldt smiled, a little. "Well, Emmy—"

"Emile."

"—it started out as a fairly standard contact. A gammaseries ramscoop dropped a hole around this dinky little K1. First Team found an interesting planet close in, about half an AU."

I did a rapid mental calculation. "Sounds a bit hot. Maybe twenty percent more light than—"

"Asshole. I *wish* you wouldn't do that," Norfeldt said. "You telling this, or am I?"

"Sorry."

He looked at me for a long moment.

"Sir."

"Better." The Dutchman pulled a cigar from his pocket, unwrapped it, and bit the end off, chewing contemplatively for a few moments before gently spitting the gobbet in a slow parabola toward the far wall, where it stuck. He wouldn't have been quite that sloppy aboard our scout, but the Dutchman always liked to leave something behind for the Navy files to clean up.

He pulled his lighter from his pocket, fired it up, and puffed the cigar to life, blowing smoke my way.

"So," he said, "First Team got into the orange-peel orbit, did the photo-sweep. Things look to be not that bad. Three decent-sized landmasses. The two smaller ones— 'bout the size of Australia—hug the equator, but the most northern looks like it might be okay. Dirtball's about three-quarters seas, alternates between heavy vegetation and desert on land. Some animal life, but no sign of civilization. Laser spectroscopy picked up some metals—

iron—looks like good hematite—bauxite, and maybe some silver, gold, etc.''

He looked pointedly at me. That last had to mean germanium, but the Dutchman couldn't say that in front of Bar-El or N'Damo. Comm officers can never qualify for the Three Monkeys, and the Metzadan had never fully taken to conditioning. They would never have been told that germanium is the only element a grabfield can get enough of a grip on to squeeze into a quantum black hole, the core of a Gate.

I didn't know how much of the stuff went into the making of a gate. Tonnes, certainly, presumably tens of tonnes, possibly thousands. I might have figured it out—I'm not particularly weak in math—but most of what's known about barrier physics, transitional mechanics, and five-space rift topology is tightly wrapped in a high-security blanket.

Norfeldt blew another cloud of cigar smoke my way. ''So, Second Team went in.'' He sat back, silent.

I was about to set myself up as the straight man—as usual—when Donny saved me the trouble.

''They didn't come back?''

''Very good guess. No, they didn't come back. Therefore, no report. Any further dumbass questions?''

I shrugged. ''I don't see what you're so worried about, Major. There's only three possibilities. One''—I held up a polite finger—''Second Team blew it, somehow or other. Accident, equipment failure, the pilot slammed the scout into a tree, something. Two'' —another finger—''there's some sort of serious problem. We find it, we duck it, and we get out alive. Blow the Gate on our way home.''

''And three?''

''Easy. We screw up, and die. Is there a fourth?''

He had that smile on his face. Again.

''You're a good kid. Emmy, but you're still green as all hell.'' It was one of the few times that I'd heard a patient tone in the Dutchman's voice. He took his cigar out of his mouth and tapped the soggy end against the gold oak leaves on his collar. "I'd like to dip these suckers in silver someday, Emmy. Or maybe even get myself a nice silver chicken. Forgetting the bullshit First Team Stuff, how many contacts have I run?"

"Eight, that I know of, if you don't count—"

"Precisely. And how many were Drops?"

That wasn't his fault. Luck of the draw. Norfeldt was a drunkard, a smoker, and a boor—but he was also the best Contact Team Leader that there was. Period. "Hey, that isn't your fault, Major—"

"Don't you fucking dare try to comfort me, you little Prussian asshole! *Pfah*." More work for the Navy files. "Say that I'm unlucky. Maybe the powers-that-be'll decide I'm too unlucky to ever get promoted." He tapped at the spot on his uniform where General Dupres had pinned his DSD. "I got a trunkful of medals; I'd like a fucking *promotion*. I can't afford to keep losing contacts, not even if they're legitimate Drops."

Donny N'Damo started. "But—"

"Shuddup, suntan. So, we're going to take your fourth option, Lieutenant von du Mark. If this is a Drop, we do not drop it. We either fix the fucking problem, or we come up with a recommendation to fix it. Understood, Mister?"

He'd said it. It hung in the air. In the back of my mind, I was composing a memorandum to General Dupres.

Subject: CONSERVRULREGPROP, Gross and Indecent Violation of by Major Alonzo Norfeldt, TWCS. It has come to the attention of the below-signing officer that . . .

The Dutchman would be broken out of the service, maybe; riffed, at best.

And then I thought about it a bit more. About getting a new Team Leader, someone with a bit more civilization than the Dutchman. But maybe a little slower, maybe a bit more obedient to the rules, some Regulation Charley asshole who was more interested in seeing that the job was done by the numbers than that it worked. Somebody without the brains or balls to play roll-the-dice on *Magellan*'s bridge.

I looked over at Bar-El's ugly face. He was smiling.

It wouldn't have been convenient to have a different Team Leader on that Xeno operation, his smile seemed to say.

Right. We would have done things by the numbers, properly, and been properly blown into small bits.

"Well?" The Dutchman raised an eyebrow. "What's it gonna be, N'Damo?"

"I just peep, Major. I don't . . . get involved in anything else."

"Emmy?"

"Emile." I threw up my hands. "Shit, Major. I don't like it, but count me in."

In triumph, he turned to Bar-El. "Well?" The Dutchman had probably read Bar-El's smile the way I had:

Wrongly.

Bar-El opened his mouth, then closed it, and shook his head. "I suggest that you find an appropriate excuse to keep me aboard *De Gama*, Major. I'm not going with you."

II

A scout sleeps four.

Da Gama's aft hold was at the boundary between the quarantined section and the Navy's clean part of the ship. Through the plexi window, I could watch the Navy files swarming over the scout. They reminded me of a bunch of roaches on a dead rat.

Although that wasn't a fair comparison. The scout was a trifle cleaner when they were done, and clearly I'd rather have it tested and fueled than not.

But a scout sleeps four.

Bar-El glided into the compartment, moving carefully,

precisely, as he anchored himself to a stanchion before throwing me a precise salute. "You wanted to see me, Lieutenant?"

I returned the salute. "At ease, dammit. This isn't a zero-gee parade ground."

He nodded, reaching out to turn up the outflow as he pulled a slender tabstick from his shirt pocket and puffed it to life, savoring each puff individually. "Thank you, sir."

The tradition in the Contact Service is that second lieutenants don't call first lieutenants "sir", unless the first john is his commanding officer—a CO is always sirred. But Akiva Bar-El tended to ignore the tradition, and often sirred me, either unconsciously or insolently. I guess I should have straightened him out, but it really didn't bother me; besides, this wasn't the time to go into that.

"We go in two hours, Akiva." The air currents pushed us around just a little; we waved like two fronds of seaweed. It made him look as though he had been drinking. "Three is not a Team."

He looked uncomfortable, and then angry. "We're supposed to have the option to Drop."

"A Contact, or the Service? You dropping out of the Service?"

"No, sir. I don't think I have to. I don't think Norfeldt can give me the choice of either going along with his rule-breaking or dropping out of the Service."

"So you're dropping Norfeldt?"

He grinned a little, but it was only a facial expression. There was no feeling behind it. "It's a question of who drops who first, Lieutenant."

"We don't have time for a lot of discussion, Akiva. You can't drop it now. Seven weeks ago, sure. Or even a month ago, when we could have switched off with a team on Nueva. But now, now's a damn fool time—"

"Now?" For a moment, anger flared behind his bushy eyebrows. "Now's a damn fool time for Norfeldt to throw this at us. At me. Turning a Contact into a Drop is about as important a weapon as we've got, sir. The Dutchman is trying to take that away, sir, and asking us to stick our necks out.''

''He's sticking his neck out, too, Akiva. Any one of the three of us could send in a report—''

"I understand that, sir. Don't think I haven't thought about it. But that is not the point. The point is that if there's trouble out there, it would be suicide to go, under Norfeldt's conditions. Maybe he should just think about scrubbing—three isn't a team, after all.''

"He trusts us.'' Little beads of sweat bobbed in the air in front of my face. One of them touched my eye and became a tear.

"And Metzada trusts me. As I have reminded you, sir, I am in the Contact Service, First Lieutenant von du Mark, for the good of Metzada. For the offworld credits that my salary brings if I live—''

"Noble.''

''—or for the insurance policy that the Thousand Worlds will pay off on if I die in the line of duty. Not for Norfeldt's glory.'' He took a last puff from his tabstick, then flicked the ash toward the outflow before wetting his thumb and forefinger and crushing the butt out.

"And not for your glory, either, *Deutscher*,'' he said quietly. "Do you understand me, Emile von du Mark?''

In that moment he could have killed me without hesitation or regret. It wouldn't have mattered in the slightest that I was an Austrian national, and that my family had been Austrians for two centuries. It wouldn't have bothered him that what he called the Holocaust had ended more than two and a half centuries before I was ever born.

None of it would have made a difference; in that moment, his people's history was a very personal matter between Akiva Bar-El and me.

But the moment passed.

"This isn't a noble mission,'' he said. "Its purpose is to get Norfeldt some light colonel's leaves. And perhaps to get some captain's bars for First Lieutenant Emile von du Mark?'' He said that last without any rancor, as though it wasn't an insult. Bar-El was just idly considering what my motives really were.

He shrugged as he remembered that he didn't give a damn what my motives really were.

"Stay in the scout," I said.

He looked at me.

"We'll all four go down, but you just stay in the scout. I'll . . . explain it to the Dutchman. You just sit tight, and hit the panic button if things go to hell." I shrugged. "If there's anything. Second could have blown it; it could be a walk-through."

"Norfeldt would let me?"

I snickered. "No. He'll ride you unmercifully. But he couldn't report you, not under the circumstances. And how would he make you go out? Do you think there's a chance he'd pull a gun on you?"

Bar-El smiled vaguely. "Not twice." He looked out through the plexi window for a moment.

And then he said, "Interesting."

They let us into the hold a short while later. Donny looked surprised when he climbed into the scout and saw Bar-El strapping himself in his couch. It took him a lot of effort not to say anything.

Bar-El just lay quietly, endlessly stropping his Fairbairn knife. Which may explain why the Dutchman didn't say anything.

Then again, it may not.

Da Gama split her gut and pushed us free.

I let the scout tumble for a few minutes before I hit the gyros, and then impatiently canceled most of the rotation with the attitude jets.

We waited while the battlecruiser slid away, an antennaed, blistered expanse of steel and aluminum hundreds of meters wide and long.

The Dutchman nodded to me. "The auto checks. Engage."

I hit the autopilot—"Engaged"—and then sat back to enjoy the view.

Alpha burned distantly in the aft monitor as AlphaCeeGate grew in the forward screens, filling the forward view.

Appearances were deceiving.

I wasn't looking at AlphaCeeGate through a curved transparent port on the scout's command deck, but through a monitor that could show me the starscape in hues of radio, gamma, or IR, or, as now, just relay the visual spectrum, brightening reference stars.

And the Gate wasn't an immense solid cup, though it was both immense and cup-shaped. The aluminum power-screens surrounding it for a thousand klicks were so thin that the entire silvery disk could easily have been folded up and packed into the back of my old Hummingbird. Unfolding it would be another matter.

Somewhere, at the center of the disk, was a naked singularity, a true hole in space, carefully maintained by a field generator. The scout slipped unerringly into the approach that would put us through the hole, and out through the right Gate—

I hoped. Fervently.

The Dutchman sat alongside me, N'Damo behind us, and Bar-El in the pit alongside N'Damo, still honing his sticker. Norfeldt turned to N'Damo. "You going to need a sickbag, N'Damo?"

"Yessir."

Norfeldt passed him one; Donny taped it into place.

"You, Emmy?"

"That was just the first time, Major." It's ridiculous, absolutely ridiculous. I can eat a meal of squid salad, snap a trainer through an Immelmann on instruments alone, and then land it and hang upside down while munching on caramelized sweetbreads—but I can't go through a goddam Gate without getting nauseous.

Unless I'm loaded to the gills with Paradram. "I'm just fine, Major," I said, palming another pill and swallowing it.

"Here it comes," he said. He folded his hands across his belly and cracked his knuckles, rubbing his Team Leader's ring against his class ring.

As he spread his hands to grip the arms of his couch, the light flashed off something I'd never noticed before, a bezel on the palm side of his Team Leader's ring.

A bezel. If he held his hands right, he could read the faces of the cards that he dealt, using it as a shiner.

An expensive bezel. Any disreputable jeweler would have ground the bezel into the ring for less than a quid. It had already cost me six months' pay.

To hell with Major Alonzo Norfeldt's lieutenant colonel's leaves.

The Gate rushed up toward us, until all we could see was a gleaming expanse of metal. I had to keep reminding myself that it was mostly just thinly aluminized nothing.

"Here it comes, children," he said. "Standby for im—"

"—pact." The main screen was full of stars. I keyed in the aft monitor. As the new Gate shrank in the distance, we could see the new sun behind us, huge and red.

"I thought you said it was a small star," Donny said.

The Dutchman growled at him. "Shut up."

"It is, Donny, but we're close up." But he wasn't listening anymore.

I hadn't heard a sound from Bar-El, and when I turned to look at him, he eyed me neutrally. Kind of strange, really; if I'd been raised under Metzada's high gravity, I would have found low-gee hard to get used to.

My own stomach was churning, a condition that didn't improve as the scout quivered, spun slowly on its gyro, and started to accelerate at about a tenth of a gee.

The Dutchman turned to me. "Mister von du Mark." He leaned back, his thumbs hooked over the only fastened button on his uniform shirt, just above his belly.

Damn him. Here he was, looking more like a vagrant than a CS officer, and he wanted to get formal.

"What is it?"

He eyed me slowly, deciding whether or not to straighten me out. On the negative side, I already had enough on him to get him cashiered.

But on the positive side, it was his Team. "What did you say, Mister?"

"Sorry, *sir*. What is it, sir?"

"Better. Now . . ." He punched a few keys on his panel, then raised an eyebrow. "I have it as just about four days until we're in orbit around the dirtball. Does that square with your calculations?"

"Yes, sir." I could read ETA TO ORBIT 97:32:15 as easily as he could.

"You think you can handle things for a watch?"

Piloting in an atmosphere can be tough; sitting around watching a computer match velocities with a planet isn't. A dog can handle a vacuum-side watch. "Yes, sir."

"Then I will retire to my quarters," he said, unbuckling himself from his couch. "You have the conn. Wake me in eight hours."

"Aye, sir."

He nodded to N'Damo on his way out, who threw him a startled salute.

Bar-El eyed him levelly, but neither of them said anything.

III

"Where you want to put her down, Emmy?"

"Emile, sir. And I don't know. Two obvious possibilities: near Second's scout, or as far away as we can get."

It seemed mostly green down there. While the ratio of land to water was about the same as Earth's, all of this land was concentrated in only three landmasses, all on the same side of the planet.

And a lot of it forested. That's what First Team's report had said. It hadn't seemed so significant when I'd read figures off a screen. Looking down on a forest as large as Asia, wreathed in cloud, lapped by a turquoise sea, the planet looked choked, like a diseased fruit.

"N'Damo?"

Donny tapped three times at his panel; a point on the screen pulsed red once, twice, three times, and then went green again. "Just the echo transponder. Nothing else."

The Dutchman tapped his temple. "Anything up here?"

"Sorry, s-sir." N'Damo shook his head helplessly. "I'm just an esper, Major, not a psychic. If there's anybody down there, they're a good thousandth of a light-second away, and we're not in a close enough frame to communicate by psi. Unless you believe in simultaneity."

Norfeldt snorted. "I'll believe in any damn thing if believing'll let me communicate—never mind, never mind." He turned back to me. "What do you think about aiming for the transponder?"

I thought about it. Again.

"Well," I said, "plus side: we know Second's shuttle got down there. Add a bit for the transponder still being active, add a bit more for the desirability of seeing if any of Second are still alive, and then subtract a *hell* of a lot for the fact that they almost certainly aren't."

"How about an LZ?"

I didn't like the fact that I couldn't find any decent-sized clearings groundside. When I run for God, one of my campaign promises will be that every world gets a lot of plains. "We may have to burn our way down the last few meters. And that's tricky."

A shuttle has to make an almost totally unpowered landing; you kick in the belly jets not much more than a klick out. Use too much juice in landing and you won't have enough to rendezvous skyside.

"Or deadly." The Dutchman decided. "Okay, we'll try

for their neighborhood. Gimme some mag and show me where you were thinking about doing it.''

I zoomed in and tapped the surface of the monitor. "Right about there. Visual shows solid forest, but I'm getting some anomalous IR reads—well, actually it's IR absence—like there's a swath of cool air nearly a klick wide and a few hundred klicks long.'' I punched up the IR overlay and let him see for himself.

"Like a river. Except that we'd be able to see a river.''

"Right. And here," I said, pointing, "we've got some kind of heat concentration.''

"A fire?" Donny asked. "Or a volcanic vent?''

"Again, nothing on visual. Be a damn funny volcanic vent—too diffuse. Reads about forty-five degrees.''

"Could be an inversion layer or something. Any other ideas?''

I shrugged. "I've seen villages that look that way from orbit. Not alien, but a Hmong one, back in Siam.''

Norfeldt chewed on his cigar for a long moment. "You're assuming the danger is natives.''

I spotted that trap. "I'm assuming nothing. But you're the one who taught me that it's almost always the sapients we've got to watch for.''

"I did, at that. Any other concentrations like that one?''

"Yes, but that's the most distinctive.''

He grunted. "All right. Do it.''

We burned the air on our way down. The early part of a reentry is almost as simple as point-to-point in space, but by the time you brake down to about Mach 2, the artistry comes in. There's always something unexpected.

This time, it was some sort of jet stream at about fifteen klicks up that tried to carry us away from the area we'd decided on as an LZ. I had to light the engines to get us out.

"I don't see any clearing, Emmy," the Dutchman said.

I glanced at the monitor. "There isn't one." I reached my left hand over to the small joystick mounted between the Dutchman's panel and mine, brought a cross of light onto the screen, put it where I wanted it, then punched for a probe.

"But give me a minute," I said over the roar of the probe blasting away. I banked into a turn gentle enough that it wouldn't force the belly jets on.

"Emmy—"

"Shut *up*, sir." One of the few privileges of a pilot has is to get the damn shuttle down or up without having his elbow unnecessarily joggled.

I held the turn for a full one-eighty, then took a quick glance at the energy display on the monitor. The max range line fell short. I spread the wings fully open and the line lengthened, but it didn't quite touch the probe's destination. Damn. Not enough energy to make it to where the clearing was going to be in a moment.

"Hold on." I slammed my left fist down on the ignite button, gripping the stick tightly as the nose intakes wheezed open, then let the rams roar long enough to bring the line forward to where it was supposed to be. "We're right on target, Major."

I shut the engines down to a quiet murmur.

Despite the fact that the shuttle is a variwing and not a rotary-wing, landing a Service shuttle is more like a hot copter landing than anything else.

In a copter, you make a hot landing by skimming in just a few meters over the ground toward the LZ, the swinglocks off the stabilator so that you can bring the nose way up, and then, at the last second, you pull back hard on the yoke, while you kick in every last bit of throttle and pitch your rotors can take.

Do it just right, and—assuming that you don't have what's appropriately named a "catastrophic rotor failure," in which case you're dead—the nose of the bird will pitch up while the fast-milling rotor, now almost perpendicular to the ground, will quickly slow your forward speed to nothing.

After that, you have to push the nose forward and down, while you ease off the throttle just right.

Do everything perfectly, and in just a few meters you can go from skimming quickly over the ground to settling gently down on it.

Do anything wrong, and you *will* dump the bird.

That's with a copter. There are some big differences when you're landing a shuttle. A rotary-wing craft doesn't have a stall speed in the way that fixed-wings and variwings do; stalling happens when your rotors aren't spinning fast enough for their pitch, not when the craft isn't moving forward fast enough. You can learn by trying a wimp version of a hot copter landing; hell, a normal horizontal landing *is* a wimp version of a hot landing.

But a variwing shuttle can stall just as easily as a fixed-wing craft; you practice a hot shuttle landing the same way you execute one:

At better than four hundred klicks per hour.

We came in low over the forest, the shuttle's wings fully spread. Less than a klick ahead, the smoke from where the probe had detonated puffed its way upward into the sky.

At just under three hundred meters out, I hit the program button to shut down the mains and fire up the belly jets.

My right hand on the stick, I curled my left hand around the throttle as I pulled back hard on the stick, pushing the throttle almost to the wall.

The belly jets roared, better than three gees worth.

As forward speed dropped off to nothing, I pushed the nose down and pulled the throttle back, balancing her down on her belly jets. You hear how hard it is to pull off a hover in a copter; I *never* want to hear any of that bull from someone who hasn't tried it in a shuttle.

"Not too bad," the Dutchman said, as we dropped toward the smoking clearing. "Not too bad at all."

Vines and branches scraped across the hull. Leaves

bloomed in a silent explosion. Something orange, with wings and two huge, startled eyes, flapped across the monitor's field of view.

Our rate of descent slowed, but I couldn't see anything on the monitors.

"Radar, Major."

"One hundred meters, Emmy."

But one hundred meters to what? I glanced at the radar display, but all it showed was flatness. "Okay, here we go." I eased up on the belly jets. "Give me landing pods, full extension."

The Dutchman snapped a toggle; the pods ka-*chunk*ed into place. "Got 'em. Fifty. Forty. Thirty. Twen—ten."

I pushed the throttle forward again, hard.

Steam geysered as the scout dropped lightly to the muddy riverbank and settled itself firmly into the mud.

IV

"River. A fucking *river*." Inside the bubble helmet of his environment suit, the Dutchman, chewing on an unlit cigar, shook his head. "Ridiculous. Who ever heard of a forest canopying over a whole fucking river?"

Well, that explained the inversion layer—it was the cool air flowing over the river and its banks.

He turned up the floodlight and pointed it toward the river.

"I've seen ugly," the Dutchman said. "But this is fucking *ugly*."

Off to port, the river undulated gently in the light from the floods. The carpet of green microorganisms layering it was unbroken from bank to bank, and for as far upriver as our lights reached. The trunks of the trees rooted on the riverbanks were white as freshly cleaned bones. There seemed to be several different species, but the leaves of each were variations on the same theme: pale filaments waving from slightly thicker stalks.

By the time sunlight reached down here, it was about as strong as moonlight.

"*Look* at this place," the Dutchman's voice came over my headphones.

"I've got a bad feeling about this," I said, kicking at the mud against the scout's side.

"I've heard that before," the Dutchman said, standing beside me. "Biogel looks okay, though," he said, tapping at his compboard.

"Then you want to do without seals?"

The Dutchman snickered. "No, thanks." Biogel is, chemically, a very close approximation of human tissue, and it is subject to damage by almost all biological and chemical contaminants that can hurt you and me. But the key word is "almost."

"How are we fixed for takeoff?" he asked, as though the notion of fix-it-or-else was gone.

"Not good," I said, lifting myself up into the airlock and holding out a hand to help the Dutchman grunt his way in. "Not good at all."

The lock closed; the Dutchman punched the wash button and jets of blue soapy water, amply laced with biocides, dissolved our oversuits and washed them and the dirt away, leaving our E-suits and his compboard gleaming.

"Except from my point of view—the belly jets are badly clogged." If they were free, a light blasting might clear them, but with all the weight of the scout pressing them into the mud, trying to blast free was just asking, begging for a backblast explosion.

There was another choice. "I can flip up to vertical by blowing away the landing pods, and then fire off the main engine."

"Yeah? So what's the problem?" The soapy spray ended

and the first rinse cycled quickly on. I felt like a pair of pants.

I closed my eyes as the UVs and IRs came on, killing, I hoped, any residual bugs from outside. Even through the insulation of the suit, I could feel the heat waves play across my skin.

"Well, Emmy?"

I shrugged. "I've only done it in practice; I don't know of anyone ever using the panic button to do it. I could check the program, I guess."

The inner door swung open, and we stepped into the scout, slapping away the residual water, removing our bubbles and backpacks and enjoying the smell of sweet, conditioned air.

"I see what you mean about how that's good for you. You just became about as expendable as the whole Team." The Dutchman considered it for a moment, patently thinking of trying to force Bar-El into going out. "Well, lucky for you the whole fucking Team's expendable; wouldn't want you to feel left out. How far away do you say we are from Second's shuttle?"

Since my hands were busy, I nodded to N'Damo; he tapped a query on his keyboard. "About eighty klicks from the scout. About two from the heat source."

Taking a bulb of coffee and putting it in the heater, I glanced at the screen. Right now, the only clear and present danger to us seemed to be dying of depression. Nothing was moving out there but the river's algae carpet and the occasional falling leaf. The birdlike creature I'd seen lived up above, where it was green and the sun shone very bright.

Donny opened the heater and handed me the bulb.

"Thanks." I sipped it. Presugared and precreamed, it tasted like it was predrunk. "You getting anything?"

Donny scratched his head. "Just a trace, off that way." He pointed; I glanced at the inertial compass. South.

He gestured vaguely. "Animals sound like that, sometimes."

"That where the heat source is, Emmy?"

"Emile. And yes, sir."

"All right, we'll take a walk that way. Have the skimmer—" The Dutchman stopped himself. The ground-effect skimmer with its mounted recoilless was a finicky piece of hardware; it was too likely to get its fans caught up in the muck outside. Besides, it was Bar-El's job to run the skimmer.

"Okay," the Dutchman said. "N'Damo, get three lifters and three cutters."

He thumbed the weapons case open and pulled out his forty-four and a utility belt filled with plastic quickloaders.

"I'll get them, Major," I said. "I want to get a pair of floating lamps and a sample kit."

"What do you want all that shit for?" The Dutchman took two oversuits out of the disposables locker and tossed me the smaller one.

"Because we don't have a Second Team report and I don't like working totally blind." I shrugged into the olive-drab oversuit, then reclaimed my pack and let Donny help me on with it.

"Fine. Long as you carry it."

My point.

I walked into the middle compartment. The curtains to Bar-El's cubicle were open, and he was stretched out on his bunk. He sat up and looked at me.

"This is ridiculous," he said.

"Get me three lifters," I said, walking to the blades locker and pulling out three wirecutters. They looked like broomsticks with griphandles, but when the wire was running along their sides, they could cut through brush and light wood as though it wasn't there.

Bar-El had the lifters ready when I got back to the airlock. Take one each monocrystal-iron lox and hydrogen tanks, add a rocket nozzle, belt controls, a packframe, and a few integrated circuits: instant, if very short-range, air power.

"I should not have let you talk me into this," he said,

helping me into one, then handing me the other two packs. Theoretically, lifters are made to be used with E-suit backpacks and filters.

Theoretically.

"I didn't talk you into anything. You wanted to come." After a while, we sorted the lifter straps and the suit straps out and got everything reasonably tight. "Or maybe you didn't, eh?"

"What is that supposed to mean?"

"Nothing."

"You'd have had the most to lose if we Dropped this one, sir. Even more than Norfeldt. He already has a reputation, a TL ring. But you're a bit of a jinx, aren't you? On your First Assignment, you lost half your team."

"It happens. But it wasn't my team. Not exactly. Since we're into personal revelations, just maybe up there you were just plain scared." I jerked a thumb skyward. "Maybe you still are. But you're a hotshot weapons officer from Metzada who can break board and bones with your bare hands, and everyone you care about would shun you if you turned coward, so you can't afford to admit that you're just plain chickenshit *scared* of a new world, Akiva."

I kicked the door that led to the compartment housing the skimmer with its recoilless. "Which is why I've got to slog through the mud instead of riding that. Doesn't exactly thrill me."

I walked back into the forward compartment. For a moment, I was sure that I'd played it right, and that he'd ask me to wait.

But the door closed, and he hadn't said anything.

Like the Dutchman says, don't make assumptions.

V

We had been working our way along the river, hacking a crude path in the direction my radiocompass indicated, when it struck me, and I chuckled.

"What's so fucking funny, Emmy?"

"Nothing." I shook my head. I had been thinking how, with the white trunks and rattling leaves, the twilight and diffuse shadows, this looked like a ghost forest . . . but that we were the spooks, clattering our way along the mucky forest floor.

It would have lost a lot in the telling, and it wasn't funny to begin with. Not really.

But for a few moments it chased the realization that Second Team was down here, and had been for a while.

Idly, I wondered if Bar-El was listening on the open circuit I maintained with the scout. If we got into trouble, maybe he'd decide to bring the skimmer out and pull us out of it.

Maybe. But that would take time, even skimming along the algae-covered surface of the river. Too much time, probably. Trouble is usually on a quick schedule.

"Hold up for a second." The Dutchman's cutters whirred, as he carved himself and N'Damo a relatively clean place to sit on a rotting fallen log.

I did the same for myself. It was good to get off my feet.

"How do you figure it, Emmy?" I could hardly hear the Dutchman above my own panting. Even with the wirecutters to hack a path, the ground was still soft and squishy; each step was heavier than the last.

Of course, we could have used our lifters, but those

were supposed to be for emergencies. I had only about three minutes of flight time—Donny had a bit more, the Dutchman had quite a bit less.

"Sir?"

The Dutchman's gesture took in the whole of the surroundings. "This shitheap."

"I think I know what it is, but I'm damned if I can figure out how it got this way." My headband was soaked; I reached down to my belt and turned up my helmet blower to push the sweat away from my eyes.

"I don't see how this could be a balanced ecology. We're in some kind of transition phase, maybe a real short one. These sickly plants down here look like they've lost the battle for sunlight. When they die, they fertilize the winners, the giants. But how they've kept going for more than a few generations I can't figure. And it must take more than a few generations to grow some of the giants. We hit the first level of vegetation a hundred meters up."

"I don't give a rat's ass for the fucking plants," the Dutchman said. "It wasn't anything we've seen that killed Second Team."

Donny swallowed hard. It was the first time the Dutchman had admitted out loud that Second Team was dead.

"What about animals?" the Dutchman asked.

I shrugged. "Sarcophages down here, maybe. But I doubt it—plants do that better. Up above, sure. We could find a pretty diverse ecology in the treetops, where there's light to drive an ecology. Down here's a dead-end street."

"Hmm. This is the bottom of the heap and not the base of the pyramid, eh?"

"It feels that way."

Using a pale tree as a crutch, the Dutchman got to his feet. The trunk bent and compressed like wormwood where he leaned against it, and a pale sap oozed out. "But tell me, how do you explain the heat concentration?" He glanced down at his wrist. "Up ahead about two hundred meters."

Donny got gingerly to his feet, as if he wasn't used to using them for walking.

Opening up the sample kit, I used a scoop and a siphon to get a few cc's of the tree sap.

"How many of those do you have filled?" Donny asked.

"About half." I thought he was going to offer to take over sampling for a while, but he didn't, and I didn't feel like asking. He turned his radio off and butted his membrane helmet against mine.

"What do you think?" he asked, in a whisper.

I didn't bother shutting my mike off as I looked around. "I think I'm going to advise my father not to open up a spa here."

"No. Second Team."

I shrugged and turned my mike off. "Dead."

"How?"

"You're the esper. Mmm, lift your hand up. That looks interesting." He lifted his hand from where it had been, out behind him, taking his weight.

The plant across the back of his glove was star-shaped and about five centimeters across. I picked it up with a long pair of tongs and dropped it into a sample bag.

Donny was still looking at his hand.

"Donny?"

"*Listen*," he said. "Listen, *listen*, listen."

I cocked my head. The bubble was a good transmitter of sound—a bit better than air, in fact—but all I heard was rattling leaves, my own breathing, and the quiet whirring of the Dutchman's cutter.

"No. Not here, here." He tried to touch his head through his membrane helmet. Then his eyes widened, and he smiled.

"I . . . hear them upsides. They're coming."

"Major."

The Dutchman was holding his cutter in his left hand, and his Colt & Wesson forty-four Magnum in his right. It occurred to me, not for the first time, that the cutter might make a decent hand-to-hand weapon. "Intelligent?"

"I'm . . . getting words, words, words," Donny said dreamily. His eyes closed, and he started to slump down, so I gripped the back of his lifter to steady him. "But not . . . like us. Everything is . . . together. Everything is now. Everything is here, part of here, now, upsides, here."

I shook him. "Easy, Donny." He straightened, which gave me the chance to let him go and draw my wiregun, all the while wishing that Bar-El and the skimmer were here, together with its recoilless.

"No, togetherhere, togetherhere, they're *friendly*," Donny protested. He put his hand on the wiregun; I jerked the pistol away. "Friendly."

"You sure, N'Damo?"

"Positive. Major, I am. Togetherhere. *Upsides*," he insisted.

"Just tell the buggers to keep their fucking distance," the Dutchman said.

He squinted through the gloom. He was probably thinking the same thing that I was, that as a tactical situation this absolutely, unconditionally sucked—that's a military term for when you have only hand weapons, no support, and lousy terrain. Except when I looked up and down the river, I couldn't see more than thirty meters in any direction, and the muck underfoot hampered my movements.

The Dutchman reached over and snapped a switch on Donny's belt, slaving Donny's lifter to his.

"You sending?"

"Trying, trying." Donny shrugged. "Trying. I am."

The Dutchman's mouth worked for a moment, then he gestured with his cutter. "Make a clearing, Emmy."

I thumbed my cutter on and had started to cut through the brush when a black shape flitted overhead. Then another. And another and—

"Easy, Emmy."

They settled in low-hanging branches. Three, four dozen of them.

"They are . . . very glad to see us," Donny said. "Glad to see us."

They looked like bone-white bats.

They eyed us from the spongy limbs of the surrounding trees. When one shook its wings out I saw that the wing-span was three, maybe four meters, but they kept them tightly folded, accordion-style, against their backs.

Their vaguely canine heads were comically large, as were their taloned feet. The claws were hooked, some blunt as though more for grasping than tearing, some sharp enough to sink into the wood as they hung there. They were each about a meter high and massed maybe fifteen, twenty kilos, max.

"They dangerous, N'Damo?" the Dutchman asked.

"No."

"You sure?"

"You can't lie with your mind, your mind, Major Norfeldt, the Dutchman."

Their faces were broad, with huge eyes and large cupped ears; the eyes were a fathomless, solid black. It felt like they were following my every move, but there was really no way to tell.

"How intelligent are they, Donny?"

"They are aware, aware." He opened his eyes, and his body stopped its weaving.

I didn't like this, not at all. "What say we lift out of here and try again later, Major?"

"Look up, krauthead. We aren't going anyplace right now."

I looked up. The canopy formed by the branches laced together over our heads bent with the weight of the things. And beyond, above them, were hundreds more; at least a thousand, all together.

If the Dutchman had had a cigar in his mouth he would have chewed on it. As it was, he just grunted, reflexively fondling the butt of his pistol.

It was an archaic device, lacking the sophistication and spraying power of my wiregun. But one Glaser Safety

Slug spewing out of the barrel of that ancient piece of steel had more immediate stopping power than all the wires in my gun.

Trouble was, it was a six-shooter, which looked to be at least nine hundred and ninety-four fewer shots than a combat situation would call for.

"We'll stay a bit, Emmy," the Dutchman said calmly.

Some of the tension went out of my shoulders when I saw him holster his Magnum. I did the same with my wiregun. But while the Dutchman thonged the weapon into place, he had left the flap open, and so did I.

One of the chiropterans dropped off the tree, wings outfolded to break its fall, then shuffled and splashed forward until its head was under N'Damo's hand. Donny rubbed the broad head absently, as though he was idly petting a cat, that distant look on his dark face again.

"I'm waiting for word on how smart these chiropterans are, N'Damo," the Dutchman said, looking down distastefully. One of them was rubbing up against his thigh. "They sure as hell don't look bright enough or vicious enough to have taken out Second Team."

"I see a nest, a nesting place, a nest," Donny said. "But they look at us and see them, overthem."

"What the fuck?"

Donny shook his head violently. When he spoke again, he sounded awake. "There's no . . . perception that we're alien, Major, just different. A new, a new species in the forest. They know the trees, the water, themselves. But no abstract concepts—I think they've got a leg up on chimpanzees, but it would be a close call."

"No hands," I muttered.

"Huh?"

"No hands, Major." All the brains in the universe don't do you any good if you can't alter you environment. So there's only a slim evolutionary edge in becoming intelligent if you don't have hands or equivalents. It doesn't take much brains to sneak up on a leaf; it takes a lot more to sneak up on a leaf-eater.

"I noticed." The Dutchman paused. "So where the fuck are they, eh?"

Donny leaned closer to me. "They?"

"Whoever killed Second Team, asshole." To the Dutchman, the threat was always a *them*. Like the other old saying goes: personifiers of the universe, unite—you have nothing to lose but Mr. Dignity.

"They've got a village, Major," Donny said.

"What? You said they were stupid."

He looked embarrassed for a moment, but then his eyes went glassy as he retreated into communion with the locals. "Not a village, really, not a village, Major, village. Not really—"

"Go easy on him, Major—"

"Shut up."

"—more of a rookery? A rook, rook, rookery." He pointed. "Over there, it is over there."

"That's where I spotted the heat concentration, Major."

"Thank you, Lieutenant von du Mark. Take two brownie points out of petty cash."

He stood silently for a moment, eyeing the creatures, who were busy eyeing him eyeing them.

I shrugged, and eyed all of them. It seemed to be the thing to do.

The Dutchman nodded. "Okay, let's go." He pulled his hand controls off his belt. "Airborne, after me. First the spook, then the kraut."

His lifter started with a loud roar. Kicking up mud and leaves, he rose into the air like a fat balloon. In a moment, Donny followed him.

The noise and rush of heat didn't seem to bother our local audience. A few dozen flapped after each of the other two, but the rest stayed to trade stares with me. I didn't like that, not at all. There's only two possible explanations for a wild creature that doesn't run at a strange loud sound: either it's dogshit stupid, or it's the toughest bastard around.

I hoped the chiropterans were stupid.

I stowed my cutter and triggered a beep on the scout's freak. "Bar-El? You catch any of this?"

No answer.

"We're going to check out the village now."

I pulled on my lifter controls, thumbed them on, and rose into the air.

We came down in a bona fide clearing surrounded by real trees. None of the pale, spongy, phony trees grew within twenty meters of the woody giants which thrust upward, vanishing into the canopy, into the gathering twilight.

Pale vines laced the trunks, which were thirty to fifty meters around. Woven baskets hung from the grassy strands. Hundreds, thousands of pairs of beady eyes peered at us, from tree limbs all around us.

"Some village," the Dutchman said, snorting.

Donny looked very uncomfortable.

"It's all right, N'Damo. You're doing fine." Norfeldt turned his back on Donny, so he missed the pleased and surprised look on the kid's face.

Like a puppy patted on the head. Espers can be like that.

I went over to the Dutchman. "What now, Major?"

"Damned if I know. So far, so good, eh?"

"We're alive, if that's what you mean."

"That's it, Emmy. Take some samples—then we'll hit the air and get back to the scout, have a good night's rest, and check out Second's scout tomorrow."

Beyond the circle of light, all I could see was shadows and eyes, watching. The tree bulked comfortably at my back.

When I poked at one of the woven-basket nests, one of the chiropterans flittered out and took to the air almost silently. I shook the next to be sure nobody else was home; it rattled like a bag full of sticks.

When I poked my flash inside, it gleamed against dry bones.

They were split lengthwise, and the insides were still faintly wet. Feathers lined the nest. It looked as though one of the brightly colored flyers from up above had come down, slumming, and paid for it.

I checked another nest. Same procedure, except that this time there was nobody home. More bones, though, and more feathers, and parts of a pelt from a creature I hadn't seen before. It had died sloppily, and the chiropterans weren't done with it yet. The brain was still in the skull, and some of the viscera were still present, uneaten.

My stomach was starting to protest, and I couldn't get the sour-vomit taste from the back of my mouth. Enough for now, I decided. I could swallow some Paradrams before the next time we went out.

I looked around.

All I could see was eyes. Donny and Norfeldt were gone.

"*Major*—"

"Shut the fuck up, Emmy," the Dutchman said, his flash blinking about fifteen meters away. His collar lights came on for a moment, and I could see his face. "What's the problem?"

"I couldn't see you."

"Well, I sure as hell can't see you now, either." He shut his collar lights off. "Whatcha got?"

"Their eating habits. They're not herbivores. At least some of their prey is pulled down out of the upper levels of the forest, up at treetop level."

He frowned.

Something brushed my membrane helmet, like a flurry of dry leaves, but with some weight behind it. I took a step back and brushed it away, but there wasn't anything there, not anymore.

"Nightfall," the Dutchman said, and I swear I *heard* him smiling that smile that said, all of a sudden, that he knew something that I didn't, something that was about to become awfully important.

Or fatal.

"Condition Blue," the Dutchman said. Attack expected. "Get your weapon free."

Something hit me in the back, not very hard. I turned. Something else thwocked off my membrane helmet again.

Something bounced off my hands.

My leg.

My back again.

And then my helmet. Batting at the vague bodies, I turned the floods up full.

The air was filled with them. They boiled out of the nests, off the vines, down from the trees, and blew into the air like an explosion. They bumbled against my membrane helmet, not very hard, but a dozen times a minute.

I fetched up against the tree, hard, and was batted down to my knees.

"Emmy—"

"Here, Dutchman. I'm over here."

But I couldn't see where he was.

They cut through the light and then fluttered away. My membrane helmet was laced with scratches. The air rumbled from their beating wings. I felt the sound more than heard it.

One clamped itself on my shoulder, but an explosion to the left shattered it into blood and gore that covered my helmet completely.

I got to my feet again, felt a weight on my right arm, and clapped my left hand onto my forearm.

When I jerked the chiropteran free, the talons took a small swatch of my oversuit sleeve and ripped through, into my E-suit itself. I felt another hand on my arm, grabbed for it, and felt a gloved human hand.

"It's me, Emmy. Let's get the fuck out of here," the Dutchman said calmly. "And don't you *ever* call me Dutchman again."

Fine time to be worrying about that. "Suit breached."

"Better hope that the biogel wasn't misleading us. N'Damo? Where the fuck are you?"

"Here, Major," he said, from somewhere. I couldn't see a damn thing.

We linked hands and started walking. I fell down a lot in the next twenty meters. The last time I didn't bother getting up.

"This isn't going to work," I said. My throat burned from the bile I'd held back. My gut was clenched like a fist against the sickness. Primeval reflex: dump excess baggage and run. But letting go in a closed suit is not exactly a survival-oriented behavior.

Norfeldt and Donny each took an arm and hauled me to my feet.

"I can't see anything—" I started to say.

"Doesn't matter," the Dutchman said.

"Use the lifters. Have to slave mine to yours—"

"No way. We'd get knocked out of the air before we went ten meters. Safe and sure on foot, Emmy. Come on, N'Damo, they're not going to wait for fucking ever—"

It was about then that Donny grunted, hard.

He lost his grip on my arm and went down.

"Donny?"

"Clawed—suit breached—"

Then they hit me, like a white-hot nail driven into my back, through the outer insulation, cooling/heating tubing, and my uniform coveralls, straight to flesh.

I yelped and bit deep into my lower lip.

The report of the Dutchman's Magnum hammered in my ears, and even through my gore-covered helmet I could see him standing a few meters in front of me, cloaked with the flesh of the aliens. The Magnum spat lightning again, and spattered chiropteran pate into the night air. Another, caught by the blast, tumbled to the ground in miscellaneous pieces.

One clamped itself onto my leg. I slapped it backhand without thinking and then kicked it hard in the head. It flopped into the water, twitching. It was easy to kill them, but there were millions of them and only one of me, only one of me.

I started fumbling for the straps on my lifter. A lifter's

pack was designed for security, not for easy disposal; it seemed as though there were about two dozen fasteners.

Norfeldt's Magnum went off five more times, then it went silent as he reloaded. I wanted to shout for him to be sure to save a shot, but my teeth were stuck in my lower lip.

I got the sample pack off, dropped it and a couple hours' of work into the swamp water.

"Major."

Dimly, I saw him turn my way. I hoped to hell his helmet allowed him more visibility than mine allowed me as I fumbled at my lifter's buckles.

"Fucking kraut's a genius—*do* it."

I gripped the lifter by one strap and threw it as hard as I could. It splashed down all of five meters away.

I didn't have to say anything; the Dutchman squeezed off two quick rounds. The pack exploded.

The concussion knocked me off my feet, while the heat of the explosion raised blisters on my exposed forearm. Carbonized bits of wood and flesh struck me in a sudden rain.

I forced myself to my feet. I could see, a little. My membrane helmet was scratched cloudy, but I could see where Donny was lying, almost at my feet. I hauled him out of the water, the Dutchman took hold of his other arm, and we started wading, unfastening his lifter from his back as we did.

Behind us, the fire flickered dimly. Above it, a thousand chiropterans orbited. Maybe we could get out while—

The flock shattered in our direction.

"Not enough." My lungs were burning. My strength was leaking out, slowly, like the air hissing out through the suit.

"Stop your—"

His words were lost in thunder. And red-hot lightning.

"*If you move, you die.*"

The thunder and lightning moved closer. The needle of flame, hot and bright as the sun, played through the trees.

* * *

Walking an automatic recoilless onto a target is relatively easy. You work the controls in your left hand, aim it as close to the target as possible, pull the trigger, then use it like a garden hose as you correct the spray. Even if you're controlling a hovering skimmer with your right hand and feet, it's not all that difficult.

Of course, it's not quite so simple when the skimmer is moving at something better than forty klicks an hour, and when you yourself are under attack by hundreds of flying chiropterans.

And when there are three nontargets right in the middle of your field of fire, three separate points that you don't want that deadly hail of lead to touch, it's practically impossible.

And when your targets are thousands of airborne chiropterans who *have* to be knocked out of the sky while your three Contact Service comrades aren't to be touched, it's absolutely impossible.

Check the manuals; ask anyone.

I guess Akiva Bar-El hadn't read the manuals. He swung the recoilless around, firing it continuously, burning down the chiropterans. The vegetation blew into flinders beneath the deadly hail; pieces of aliens were chopped and shattered into a gory rain.

Even through my suit, I could feel the whip of bullets coming within centimeters—

—but not a one touched me. Or Donny. Or the Dutchman.

"*When I tell you to, make a run for the skimmer.*" The water around us came to a boil and shattered into the air, but the thunder went on and on. "*Wait for it, wait for it, wait for it . . . and . . . now.*"

"No time for a nap, Emmy." The Dutchman shook my shoulder roughly. He and Donny helped me sit up.

"You okay, Donny?"

"Sure," he said, dazed.

The Dutchman pulled a pair of syringes from his medikit

and jabbed me in the thigh. "I'm going to give you a broad-spectrum cocktail, kid—and," he said, jabbing another one viciously, "a bit of Afterburner. We gotta get airborne."

My head started to clear; I looked around. I was sitting on cracked, powder-dry earth. For a few hundred meters all around, scatterings of wood shards and smoking ashes marked where the smaller trees had stood.

The larger ones were still there, flayed and blackened, oozing sap.

Farther away, fires licking skyward were already going out.

The scout sat a short distance away. Akiva Bar-El stood on its roof, the recoilless now mounted abaft the weapons turret, the backblast tube resting on his right shoulder. Scattered around on the ground outside it were at least thirty chiropteran bodies.

They hadn't been shot; they looked like they had been batted out of the sky, caught and crushed in a giant's hand.

"Can you fly?" the Dutchman asked.

"It's a day for miracles." I nodded. "Get me to the couch."

VI

"Let's get out of here," Norfeldt said. "This place depresses me."

I had a tear twenty-five centimeters long extending from just above my right kidney down across my right buttock and a short way down the back of my leg. It wasn't very deep, and it had clotted over before I dropped into the pilot's couch.

It just hurt like hell.

"Everybody strapped in?" I asked, running through the main engine's start sequence, setting the throttle to minimum before punching the ignite button.

"Here goes." I punched for the combination that would blow the restraining bolts on the landing pods, then hit the start button.

The scout reared up on its hind pods; I shot the throttles forward just as the nose reached vertical.

The engines roared.

Weightless, docked with the orbital stage, burn ointment covering my right forearm, local anesthetics taking care of the pain in my leg and butt, I started to feel better. Anyone can free-space-navigate from orbit to a Gate.

"Right about sunset," Akiva was saying, "I lost the beeps from your personal transponders."

"All at once?" The Dutchman raised an eyebrow and puffed a cloud of smoke toward the outflow.

"Yes. Which seemed strange, so I suited up and popped the topside hatch. I had about three seconds to notice that the antenna had been chewed through before they were all over me."

Norfeldt raised an eyebrow. "You telling me you took out two *dozen* of them without your sprayer?"

"Yes, sir." He didn't wince as Donny pulled the bandage away from his forearm. "I knew there was a reason that God gave me hands."

"Right." Norfeldt shook his head. "It's all my damn fault. Teach me to trust an esper. Idiot."

Donny started to open his mouth, but Norfeldt waved him to silence. "Not you, shithead—me. I'm the bloody idiot. You were so sure that the aliens weren't hostile—"

"They *weren't*. Honest, Major. You can't lie with your mind."

"—that I believed you." He looked over at me. "Any bets that that's not what happened with Second? I swear, that's the trouble with having a decent-rated peeper around—

when the locals are psi-positive, you're tempted to trust him. You can't lie with your mind, right?''

Bar-El shrugged. "So much for fixing this, Major." He looked around. "It's going to be a Drop, no?"

Norfeldt started to say something, but I beat him to it. "I think when we get a properly equipped lab down there and study the chiropterans, we'll find that when the sun goes down it triggers some kind of hormonal change. Their color changes and they get more aggressive. Which is when they go hunting."

"For what?" Donny asked. "There's not enough animal life down there to keep a few of them alive, let alone the concentrations we saw."

"Down below, no. But upstairs, in the treetops, there's an ecology more like the ones we're used to. Photosynthesis on a large scale, arboreal herbivores, carnivores. But you need sunlight to drive the whole process, and a lot of it. All there is downstairs is a sarcophagy, which probably provides the minerals for the giant trees, but damn little else.

"In the lower regions, near the ground, the plants live off what little sunlight they can get, and they live off their more successful big brothers. I'll bet that if you dig out the root system of one of those giants, you'll find the vegetation for a klick around hooked into it, feeding off it."

"And the chiropterans feed off the more successful animal life," Donny said.

I nodded. "Night falls, the life processes up above slow down a bit, and the peaceable lower-level carnivore adopts the right temperament for feeding."

"Great," Akiva said. "If we can keep the sun from going down, they'll all starve to death, and the planet is ours. Sounds simple enough." He snorted.

"Nothing that drastic," the Dutchman said. "Not necessary. Now that we know they're dangerous, they're *not* so fucking dangerous."

"We might be able to gimmick up some counteragent for their aggression hormone, and maybe let them move or starve."

"We'll do it with mirrors," the Dutchman said, his right hand folded over his left, which was knotted into a fist.

Akiva and Donny were surprised. I wasn't.

"Bring in some powerscreens and set the suckers in orbit over our installations," Norfeldt said. "The old Solares trick. You put it in the right orbit, aim it right, and they'll catch the sunlight and direct it downward. The sun never goes out, so the bats move elsewhere."

"Could you match the candlepower of full sunlight?" Akiva asked.

"You can better it, if you have to; you can make powerscreens huge, jewboy. But I don't think it's necessary, not if Emmy's right. All we'd need is enough to fool the bats." He looked at the green world, full and round in the aft monitors.

"Drop, *shit*," he said.

VII

I knocked lightly on the curtain rod. "Akiva?"

He slid the curtain aside and let me in. Like me, he had a bunk, a closet, and a few plastic web-covered shelves under the air-conditioning unit. Only a couple of spare uniforms were on the shelves. There were no pictures, no letters on the gleaming walls. Nothing to make the cubicle personal.

It was the first time I'd been in his cabin.

"Yes, Lieutenant?" His eyes were dark and fathomless.

"I came for a couple of reasons. For one, to apologize," I said. "And to thank you."

He eyed me carefully. "Your apology is accepted. And you are welcome. And if that's it—"

"That was one reason. The other one is Norfeldt."

He looked me over. "I doubt that it would do much

good to turn him in, at this point. The unwritten law, and all—he *is* good on the ground, it seems.''

"But you're going to do it anyway." Just because something wouldn't do any good wouldn't stop a man who would take on a couple dozen chiropterans barehanded, and then push a skimmer hard enough and fast enough to arrive in time to pull a miracle with powder, lead, and steel.

"I can't let him get away with it. I . . . understand that winning is everything to him, and that he has no sense of decency, no sense of proportion, but I will not let him get away with it.''

"We won't," I said. "But let's punish the bastard, not just report him.''

"Excuse me?''

"He cheats at poker, Akiva. He has a flasher carved into the bottom of his Team Leader ring—he reads the cards as he deals them.''

"So?''

"So, he only deals a quarter of the time," I said, pulling my reader out of my blouse pocket and tossing it gently to him. "According to Mr. Scarne, two partners working in tandem are a lot more dangerous than an occasional peeker. Study up—we've got a few weeks until we're back home.''

He looked at me for a long moment, and then he broke into a smile.

By the time we were home, the Dutchman was down a full two years' pay, and had resolved to give up poker forever.

Not that I got heavily into Qualifications Courses; the Team just switched over to bridge. In order to get anywhere cheating at bridge, you have to have two partners working in collusion. I was sure that the Dutchman wouldn't suggest it to Donny N'Damo, or to me.

Or to Akiva Bar-El, whose smile had become a permanent fixture on his ugly face.

Interlude

Destination: Captain Manuel Curdova, TWCS
                      Contact Service Administrative
                      Bureau
                      Building 4, Level 3
                      VNYC

Routing: 1800RQW5R52EE83

Origin: First Lieutenant Emile von du Mark,
                      TWCS Aboard TWS NEIL ARMSTRONG
                      (#LC3369)

Subject: Personal

File Created: 2 January 2247

Dear Manny,

Insert some sincere applause here, amigo. Nicely done, Captain.

As you might have gathered, I've been reading the A/A reports on your field trip. I gather they're going to give you the DSD and a cluster. As to the promotion that's undoubtedly in the wind, I have mixed feelings about the salutation above; it's unlucky to anticipate too strongly, but I hope you've gotten your oak leaves by the time you're reading this.

I'm only partly jealous. I don't want to ever *AHEM* luck into a TL ring that way, and I don't know if I could have handled anything like the G'Reeeth situation on my first time in the field.

Which isn't meant to be patronizing; I'm not willing to claim I could handle it now. After all, I only went out on First Assignment a bit less than six years ago. I swear it feels like yesterday.

Although, I have to wonder why I feel so old, Manny, so old....

But never mind that.

To repeat, I am very jealous—of your results,

dammit, not what you had to go through to get them.

Now, will you listen to some advice from, granted, a junior officer, and someone who's yet to earn a TL ring—but one who is, nevertheless, still up a bit of field experience on you?

Take your TL ring, mount it on the plaque, put the plaque up on the wall behind the desk in your office, get the hell back into your office, and stay there, Manuel. I have the feeling that Veronica won't say that to you, but you and I go way back, and I have to say this.

Nobody's doubting your courage. But the simple fact is that anyone in fieldwork is living on borrowed time. Team Leader is not a job for a man with a wife, and most particularly not for a man with a wife and two children. I want you to think about what it would have been like for Emilita and most particularly Arturo, if you'd been just a little slower—he never would have known his father.

Think about it, dammit.

Yes, I got your message. Would you try to explain things to Janine? I don't see a lot of point in continuing on, all things considered, in light of what I'm suggesting to you. I know, I know I should say something to her myself, but the woman just doesn't listen to me.

People not listening to me seems to be an ongoing problem.

I've got a really bad feeling about this Pon business, and the Dutchman and I are going into it alone, without the rest of the Team. I can understand leaving N'Damo out—the poncharaire are completely psi-neg, after all—but I wish we could have gotten Bar-El.

I don't have any good reason for that feeling, granted, but I do.

Oh, by the way, as long as I keep an eye on him and whip out the calipers every now and then to check the dice, the Dutchman plays a good game of backgammon.

Which is to say that I'm way up; and the best part of it is that the Dutchman won't quit. I don't give a rat's ass about the money.

But I do like beating the bastard.

I guess that's all for now.

Best wishes,

Emile

File Transmitted: 9 January 2247

In the Shadow
of Heaven

I

By the time I'd finished vomiting and had gotten my shaking under control and my freezing body back into the relative warmth of the drafty stone igloo, the Dutchman was practically green.

Not with envy—while the pureed-*akla* gruel that was the mainstay of the poncharaire diet wasn't quite poisonous, it did contain a compound or two that was, for humans, a powerful emetic. And despite my suspicions, the Dutchman was human, after all.

<How nice is of thee to returns,> the Dutchman said in the awkward pidgin that he thought was a fluid mastery of the guttural poncharaire language, then switched back to Basic. His tone was calm, even friendly—that was for the benefit of the two poncharaire in the single-room hut with us. "But keep a hold on that famous glass gut of yours, Emmy—"

"Major, my name is Emile. Emile von du Mark. Not Emmy."

"Listen, shithead," the Dutchman said gently, "and listen good." His smile broadened; his tone became even more affectionate. "If you ever raise your voice to me again," he said as he nodded and smiled, his jowls and extra chins waggling in rapid syncopation, "I'll choke you to death with your own small intestines, *Lieutenant*. Understood?"

"Yes. Sir."

The Dutchman settled back into his wooden chair. If I hadn't disliked him so much, I would have had a bit of sympathy for the way he was holding up. The plus-twenty-percent gravity of Pon added only about fifteen kilos to my

weight; it added a full twenty-five to his, and made his
muscles—which would have included his heart, if the
Dutchman had one—work much, much harder carrying his
already ample bulk around. Even sitting up must have
been a chore.

The larger of the two poncharaire raised his head from
where he knelt beside the low table, then froze into position. That's one of the things I'll never get used to about
them: sitting statuelike for a full minute's contemplation
before speaking is strictly *pro forma*. They think humans
are impetuous.

K'chat's body was of the hexipedal, centauroid form
common on high-gee planets, at least among sapients. On
worlds with gravity much greater than Earth's, creatures
with only four legs never seem to free the front pair from
the task of fighting gravity. And without manipulative
members—hands—you don't get sapience.

Please don't bring up cetaceans and airybs: the first gave
up their hands to go back to the sea; the second are sapient
only if you're not fussy. I'm fussy.

Hmm . . . maybe calling the poncharaire centauroid was
an oversimplification. I'm not claiming that either K'chat
or Ahktah looked like an improbable mixture of human
and horse; they looked much more like wolves. A poncharaire's long body is all of one piece, covered by
soft brown fur from the top of its cloven hooves to the
wrists of the six-digited hands with their paired, opposable
thumbs.

I couldn't read K'chat's lupine face. I'd had enough
trouble learning the language, and I'd yet to make a dent
in their nonverbal cues. I didn't have much hope to; I was
trained to be a Team's pilot and second-in-command, not a
combination substitute psi-neg comm officer and ersatz—
and very expendable—diplomat.

K'chat reached out a thick-wristed hand, conveying a
smidgen of gruel from the bowl on the table to his mouth.
<In thy absence, Ehmillfundoomark, we accomplished

very little. Have thy short moments of contemplation brought thee much insight?>

I'd never really thought of vomiting as meditation before, but claiming such as the purpose of my leaving the room had been a reasonable excuse.

Besides, it was the sort of thing that the poncharaire wanted to believe; much better to accept the need for me to take a moment away in meditation than to believe I was out upchucking the delicious meal that they had sold the Dutchman and me.

As I tried to phrase a polite negative, the other poncharaire snapped his toothy jaws.

<There is no insight to be gained,> Ahktah said to the Dutchman and me, not bothering to acknowledge us as equals-or-better by eating. He dipped another smidgen of gruel and turned back to K'chat. <There is none, leader-of-the-clan-of-clans.>

<There had best be, Ahktah. There *must* be some insight to be gained.> K'chat waved his left arm—the noneating one—in a circle. <If we do not find a way in which it will be permissible to deal with the hoo-mans, soon there will be no more villages. No more people. No more offerings to the gods. Will that please them, priest?>

Ahktah stroked the center of his face: a poncharaire shrug. <The gods will tell this one what pleases them. Perhaps they will cheaply give their blessing. Perhaps they will give it not at all.>

The Dutchman's face was somber and emotionless as he tasted the gruel before speaking to Ahktah. <This is understand. I asks these of thee: what, if anything, can we does so that thy deals with the gods will bring the result thy people does needs?>

<This one . . . does not know. The gods are . . . conservative, unliking of change. It may take more wood and food to buy their blessing than can be spared.>

The hypocrite. "More wood and food than can be spared," hah. It wasn't the gods that were twitchy about dealing with humans, it was the priest. I was sure that the reason that the gods' blessing might prove too expensive was that Ahktah was afraid that any changes would endanger his power. Look at history: shamans are like that; they've preached against things as trivial as lipstick and something as vitally important as spaceflight.

K'chat turned again to Ahktah—speaking to someone one is not facing is one of several things that the poncharaire consider a very serious insult. An offer of charity is another—which was a large part of the poncharaire's problem.

And the Dutchman's and mine, for that matter.

And one of the reasons I very much missed large, ugly Akiva Bar-El.

<Thy sledge is loaded?> K'chat asked.

<It is.>

<Then, let this one ask thee this: When will thee go next to Heaven to bargain with the gods?>

<Tomorrow. But this one doubts that he will be able to purchase their blessing. The gods are wise traders, and not likely to—>

"You're a pious fraud!" The words leaped out of my mouth. In Basic, thank God.

Ahktah turned slowly toward me. <What did those words mean?>

I couldn't help it: I *liked* the poncharaire. And Ahktah's prohibition of any extensive dealings with humans meant their extinction.

"Emmy." The Dutchman smiled kindly. "Assuming the nice doggie doesn't rip your throat out, you're about three fucking seconds from buying yourself a court. Now, sit down, please. We're not going to make any progress with you venting your spleen all over the place—if your spleen needs venting, I'll do it. With a butter knife, not a Fairbairn. Understood?"

Without waiting for an answer, he scooped a bit of the gruel to his mouth and turned to Ahktah. <This one's . . . friend say he hope that thy not-know is wrong, though he

also say he much respect thy sincere, as well as thy skill as bargainer-with-gods.>

K'chat's eyes twinkled as he tasted the gruel, then spoke to me. <So *much* meaning in so few words! This one hopes that all our wishes are fulfilled—not only will my people live, but perhaps this one may have the chance to learn such a . . . delightfully compact way of expressing oneself.>

He gestured to the black, thumb-sized heaters scattered around the room. <As well as having such wonders, not having to suffer so in this time of freezing.>

He used a form of the poncharaire word for winter, but it really wasn't winter; we were, technically, in late summer. But Pon was a thousand or so years into an ice age, and the poncharaire, who had evolved in warmer times, weren't ready for it. Which is why their population had shrunk, from the millions that had covered the southern continent like a blanket to a small clustering of settlements, the total population perhaps as many as a hundred thousand.

Ahktah took a taste of the gruel, and stood. <There is no point in further talk. Tomorrow, this one will go to Heaven to deal with the gods. And then the matter will be settled.> He left, not bothering to latch the door behind him, his hooves clattering against the ice outside.

The cold north wind blew in; I went over and closed the door, then reached down to my belt and turned my rubbery coldsuit up a notch.

K'chat sighed. <This one does not blame Ahktah for being frightened. It is just that he is new to the priesthood— his mother, Ehlat, froze on her way back from Heaven just this past winter.>

"Major, can I—"

"Might as well." The Dutchman shook his head. "You may already have blown it." Norfeldt let himself sag back in his chair.

<K'chat, this priest of thine—>

<Is young, and a bit . . . impetuous. Somewhat like thyself, no?>

<*No*. This one is trying to help—>

"Emmy. Go easy, there."

Damn, he was right—that was starting to sound like an offer of charity. <—that is, to trade with thee and thine, to our benefit and to yours. Ahktah can't be allowed to interfere. The True People will die.>

K'chat stroked the center of his face, both thumbs trembling slightly. <If the gods so will . . .>

<It already begins. This one has been partway up the slopes of Heaven, has seen the old True People there, freezing slowly to death.>

<There is wild root up on the slopes, although the wood is gone. And they are closer to the gods. Wouldst thou prefer that the old ones live down on the plains with us, gathering enough wood, but with their rootbins empty?>

<But it is not *necessary*.>

The Dutchman raised a palm. "Not your job, Emmy."

I guess he was right. It wasn't my job to explain to K'chat that it was well worth it to the Thousand Worlds to trade ten-for-a-quid heaters for mineral rights. It would have sounded like I was making an offer of charity. Under normal circumstances, a subconscious psychic explanation could have been made by a comm officer, but the poncharaire were all psi-neg. Explaining that we were offering a fair exchange, not charity, was a job for a Commerce Department Trade Team negotiation expert.

It wasn't our job. All we were supposed to do was to pave the way for the Commerce Department mission.

But we weren't having much success. I tried another tack. <K'chat, dost thou know what would have happened if we had arrived in another few sixes of years?>

<Thou wouldst have found but our bones, my friend. This one knows.>

And that would have been too bad, even from the Dutchman's point of view. It's almost always cheaper to hire natives than it is to import even mechanical labor.

<That is correct. But if we can't persuade thy priest to let us walk among thy people, teaching them of our ways, trading with them, value for value . . .>

<Then we die.> K'chat rose, his eyes clouding over. <This one knows that, Ehmillfundoomark. For our sake, and for thine, it would be best that thou persuade Ahktah that we should deal with thee so that he goes to deal with the gods knowing that dealing with yoo-mans is best for us, the last of the True People. Is that not so?>

K'chat didn't wait for an answer; he gestured a goodbye and then left, shutting the door gently but firmly behind him.

Just ahead of the Dutchman's explosion.

"You stupid, *brainless* asshole—you came damn close to threatening Ahktah just now. And then you talk reasonably with K'chat? Fucking *idiot*."

"And what was wrong with that, Major?"

"I thought you were supposed to be a first john, not a greenie."

"Major, I've been in the service for almost six years—almost ten, if you include Alton." I was still a first lieutenant. Now, while promotions don't always come fast in the Contact Service—the Navy gives out new rank the way my mother's Aunt Anna used to hand out Christmas kroner—six years was none too soon to be promoted to captain. Hell, Manny Curdova was likely to get his major's leaves.

I didn't begrudge Manny his promotions, mind; I just would have liked a pair of bars and a TL ring of my own.

The Dutchman eyed me levelly. "If you're so fucking salty, Emmy, why are you acting like such a greenie?" Norfeldt propped his chins on his hands. "Talking reasonably with K'chat, trying to sell him, it doesn't make sense because he *is* reasonable—you were just preaching to the converted. You could have blown the whole play by yelling at Ahktah. Think about it."

"I don't know, Major. Maybe you're right." I walked

over to my cot and stretched out, pillowing my head on my hands. It was hard to think straight; I was just too tired, feeling too old. Maybe my extra weight didn't bother me as much as the Dutchman's bothered him, but I didn't like it much. It would have been like home for Akiva Bar-El, who had been raised on Metzada, after all. But the Commerce Department people had decided that we didn't need the big weapons officer along.

Well, more accurately, they suffered from the misconception that someone who made violence his profession and specialty was a bomb always ready to go off. Now, it can work out that way—that was Kurt Buchholtz, all over—but Akiva had more self-control than anyone else I knew.

I stared at the rough, curving walls overhead. "I can't stand the little bugger, Major. 'Let's see what the gods say'—the damned hypocrite."

Norfeldt chuckled hollowly. "So you don't believe in their bullshit gods?"

" 'Course not. It's idiotic."

"Not idiocy, kid: hypocrisy. But hypocrisy, greenie, is a fine social lubricant, suitable for many squeaky situations. You think K'chat believes in their gods?"

"He seems to."

"Precisely. And he may. But has he ever seen them?"

"No. Only Ahktah—oh."

"Right. Only Ahktah. Ahktah is the priest, Ahktah climbs Heaven, tracking the village's tithed wood and food—"

"Not tithed. It's one-twelfth. Base six, remember?"

The Dutchman dismissed the distinction with a wave of his hand. "Don't get technical with me, krautbrains. The point is that he trades a portion of their harvest to the gods, in return for their blessing. Understandable, considering that they must have had a vigorous trading culture before the freeze."

"It does *not* make sense, their giving away hard-found food and wood—and for what?"

Norfeldt shrugged. "Don't ask me. I'm not a believer. The question is, is Ahktah?"

"I suppose so."

"You really *must* have sauerkraut between your ears. You really think he just drags his sled up there and hands over the stuff to the gods? 'Here you go, nice godsies, and can I have a fucking blessing, please?' 'Why sure, Ahktah.' You think it happens that way?"

"Well, no."

"Finally, you're showing a bit of intelligence. Not much, mind, but some. Of course he doesn't, *because there aren't any gods*. He probably stashes the wood, has himself a nice warm fire and a good feed each trip."

Slowly, Norfeldt got to his feet and rummaged around the floor, looking for a fresh wine bottle among the empties. "Aha." He uncorked it and drank deeply. "Shit. I'm forgetting my manners." He held it out. "Want a hit, Emmy?"

"I don't drink that swill." Not that I'd turn up my nose at a nice Moselle, but the Dutchman seemed to think that the cheaper a wine was, the better it was. Hell, if I'd substituted wine vinegar mixed with Everclear he probably wouldn't have noticed. "I don't get your point, Major. You just confirmed what I'm saying, that he's nothing but a hypocrite."

"Right. And you, asshole, you keep threatening his power." He waddled over, dragging a chair along with him, and sat down. "Not that it would make much difference if you'd been clever enough to try to wheedle him instead of threatening him—the little bugger's smart, alas. Shamans always have to resist change; any change in a shaman-controlled society *has* to threaten their power, their position."

"Not al—"

"*Always*. Look at what the Catholic Church put the early Lutherans through. They had to: prospering Protestants proved that the Holy Mother Church didn't have a monopoly on capital-fucking-R Right. Or look at the way the Imams slaughtered the Bahais, for godssake. Or consider what the Fundamentalistas put the Humanists through. Emmy, the only shaman-oriented group I can think of that's *never* persecuted nonbelievers and outsiders is the Bahais, and they've never been in a majority in any room larger than a WC.''

He took a slow swallow from the bottle, then belched disgustingly. ''Ah. That feels better. Mmm, it would have been a lot easier if the poncharaire were either hostile or psi-pos. If they were nasty, we could just flatten 'em—and to hell with the economics of bringing in offplanet labor.'' He considered with relish. ''And if they'd been psi-pos, a good comm officer like Ari McCaw or even that little suntan N'Damo could have persuaded Ahktah that the gods wanted them to deal with us—without Wolfie ever knowing.''

''That would have been nice, but they aren't warlike, and they are psi-neg, and Donny isn't here, and . . .'' I stopped myself. I'd been about to say that Ari McCaw was dead, killed in the line of duty, more or less.

But it's a custom in the Contact Service that you don't mention dead comrades, except when it's strictly necessary or when you're toasting their memory. It wasn't strictly necessary, and I didn't feel much like drinking. I felt more like vomiting.

''So?'' I finally asked. ''What are we going to do? We can't persuade Ahktah—''

''So, Emmy, we use more . . . primitive means.'' The Dutchman's heavy gunbelt landed on my cot with a solid thump. Our orders had strictly forbidden us firearms, but Norfeldt had violated them, as usual. Had he disobeyed the orders because he really wanted to have his Magnum handy, or was it just for the sake of disobeying orders? I'm really not sure; maybe even Norfeldt didn't know.

''If you can't reason with him,'' Norfeldt said, ''then I'm sure you can figure out a way to keep Ahktah out of our way, *nicht var?*''

''Wait a minute—''

"Tomorrow, you follow the bastard up the slopes of Heaven, armed with both pistol and camera. You take holos of him snacking on the offerings, and then you flash him same. If he doesn't give in, if he doesn't agree to report that the gods *strongly* favor dealings with humans—"

"No."

"—the gods get themselves a four-legged sacrifice." The Dutchman wrinkled his brow. "What's the matter? Squeamish?"

"How about *you* doing it?" I don't like killing, particularly when it's not in self-defense. Maybe Akiva Bar-El could have handled it easily, but not me.

Norfeldt shook his head. "God save me from greenies—"

"I've been an officer for—"

"—and those supposedly seasoned officers who still *act* like motherfucking greenies. Look: if we don't deal with the locals, they're going to die off, right?"

"Right, but—"

"Shut up. And if Ahktah interferes, that interference has to be stopped. I've got a few years and more than a few kilos on you, Emmy. I can't climb up Heaven; my heart probably wouldn't take it." Slowly, painfully, he pushed himself to his feet. "Now, since it's got to be done, and since one of us has to do it, and since you're the only one who can do it, you will do it. Understood?"

"Yes, sir," I said sullenly.

"And now, if you'll excuse me, I've got to go empty my gut. Something around here seems to disagree with me. Maybe it's the damn gruel; maybe it's a lieutenant whose first objection to a messy spot of killing was that he was going to have to do it."

He paused at the door, bracing himself in the doorway. "I didn't hear you acknowledge the order, Lieutenant von du Mark. Either you come to terms with Ahktah, or you blow him away. Acknowledge, scumbag."

"Aye-aye, *sir*." I tried to load my voice with sarcasm; either the Dutchman didn't hear, or he just didn't care.

Or both, of course.

II

It was easy to tell that it was the morning of a Heaven Day, as the poncharaire called it. On other days, they spent as much time as possible indoors, huddled around their fires, coming out only to gather wood from the stunted forests, reap a twelvedays' worth of food from the *akla* fields, or check their traps and deadfalls for the small animals that they used for leather and for food.

But on Heaven Day, everyone comes out: to make mud to fill the cracks in the walls of their houses, to carry clay wastepots out to the fields, to sweep the seemingly endless village streets with a local brush that looks like a miniature tumbleweed—to generally pretty up and repair the town. The basic notion is that a prosperous-looking village gets a better deal from the gods in much the same way that a rich trader always seems to come out on top in dealings with others.

As I plodded through the middle of the village, adults and young poncharaire alike scampered out of my way. It wasn't that I looked all that prepossessing; in fact, I was stumbling with the effort of carrying the extra weight of my climbing gear around.

No, it wasn't that they were afraid of me; they weren't. It was just that this was the Heaven Day that Ahktah was to climb Heaven to ask the gods' blessing for dealings with humans, and everyone in the village was expecting the priest to relay a loud and definite no.

I was too. Too bad that . . .

"Hey, Major?" I kept my voice low; we didn't know what the local opinion was on somebody talking to himself.

It took a minute for him to respond. "What the hell is

it?'' His voice was slurred, which was strange—I'd thought that he'd finished off the last of his wine the night before.

"Maybe there is a simpler way to do this—without Ahktah's cooperation. You remember the way we fixed the chiropterans?" The last we heard from that planet, it had been named Oroga; the first colony was already safely down on the northern continent.

"Don't be silly." An overloud snort sent my hands flying toward my ears, reaching for the phones. I stopped myself and forced my fingers down to my belt, turning down the maximum volume control. "That's fine for keeping a small area bright, day and night. But take a look to the north. What do you see?"

I craned my neck back. The gray bulk of the mountain the poncharaire called Heaven threatened to fill the sky, wisps of cloud obscuring the summit.

"Just the mountain."

"What's beyond that?"

"The glacier—oh." He was right, of course. "Damn. Sorry, Major."

"Right. We orbit some mirrors to heat things up here, we're gonna flood out the people we're trying to save. I thought *you* were the xenophile. I don't particularly like these folks"—the Dutchman didn't particularly like anyone or anything except food, wine, and cigars—"and even I wouldn't want to shoot craps with their ecology. Melting ice isn't like brightening an area, Emmy. It'd take *big* mirrors."

"But maybe, maybe if we use smaller orbital mirrors, just warm up the local area and—"

"Quit trying to wriggle out of it, Lieutenant. Even if we *could* do it that way, how's that going to persuade the locals to work for us? No. We do it standard; we sell them the heaters and the suits to go with them for outdoors, and they'll want to work for us. Then we bring in some analytical medicians, introduce the poncharaire to the concept of medicine—"

"—and video and euphorics and stims, and they'll do

whatever the hell the Thousand Worlds wants, like a bunch of four-legged puppets dancing to our tune. Right? Just fucking wonderful, Major. 'Hey, Dad, what'd you do in the Contact Service?' 'Why, I helped enslave a brand-new race of sapients, son.' ''

As I rounded the larger-than-normal, less-shabby-than-normal stone igloo that I thought of as the mayoral palace, the Dutchman chuckled.

"My fucking word, the kid's caught hisself a case of scruples." A belch followed, then the disgusting sound of him slurping more wine. "Where are you now?"

"Just about a quarter-klick from Ahktah's house." I looked up at the huge red sun, which was almost directly overhead. It was redder than Sol, and actually smaller, although Pon's relatively tight orbit made it look twice the size of my native sun. "And if he sets out at noon—"

"He has to. Tradition."

"—I should be able to follow him."

"If you don't stumble over your own feet and fall down the side of the mountain."

I wasn't worried about that, but it was vital that Ahktah not spot me, not until I had the holos in the can.

A cold wind blew up from the east. The heater in my rubbery, skin-tight coldsuit compensated, sending rivulets of warmth through the wires embedded in the black, rubbery fabric.

But my face, covered only by a woolen mask, was quickly getting numb.

The northward trail ahead of me went first past Ahktah's stone igloo, then twisted its way up the slopes of Heaven.

I skirted the old ones' settlement. Its scattered houses were inhabited by aged poncharaire who lived partway up the slopes, trading freezing on the lightly forested land for the ability to gather wild *akla*. Of course, the tradition was that they lived there because it was closer to the gods; like many traditions, it made a virtue of necessity.

Like the tradition of obeying orders, maybe. Maybe that was a necessity, sometimes.

I rubbed a gloved hand across my face and quickened my step, resenting the weight and the pressure of the gun inside my suit, the butt of the pistol carving a hole for itself just over my hipbone. The Dutchman's forty-four massed better than two kilos, and he hadn't offered to take in his custom-made belt for my use of it, which left me without a holster. I could have just tucked the Magnum in my belt, I guess, but you've got to be careful with pistols in cold weather. Parts tend to seize up.

Smoke rising over a hill showed me that I was nearing Ahktah's house; a clattering in front of me suggested that I might have cut it too close. As I topped the hill, Ahktah, his heavily laden sledge hitched to his midsection, was puffing up the trail away from me.

Back at the Academy, I always got top marks in orienteering. I studied every text I could get my hands on, and put it all to work—I guess my run-in with that bastard Brubaker had some positive results, after all. I set a record on the Triple-E course—Escape, Evade, and Elude—that stood for four years. It was finally beaten by an adjusted hundredth of a second by some Alsatian.

All of which is to say that as I followed Ahktah up the trail, hiding behind stunted trees, ducking behind boulders, it's not surprising that he didn't discover me.

You follow the little bastard up to Heaven, watch him stash his haul and have hisself a nice feed, the Dutchman had said. *And you snap his picture, and then you confront him—*

Dammit, it just wouldn't work. Not the way the Dutchman wanted it. When you corner someone, he'll attack. When I proved to Ahktah that I could ruin him, he'd try to kill me, not give in.

I might as well just forget about trying to blackmail him; it would be more honest just to put the barrel of the pistol to his head, cock the hammer back, and pull the trigger—

"What did you say?" The Dutchman's voice crackled in my headphones.

"Nothing," I whispered back. That was bad. Very bad. I hadn't realized that I'd spoken out loud. Granted, there *are* a few worse things to do when you're on a stalk than unknowingly talking to yourself—like wearing a clown suit and banging on a big bass drum, maybe.

"What is it, Emmy?"

I didn't answer; Ahktah was looking around. I hadn't made much noise, but what else could he be looking for except me? All the poncharaire, even the old ones, were down in the village, prettying it up for Heaven Day.

When Ahktah started unhooking his harness, I lowered myself even further and answered, "He may have spotted me, Major." I kept my voice barely above a whisper. Let the Dutchman turn up the volume on his end. If Ahktah hadn't seen me, I wasn't going to risk it further. "He's loosened his sledge."

"Dammit, you must have spooked him. Get the gun out."

"I don't need—"

"Shut up. It works like this: I'm a major and you're a lieutenant. That means that you get to do what the hell I *tell* you to, which includes getting the fucking gun out. Now."

"But—"

"Further, he's used to this gravity, and you aren't. I don't want you to let him get close to you, Emmy. If he closes to springing distance, you point the gun at him, curl your index finger around the trigger, and then make loud noises until you hear only clicks. Understood?"

Officially, I didn't hear that; my comm unit must have slipped off and broken when I ducked down. It took only three sharp blows to make sure that I wouldn't have to disobey an order. I'll do humanity's dirty work, and I won't hesitate to kill in self-defense, but that's as *I* define it, not because some creature's closed to within springing distance. That doesn't constitute a capital crime, not as far as I'm concerned.

When I raised my head, an icy wave of panic washed across me. I couldn't see Ahktah. His sledge was still parked on the trail, the empty straps of his harness lying on the ground.

Where the fuck is he?

Blind Man's Edge is an old Triple-E technique; I took a deep breath and closed my eyes, letting the air slip quietly from my lungs, and listened.

I could hear the wind blowing through the brush, and the splutter of a dead leaf caught between two twigs . . .

. . . but that was all.

It was time to move. If he was stalking me, I might be able to lose him.

A basic principle in Triple-E, all things being equal, is to move away at right angles to the direction that your opponent is expecting you to move in, but not to spend a whole lot of time working out what direction your opponent *is* expecting you to move in. I headed for the igloo, hoping Ahktah would figure I'd run away.

Besides, it offered the best cover around.

I paused for a moment at the door, debating whether or not to go in. Enclosed spaces are a two-edged sword, but if I had to make a stand, it was best to do it with my back to a wall. I swung the door open and dove inside.

And crashed into a dark shape, sending an armload of wood and roots flying in all directions.

<*Ehmillfundoomark!*> Absently, Ahktah mimed eating. <Thou *dost* know.> His arms extended with strange slowness.

I knew that I wouldn't be able to get the Magnum out of my coldsuit quickly enough; I drew my Fairbairn knife and held it out in front of me. Light flashing off the blade, I gripped it easily.

Ahktah already had his eyes closed. He cringed, kneeling in front of me.

"What the *hell?*"

<Do not tell anyone. Please.> Ahktah's voice quavered, his head lowered, not meeting my gaze.

He had been carrying an armload of wood and food. The bastard was stealing from the old ones' bins, as though the tithes from those below wasn't enough.

<Thief. Filthy thief.> Disgusting.

<Yes. This one deserves to die. That is why thou comest here, is it not?>

I didn't answer. The sort of filth who would steal from old, starving people didn't deserve an answer.

<But I would do it again.> Ahktah's arms were extended, pleading. <They were suffering. And this one is not as . . . devout as his mother was.>

<Cease the nonsense. Gods don't suffer.>

<Of course not. But the old ones do.> He buried his wolfish face in his six-fingered hands. <They suffer so *much.*>

III

"He wasn't bringing food and wood out, Major. He was bringing both of them *in.*" I lay back on my cot, my head pillowed on my hands. It was good to be horizontal.

"Very clever, Emmy." The Dutchman's tone of voice suggested that he was thinking that a halfwit could have figured all that out. And that a halfwit had figured it all out. "You're a fucking smart little German, okay?"

Then why haven't you worked it all out, Dutchman? I thought. They can't court-martial you for what you think.

What I said was: "You know as well as I do that the von du Marks have been Austrians for—" I closed my mouth; the Dutchman was too busy laughing to listen.

"I swear," he said, "just once I'd like to run into an

Austrian-style kraut who admits what everyone else knows: that an Austrian's only a half-assed German." He waved the subject away. "But tell me," he went on, "how does all this do us any good?"

Reluctantly, I got to my feet and buttoned my coldsuit tightly. "You don't understand, do you? What Ahktah was doing was denying the gods their tithes—"

"One-twelfth. Base six, remember?"

"—spending Heaven Day splitting up the food and wood among the old ones, sneaking it into their bins. Not something even they could talk about—to suggest that Ahktah was doing it would be a deadly insult."

The Dutchman had finished donning his suit. He took a longing look at the dregs of his last bottle of wine before walking to the door. "So what?"

"So." I turned the heat control on my belt up to full. It was wasteful of power, perhaps, but I deserved a treat. "So, you've got to remember that Ahktah is basically a believer. The reason that Ahktah couldn't ask his unseen gods blessing for dealing with humans was that he was, well, cheating them—by his lights, anyway—denying them their rightful due. That's why he didn't think they'd give their blessing for dealings with humans. Instead of burning the offering up on Heaven's top—which is what he was supposed to do—he was . . ."

I held the door for the Dutchman, then followed him out into the darkening street.

"Giving charity, Captain?"

"Right. A double sin."

We started to walk toward the palace, but I stopped. "Did you call me *Captain*?"

The Dutchman smiled as he pulled a cigar out of his coldsuit pocket and lit it. "You got promoted just before we left on this one. I figured I'd rather not deal with your swelled head for the nonce, so I sort of delayed letting you know. And since—"

"And since I didn't get myself killed—"

"—and since you didn't fuck up badly enough in the

line of duty that I had to blow you away, you may as well enjoy your new railroad tracks.'' He tossed me a set of captain's bars, stuck into a piece of cardboard. "These . . . mean something, Emmy.''

There was a catch in his voice that I'd never heard before. I was touched. "They were yours?''

"No, shithead—I bought them at the PX before we left. They mean you owe me twenty quid.''

"I'll pay you later.'' *Bastard*. "We'd better hurry, Major, or we're gonna be late.''

"Right. And try to keep the stuff down until the ceremony's over. If I can do it, you can do it.''

"Makes me nauseous, Major. Almost as bad as your cigars,'' I said, stepping up the pace as I unpinned my lieutenant's bars and pinned on the shiny railroad tracks. I held the two little pieces of silver in the palm of my hand and looked at them for a moment. I'd been wearing them for one hell of a long time.

Captain Emile von du Mark, eh? I liked the sound of that. "And what are you grinning about? Sir?''

"I'm still basking in your reflected cleverness. But you still haven't told me how you blackmailed Ahktah. From the way you've been chortling to yourself, I'm assuming it was something a tad more clever than 'Geek or I'll tell on you.''

As we approached the palace, a crowd of poncharaire of all ages looked curiously at us, but kept a respectful distance.

"Yes, sir. Just a bit cleverer. I told him we were gods.''

I'd timed it just right; Norfeldt's jaw actually dropped. He tilted his head and peered over at me. "He didn't believe that. Did he?''

I shrugged. "Well, yes and no. It's an absurd proposition—but Ahktah *wants* to believe it. It gives him an out. If we are gods, then the reason I gave him for humans landing on Pon begins to make sense.''

"And what reason was that?''

"So that we can see to an increase in both our number

of worshipers and our take. See, if Ahktah believes that we heard his prayers for forgiveness as he sinned by giving charity, and that's why we came, well, then, he isn't going to give the Trade Team a whole lot of trouble, is he?"

K'chat stood beside Ahktah. <Today our priest has returned to us from Heaven, where he has traded with the gods. . . .>

I leaned over and whispered to Norfeldt. "I told him we didn't want it generally known that we're gods, and that his prayers and . . . sinning brought us. Might make it look like we're too easy to trade with. A god has to be a tough trader, no?"

"Cute. And that means that you promised him you wouldn't tell anyone about him sinning. At least, you implied it. Hmm . . ."

"So?"

"So, it means you're becoming quite a hypocrite yourself, Emmy."

"Emile."

<. . . and since our priest has returned,> K'chat said in a half singsong, <and since he has traded our food and wood to the gods, we have earned the right to know of their blessing . . . >

I suppressed a chuckle. "Hypocrisy, so I'm told, is a fine social lubricant, useful in many situations."

"Pretty fucking funny. So we're gods, eh?"

"Just to Ahktah. We gods like to keep our secrets."

The Dutchman studied my face for a moment. "But I don't understand why you didn't ruin him. Sounds like you had Ahktah pretty much broken up there. He wouldn't have had to believe anything if you'd done things the simple way—taken a few holos, threatened to show them to the locals. If they thought their priest was stealing from the gods—giving charity, of all things—"

"They would have ripped him to pieces. Literally."

He shrugged. "So? I thought you didn't like the little hypocrite."

Oh, hypocrisy isn't all that bad, Dutchman, I thought.

Depends on what you use it for, depends on who benefits. Most people lie to themselves and to others in order to line their own pockets. Ahktah did it to feed the hungry and warm the cold.

I can live with that. How about you?

Ahktah rose. <Today, this one has climbed Heaven. . . .>

I turned to the Dutchman. He wouldn't have understood. If I told him the truth, he'd just snicker at me.

"It just seemed more convenient this way," I said.

"Mmm-hmm." The Dutchman shrugged. "I guess it doesn't make any difference, Lieutenant—"

"Captain."

"—as long as it worked."

If I didn't know better, I would have sworn that the Dutchman smiled. Like he meant it, I mean.

Interlude

Destination: Señora Veronica Curdova
c/o Señor Cruz Curdova
Hacienda Curdova
Sueca, Espagne

Routing: I800RQW5ZI2AB71
Origin: Captain Emile von du Mark, TWCS
                Aboard TWS NEIL ARMSTRONG
                (#LC3369)
Subject: Personal
File Created: 1 May 2248

My Dear Victoria,

I just heard about Manuel, and I had to write and say how sorry I am.

I know that's at best cold comfort in this time of grief for you, Emilita, and Arturo. I wish I could do more.

I'd hoped to be able to tell you how Manny died. I've tried to find out, but I still don't know. As you know, the whole affair has been slapped with a Security seal, and while I've done my best to crack through, I haven't been able to.

The only thing I know is the identity and reputation of his second-in-command.

Manny and I have known Captain Moriarty from our first day in the Contact Service. "Professor" Moriarty was and is a good and competent man. Manny didn't choose his exec carelessly when he decided to go back into the field, although I'm sure he had an internal chuckle or two out of becoming the commander of someone who had been a first classman during our plebe year.

I believe that there is no possibility that Manny's life was lost due to any incompetence by his

second-in-command. While it wouldn't be wise to
go into any detail here and now, I'm sure that
you'll be hearing from the Professor once he gets
out of the hospital.

Please ask Señor Curdova not to take offense,
but I've written to my parents, asking that they
call on you and see if there is anything they can
do. While I know that the Curdova family can take
care of itself, I'd take it as a kindness if you'd
agree to see them.

As for me, I'm not sure what your feelings are
going to be toward me. Perhaps, you'll be thinking, if I'd only been able to persuade Manny not
to go back into the field, he'd still be alive.

If so, I understand. I will be thinking the same
thing myself.

Manny was my first friend in the Service; I will
miss him very much.

Please convey my regards to the Señor and
Señora, and my love to Arturo and Emilita.

All my best,

Emile von du Mark

File Transmitted: 1 May 2248

Dutchman's Price

Three friends died on Schriftalt.

No. Not friends. Brothers? Not brothers, either. More than that. Much more. . . .

If only I'd known, I might have treasured our last few moments together, paid more attention. But I didn't know. I just had a feeling, just an unfounded—and, as it turned out, plain wrong—premonition from the moment we hit Schriftalt's atmosphere.

Not that I was wrong to be worried; I was right. But I wasn't worried about them. Just about the shuttle. Just about the damn shuttle.

I

A flier has to have both caution and confidence. But the shuttle screamed all the way down, in my ears and in my mind.

I still don't know where the fear came from. Maybe it was just that I didn't like being Second Team. Better to be First, where all you have to do is build the Gate, locate any possibly habitable planets, then do the orbital survey. Better to be Third, where at least you know there's something serious out there.

But it's not fun to be Second. When you're Second, it's too easy to be a bit too slow on the uptake, or—more likely—let your adrenal glands keep pumping, pushing you until you don't know when you're firing at shadows, or don't notice when the shadows reach out with their needle-pointed, retractile claws. . . .

For whatever reason, the shuttle screamed.

It isn't supposed to sound different until we hit about Mach 2—from the high side, of course—not as long as it's coming in at the right attitude, through the right land window.

We were at the right attitude. That was easy to check and easier to verify.

To check, I glanced at my attitude display. The screen was solid green, which meant that our actual attitude was what the computer thought it ought to be.

To verify, I noted that I was still breathing. Reenter at the wrong attitude and you're dead once you hit atmosphere.

Land windows are a different matter. If the computer and I were bringing the shuttle in too shallowly, the shrill thrumming of the heat shield wouldn't stabilize; instead, it would begin to ease off, as the shuttle started to gain altitude, bouncing off the atmosphere of the planet like a stone skipping across the water. And if we came in too steeply, the skin temperatures would go above the heat shield's classified but very high tolerance, the shield would ablate, and the shuttle would become a brightly glowing cinder for a few seconds.

Either way, it wasn't supposed to sound different.

Maybe it didn't. Maybe it was just me.

The Dutchman frowned over at me. "Trouble?" he asked around the unlit cigar clamped between his teeth.

"Don't know, but something sounds funny."

"Sounds?"

"Sounds."

"Mmm . . . N'Damo, punch up an audio comparison, and analysis."

"Yes, sir." Donny's fingers beat a rapid tattoo on his keyboard. "Here it comes. . . . Nothing special, Major. External ambient sounds indicate normal atmospheric entry," he said. "As far as the comp can tell, performance of all subsystems is nominal."

That sounded good.

"I don't know, Major," I said. "Maybe it's just me. I've got a funny feeling." I punched the PROGRAM button to let the computer fly the shuttle for a few seconds while I tested the stick against the fly-by-wire computer.

Again, nothing. I took control back.

The Dutchman snickered. "Nice try, Captain von du Mark. But this horseshit isn't going to work, Emmy."

"What isn't going to work?"

"You're not going to get even with me for your Quarterly by spooking me." The Dutchman snickered. "I don't spook easy."

Akiva Bar-El gave out a sound halfway between a throat clearing and a growl. "Captain von du Mark does not operate that way, sir."

"You being insubordinate, Lieutenant?"

"No, sir. Accurate, sir."

The Dutchman snickered again.

I don't know. Maybe there was something to the Dutchman's accusation. I'll give him the point: I was hurt by the meat of his last Quarterly Evaluation: *While Captain von du Mark's reflexes and judgment are generally adequate or better, he has on more than one occasion demonstrated an unfortunate sentimentality in his behavior. I cannot at this time recommend him for Team Leader status. . . .*

To hell with him. I deserved my own Team; I'd proved it on more than one world. Pon, particularly.

Right on schedule, I thumbed for a bit of wing, and felt them take a tentative bite into the thin but fast-moving air. I pulsed the radar for a quick look downward through the clouds.

The plan called for the final approach and landing to be over the western half of the dirtball's smaller continent, the half now mostly covered by oncoming clouds chasing a slow-moving warm front. As to exactly where to land, we weren't sure; the weather was likely to mess up an approach anyway. It was just as easy to make a decision on the fly.

The screens went gray. I gave the shuttle more wing and locked the radar on as we entered the upper layer of clouds at fifteen klicks. While I don't like radar announcing my presence, I like flying blind less.

About ten klicks south of a nice-sized mountain, there was a decent-looking LZ: an extension of the western plain, bordering on what looked to be swamp. It was well within our unpowered-landing footprint.

I tapped the screen with a fingernail. "That look okay to you, Major?"

"That where you want to put her down?"

"Looks good to—"

"Then do it."

The shuttle screamed all the way down to the ground.

I've had tricky landings; this one wasn't one of them. Energy was just about perfect: the spot we'd picked out fell just halfway between the max-range and min-range lines on the energy display. At fifteen klicks out, I spread the wings fully open, put the shuttle into a nice gentle bank that gave us—and, more important, the belly cameras that we could extrude, now that the speed had dropped and the skin cooled sufficiently—a quick tour over the area around our LZ.

"Looks good, Major."

"Set her down, Captain," the Dutchman said. "Gently."

"Airspeed, please," I said. Shuttles aren't like most fixed- or variable-wing craft: it's a bad habit to take your eyes off the screen during a shuttle landing; whether or not you bump into something is far more critical than what your airspeed is at any given moment. If you drop below stall speed—just about four hundred, by the way—the engines'll light themselves, unless you tell them otherwise.

So, when it's tricky, my preference is to have whoever's in the right-hand seat read off airspeed. I know: I could have had the computer programmed to give me airspeed indications vocally. But I couldn't tell the Dutchman what to do if I did it that way, could I?

"Five hundred five," the Dutchman said.

The heads-up display was a glowing green line across the screen, just above the nose of the shuttle—

"Four eighty."

—so I pulled back on the stick with my right hand while I eased my left hand over to the panel and set the IGNITE selector to work the belly jets, since I wasn't going to need the main engines to get to the LZ. I thumbed back the cover to arm the button. We were a bit heavy in energy, so I wheezed the nose intakes open early.

"We're coming in on four hundred, Emmy. And that's fucking *stall* speed."

"So I've heard." I punched the IGNITE button to fire up the belly jets to a nice quiet idle, and dropped the shuttle down toward the plain.

"Give me landing pods, full extension."

"Got 'em," the Dutchman said unnecessarily, as they extended with a loud ka-*chunk*. "Bar-El—stand by with the foam."

"Yes, sir."

You have to pay attention to what airspeed indicators say, but don't believe them. They lie; the approach & closing radars are worse. Both swear you're slowing constantly, but the truth is the last few meters go faster than light speed.

The plain came up like God's Own Flyswatter.

I pulled the nose up more than thirty degrees past horizontal, and then shoved the throttle almost to the wall; at more than three gees, it only took a couple of seconds to kill the shuttle's speed, both forward and downward.

I pushed the nose down, pulled the throttle back, and settled the shuttle down firmly on the tall grasses, the landing pods hissing as the hydraulic system took up the shock.

"Powerdown," I said.

The Dutchman was already flipping his switches. "Bar-El, handle the fire."

Flames licked up in the monitor as the still-hot heat shield ignited the dry grasses around the shuttle.

"Foaming." Bar-El hit the foam switch. A turret in the roof snicked open and some distant piece of machinery began to whirr as the nozzle sprayed fire-killing foam over the shuttle and its environs.

"Negative," Bar-El said, eyeing his screens. "We've got some fire beyond range to port—to the south."

Moving more quickly and gracefully than a man his size had any right to, Akiva Bar-El was already out of his harness, on his feet, and halfway into his silvery environment suit, balancing on the balls of his feet like a dancer.

"Permission to go EVA and kill the fire?" he asked.

"Damn." The Dutchman pursed his lips. "Permission granted. Hop to it. Full decontam protocol, understood?" The fat man turned in his couch to trigger the outside bio-package; a little distant heat and smoke wouldn't do much damage to biogel, and the sooner we knew what biocontaminants we were up against, the better.

"Yessir." Bar-El slipped a membrane helmet over his head, sealed it to his E-suit's collar, and inflated it while he shrugged into a khaki oversuit. He threw a power rifle's sling over one shoulder, tucked an extinguisher under one arm, and slipped into the airlock, slamming it behind him as he cycled the outside door open.

The Dutchman turned to N'Damo. "Keep in touch with the jewboy. Comm or psi—I don't give a rat's ass."

"Yesss. Sirrrrrr." The sound caught in Donny's throat and turned into a high-pitched, liquid burbling.

I turned to look at him.

Pink tongue clenched tightly between his ivory teeth, he scrabbled his fingers slowly, clumsily, randomly across his panel, his eyes vague and watery.

"Sssschtannnnn?" he hissed, in a voice distant and alien, his fingers caressing the air in front of him. "No. N'vakt sssss . . . ssssschtannnnnn. Ssss." His eyes sagged shut as his arms fell limp at his side. Reflexively, I started to unbuckle myself from my couch, but then caught myself, snorted, and punched up the readings from Donny's sensors. He was breathing, his heart was pumping away, but his brain waves looked weird. Some esper thing, undoubtedly.

"*Shit*. Why the fuck do the locals have to always be breathing down our necks? Awright, Emmy, we're going to Condition Yellow," the Dutchman said, punching for the roof radar and weapons turret himself. He raised his hand to his throat. "You hear that, jewboy? We're at Yellow. Acknowledge."

"Condition Yellow, Major," came over the speaker.

The Dutchman shut off his mike. "Keep an eye on Bar-El. He's not particularly expendable at the moment."

"Yes, sir." After landing, the pilot's first priority is powering the ship down; that only takes a few moments, and most of it doesn't require full attention. I'd already hooked my right-hand display into the turret cameras and was watching Akiva carefully spray the last traces of smoking grass. He let the extinguisher drop to the ground.

"No problem, Major. He's already on his way back."

The Dutchman went over to N'Damo. "Out, but he seems okay," the fat man said as his fingers felt gently at Donny's neck and pried back an eyelid to reveal a dilated pupil.

Bar-El entered the lock and shut it behind him. Blue water ran down the window like an old-style washing machine as the lock began to spray biocides all over him and his suit.

The Dutchman sat back in his couch and folded his hands over his belly.

"Only thing to do now is keep watch until the biogel has a chance to spoil, and wait until sleeping darkie there has a chance to wake up." He wriggled himself a bit deeper into his couch and closed his eyes.

I hated it when he pretended to sleep in a situation like this. I *think* he was pretending. . . .

II

Donny shook his head. "It has to be Captain von du Mark, not Akiva, Major. Kas*ch*tkd—no." A drop of spittle ran down the side of his mouth as he swallowed three times, then started again. "He isn't a xenophobe. It *has* to be him."

Donny looked at me, his eyes begging for support. The Dutchman looked at me, one eyebrow half raised. Bar-El looked at me, his broad face impassive.

Just to make it unanimous, I glanced at myself in the mirror.

I shook my head. "You say this Histeel—"

"Hischteeel."

"—of yours isn't fully psychic, but it's sensitive enough to tell the difference between me and Bar-El?"

"Yesss." N'Damo swallowed. "It wants to—kvreahn schtann." His mouth began to move soundlessly, his tongue wriggling like a snake.

He forced himself back under control. Well, mostly under control—his fingers shook as though he had Parkinson's disease. "Sorry. I *have* to get closer, Major. I've only got *part* of the language, can think with only *part* of the mind. It's like there's part of me *missing*."

He caught his lower lip between his canines, and bit down until a fat drop of dark blood oozed up and ran down his chin. He wiped it away.

"If you won't let me go alone, *please* let Emile come with me. Got to—" He slapped his palms together. Not like clapping. Like he was trying to crush something with the heels of his hands. "Kvath iech*tef*. Got to go *now*. Got to."

"What's the rush?" The Dutchman shook his head. " 'Err in haste, get disemboweled at leisure'—that's the way I always heard it."

I didn't like the sound of that, either. The last time I'd been rushed into a decision, I'd ended up in the Contact Service.

"Because. Hischteeel says it has to be quickly. Don't know why, but we have to move quickly. Schtanns come." He bent forward and pressed his thumbs against his eyelids until I thought he was going to pop his eyeballs out.

"And it can't be Bar-El."

"Because he's kdk*chtt* . . . because he isn't psi-neg. And he *is* a xenophobe."

I looked over at Akiva.

He smiled calmly. "We all have our flaws."

The Dutchman looked from Bar-El to me. "Agreed: you're both a couple of shitheads. On the other hand, so what if the local doesn't like the undercurrents in Bar-El's psyche?" With a thick thumb, the Dutchman flipped the cylinder of his Magnum open; he eyed the loads skeptically. "If it makes too much trouble, we can handle it, either with reason or with lead."

He frowned as he locked the cylinder back into place with a nice, solid click. "What I *don't* like is the fact that this contact of yours seems to have you locked up, N'Damo. Can't say as I like that at all—if you had a reset button, peeper, I'd be punching it."

I didn't like that, either. While the radar motion detectors weren't picking up anything significant, there could have been, say, half a thousand tanks a few meters back of the treeline, and with N'Damo locked on this Hischteeel, there was no way he could even feel another alien presence.

I took another look at the printout of the biogel analysis. All in all, it looked like the local bugs weren't going to be interested in eating us. Well, maybe some of the spores seemed to be loaded with something a lot like histidine, but it was different enough that I wasn't worried about my ability to cope with the great outdoors *sans* helmet, although we'd be wearing powered filtermasks and E-suits, just in case.

I nodded cautiously. The extra oxygen might even make me a bit heady; have to watch it.

So I couldn't say no on the grounds that it was obviously dangerous out there. Matter of fact, it seemed pretty good.

"Major?" Donny pleaded.

"All right." The Dutchman nodded. "We'll do it your way. But . . ."

"But?"

"But, Emmy, both of you wear lifters, you are going to be armed with a wiregun and extra clips, Bar-El will be outside in his skimmer with the engines hot, and I'll be working the weapons turret, just in case. Keep your eyes open, Emmy, and your safety off."

"Yes, sir."

"Emmy?"

"Sir?"

"This isn't Pon. You may—*may*—have been right to go easy there, but . . . this isn't Pon. Do you understand?"

"Yes, sir. You're telling me that this isn't Pon."

He slammed his fist down on the arm of his couch. "*Listen* to me, asshole. If you have any reason to worry about this Hischteeel character, you just blow it away and we'll let Third Team clean up after us. Just be careful. If you can't be careful, be lucky."

"And if I can't be lucky?"

"Then be *very* good."

We clumped along a rough path through the woods, Donny leading the way.

Sometimes the physical conditioning that the Service puts us through makes sense. What with my jetpack, the air filters and pumps that purified the local air, plus various and sundry weapons and ammunition for same, I must have been hauling close to thirty-five extra kilos. Subtract a few for the fact that local gravity was only point nine three standard, and that still adds up to a hell of a lot of extra weight pressing down on my shoulders and hips.

But even so, there was something nice about this forest, something particularly nice. I like real forests; I always have. Every one has a different feel.

Here, a distant breeze whispered vague but sincere promises of lazy coolness and quiet rest. Majestic trees curved overhead like the arch of a cathedral, branches decorated in plate-sized leaves that were so dark green that they were almost black.

Absolutely gorgeous. I smiled; I used to look at the old picture books when I was a kid; this was something like what the Schwarzwald must have been before the Xeno War turned it into a charred plain and the name Black Forest into a sad joke.

"Emmy?" The Dutchman's voice crackled over my phones.

"Emile," I said. "And I'm still here."

I'd decided to keep the private circuit open to Bar-El and the Dutchman while I followed Donny's rapid pace—it's just plain good sense to avoid trusting espers; when they're in communion with aliens, their loyalties aren't usually clear, even to themselves. That's why they're never armed; if you're going to have a gun at your back, it's best to know that it's a friendly one.

Donny walked quickly, with a weird, clumping stride, as though his legs weren't used to bending where they did.

I was worried, and I didn't know why. I ran it over in my mind for the nth time. The contact didn't sound simple, but I'd been through worse. Physical conditions weren't bad, not bad at all. The local sun was an F8 star, a tenth larger and a third brighter than Sol, almost unbearably small and bright when it peeked through the trees overhead.

Overall, this world got just a bit more irradiation than Earth, but nothing unusual. Atmosphere was breathable straight—my favorite—although it was a bit rich in both CO_2 and O_2, which is why we had to worry—just a little—about hyperventilating.

But that wasn't really a problem, not at this pace.

There was a sudden rustling behind me.

"Donny. Watch it!" Snatching up my wiregun, I spun as something about a third of a meter long bounded across the path.

Curling a gloved finger around the trigger, I snicked the safety off my wiregun and drew a hissing line through the trees and into it, just as it leaped into the air and fell back, cut in half.

The back half fell dead, limp. The head and shoulders jerked spasmodically for a second, and the eyes tried to focus on me, but didn't make it before it died. Dark blood mixed with brown viscera on the ground as leaves, cut and shattered by the blast, settled to the ground.

I stooped over the creature, cursing myself for being a trigger-happy asshole.

"Got a sample, Major. The local equivalent of a rabbit."

It was a kind of brown, kind of reptilian kind of rabbit, but that's what it was. The ears were hairless disks; when I pried open the mouth, I could see the peglike, crunching teeth of an herbivore behind the forward tearing teeth— rabbitlike incisors, not the flesh-rending daggers of a carnivore or the compound styles of an omnivore.

Its stomach contained a putrid-looking mulch that had more than a few leaf fragments mixed among it.

A rabbit. That's all it was. I could be proud of myself: now, the local equivalent of rabbits would justifiably walk in fear wherever the brave Captain Emile von du Mark, Thousand Worlds Contact Service, trod.

"I just killed the local version of a rabbit, Major. Call it a smeerp."

"Sounds tasty." The humor in the Dutchman's voice seemed a bit strained over the phones. "Want me to hold dinner?"

"Funny, Major." Taking a sample handler—a lot like a cat-box scoop—from my utility belt, I tucked the corpse into a sample bag, pumped the air out, then hid the bag behind a fallen log, figuring on picking it up on our way back. Or maybe pulling rank on Donny and letting him carry it.

We walked on, the worry weighing even more on me.

I tried to work it out. There were a few disturbing sides to the Contact: First's orbital sweep had included pictures of sapients, about man-high, vaguely reptilian in appearance, although it was hard to tell even from the computer-enhanced pictures. Sapients are always potential trouble, even when they're at the early-agricultural level that these seemed to be.

But *was* it an early-agricultural level? The photos had showed an unusually high ratio of leafy-surface area to cultivated area, not the sort of scraggly-looking fields that you'd expect from low-tech primitives.

Maybe that was it. Without a lot of power equipment, the locals seemed to be farming awfully efficiently. But since when was that a crime—or a danger, for that matter?

Then there were the traces of RF, which meant that there was some sort of power technology going on . . . and that meant we couldn't just Drop and go. Power technology can lead to spaceflight. Spaceflight can lead to Gates. Gates can lead to wars.

One set of Xenos was more than enough. There was no particular reason to believe that the predecessors to the Sesss were the nastiest things in the universe.

"Anything yet, Emmy?"

"Nothing, Major. Taking a bearing: I have the dee ex at"—I glanced down at my tracker—"three point eight klicks, direction forty-three point nine absolute." I thumbed for my private circuit. "I'm worried about N'Damo, Major."

"Maybe you're just plain worried. You've been spooky since AlphaCeeGate."

"I've been spooky since I was *born*, Major," I said. *I've been spooky since Manny Curdova died, Major,* I thought. But I didn't say that.

"Burning out on me?"

"Maybe."

Maybe I was. It can happen to the best, and I wasn't claiming I was the best.

"Hischteeel is just ahead," Donny said, breaking into a jog, pushing off the path, into the brush.

We broke through into a low clearing, and there it was, squatting on a log.

It rose slowly. While it seemed immense, it was only a little taller than Donny, just about my height. It was naked, except for a gray skin rag wrapped about its waist, which fell almost to its bulging knees. The skin was gray and dull like a coat of primer paint; it hung loosely on the creature's frame. Its six-fingered hands writhed and shook, as though it had been infected with Donny's palsy. The forearms and lower legs were disproportionately long; the extra joints on its fingers made them look broken.

The face, such as it was, was the worst. If I closed my eyes down to slits, I could have imagined it as a burn victim: gray, wrinkled skin, no protuberances, only holes for a nose and ears, and the horrible red eyes, hidden behind massive folds of flesh.

"Contact, Major," I forced out.

The eyes burned redly into mine.

Donny stood motionless.

"Translate, *dammit.*"

Donny turned back to me, his face from the nose down expressionless under his mask. But I could see the eyes through his goggles, and I didn't like the look in them. Sort of like my cousin Stefan looked after he joined up with the Christers and went to live on Graz Beach.

"Emile my brother. This is Hischteeel. It, oh, it wishes, with all its heart and soul, oh, it wishes to join our associational-group-of-those-who-care-together."

First Contact with an alien species always tends to bring out the orator in me:

"*Huh?*" I said.

"Listen to it." Norfeldt snorted. "The Service, Emmy— it's talking about the fucking *Contact Service.* The critter wants to join the CS."

N'Damo broke into a series of harsh whispers, answered by the gray monster. "Oh, it wishes to be part of us, and with us, and of us."

This was getting seriously weird.

"That's what's going on? This old lizard wants to join the Service?"

"No, no, *no*, my friend. "No." Donny turned to me, reaching out to grip my forearms. I pushed him away; an esper in contact is always suspect.

"No," he said, "no, it is not old. It is a youngling, just into *kchtt-t-t*—just into the change. It is time for it to join a schtann, and when I touched its mind it found that it wishes to join the Contact Service, oh the Contact Service schtann."

The creature rose slowly from the log and stalked toward me, exchanging words with Donny.

"Tell the lizard to keep its distance, Donny," I said, bringing up my wiregun.

Donny croaked at it; it croaked back.

"Not a lizard, Emile. It's a schrift, a schrift it is." He turned to me. Inside his bubble, his eyes were wide. "Hischteeel says we have to get back to the shuttle. The . . . Surveyors, the schtann-of-observation must have it under surveillance, and the Artificers and Communicators will want the shuttle. There is much in it that the Artificers would want to learn about. That, that, that is why I-we had to hurry. That is all it tries to do: to warn us and join us, its brothers-and-more-than-brothers-to-be."

I didn't like the sound of that. "Major?"

"Yeah, I think you're right." the Dutchman said. "Bar-El, you'd better go make pickup, fast—"

I heard the Dutchman gasp for breath.

"Holy *mother*fucking—Condition Blue, Emmy. You and N'Damo get your asses back here. Two thousand of these lizards just stepped out of the treeline, and if those aren't rifles they're carrying—fuck the Blue, we're in Red. Condition Red. Bar-El, get that skimmer up now—"

Bringing up my wiregun, I started to turn back toward

the lizard, but it was already lunging at me. Its massive hands batted it away, knocking it out of my hands.

The schrift reached for me. I hopped back on one leg and kicked the creature in the chest, then lunged for the lost wiregun, but found my hands full of writhing schrift, as Bar-El and the Dutchman kept talking on the all-hands freak.

"Cancel that, Major—they will not make it."

Over the whirr of the skimmer's engines, I could hear the *chuffaka-chuffaka-chuffaka* of his floating recoilless firing. Idly, it occurred to me that Akiva's microphone wasn't quite tight against the skin of his throat, or I wouldn't be hearing the background so clearly.

"I am going for them," Akiva said, his voice level, a touch flatter, more expressionless than usual.

Chuffaka-chuffaka-chuffaka.

"No—"

"I won't leave live comrades behind," Akiva said evenly, as though he was reporting on an unchangeable fact of the universe.

"It won't fucking *work*," the Dutchman snapped. "Got zero chances—get the skimmer back in the bay, and then you and I are getting the fuck out of here. Sorry, Emile, N'Damo, but the train's pulling out of the station. Now."

It was interesting, the sound of the Dutchman's voice as he pronounced our death sentence; there wasn't a trace of emotion in it.

Chuffaka-chuff.

The sound stopped.

And in the distance I could hear the roar of the shuttle's belly jets.

And then:

Whoom.

III

I wasn't there for it, and the Dutchman and I never talked about it, but later on I saw the tape of the rest of the fight, captured for posterity by the shuttle's turret camera.

I may as well put it in here.

The schrift got to Bar-El just as he was bringing the skimmer around the stern of the shuttle. I guess he'd decided to break through into the forest from a different angle, away from the mass of gray flesh that was working its way through the fire of the shuttle's turret gun.

I don't know what he thought he'd accomplish. Even if he'd made pickup, there wouldn't have been anywhere to go. The Dutchman was inside the shuttle, and was getting ready to take off and leave us behind.

Take this for whatever it's worth: I *don't* hold that against the fat man.

You have to understand: that's part of the job. You can even say that that *is* the job. Getting the information back—that the locals were both organized and hostile, and had projectile weapons that could do at least minimal damage to a Service shuttle—all that was more important than the lives of any two Team members.

In fact, on a personal level, I should be grateful to the Dutchman; he erred—*if* he erred—on the side of trying to save our lives. He hadn't just punched the panic button.

Instead, he'd fired up the engines for a normal liftoff, without taking the time to adjust the belts on my pilot's couch for his greater bulk. Norfeldt lit the belly jets and started to lift the shuttle a few meters into the air, riding on ground effect to save fuel. I guess he intended to follow Bar-El to wherever the big man planned the rendezvous.

But it didn't work out that way. As Bar-El brought the skimmer around, three gray forms leaped out of the tall grasses to the floor of the skimmer itself.

The schrift I was battling with at that moment was a youngling, just into adulthood, and only barely my size. The three on the skimmer were fully adult schrift of the Artificers schtann, each half again my size, each half again Bar-El's strength.

He didn't have a chance. The tape shows him reaching for his pistol, then letting his hand drop, as though he realized that it wasn't going to work.

I never found out what he'd done to the recoilless. The mounting is supposed to have safety chocks to prevent the muzzle from pointing at the surface of the skimmer, but I guess that sometime before, Akiva had decided to remove them, to prepare for the moment when they might be in the way of what he wanted to do.

As the three schrift tried to wrestle him out of his control seat, he lurched the skimmer into a whole crowd of hundreds of the creatures.

I've gone over the next seconds of film a thousand times—at regular speed, slow-motion, frame-by-frame, computer-enhanced. But it doesn't do any good. While Akiva Bar-El was wearing a membrane helmet—he was breathing off the skimmer's air system—and I can see his face through much of the tape, at that moment there was just too much smoke in the way.

So I can't swear to it, even though I think Akiva was smiling as he raised his clenched right fist over his head in a last gesture of defiance as he used his left hand to spin the recoilless around and drop the barrel, pointing it down toward the floor of the skimmer, down toward its own ammo box.

He pulled the trigger. I *think* he was smiling. . . .

The skimmer shattered into fire.

The picture jerks after that. A piece of hot metal caught itself in the throat of the port main engine, just as the Dutchman had lifted the ship up on its belly jets, riding on the transitional lift caused by the cushion of hot gases between the ship and the ground.

The impact was like that old physics demonstration of a dry-ice puck on a smooth table; it sent the shuttle skittering, spinning across the flat ground, supported by the belly jets in transitional lift. It also knocked the Dutchman out of my couch; apparently he'd locked his leg somehow or other, and his knee snapped like a dry twig.

The autopilot kept it under control while he got himself under control and into his couch.

"Norfeldt . . . to von du Mark," he said. "Don't say anything; just listen. After I say this, I'm going off the air; I don't want to give these fuckers any chance to trace me. If they can.

"According to the panel here, one of the main engines is blocked. If I fire it, I'll blow the shuttle up.

"Not much I can do. My leg's broke; I can't get out and clear it myself. What I am doing is firing off a probe to distract their attention, then I'm taking the shuttle up the slope of the mountain, and landing it just above the cloud line. If you can, join me.

"Maybe we can clear the engine, and maybe there'll be enough fuel left to get us back topside. Maybe.

"Good luck, Captain. Good luck to us all. Norfeldt out."

I can't tell you a lot about the fight between Hischteeel and me; I was a bit too busy to take notes. It felt like it took forever, but it lasted for only a couple of seconds. It wouldn't have lasted that long, but Hischteeel was handicapped by being unwilling to risk breaking my mask or hurting me seriously.

But I didn't know that; as we were rolling around on the ground, I was doing my damnedest to get at my wiregun or get my Fairbairn knife out of its sheath, and stick either the barrel or blade up Hischteeel's nose.

It didn't work; I didn't come close. Batting the wiregun away, Hischteeel handled me almost embarrassingly easily as it wrested my weapons away and hoisted me to its broad shoulder, one powerful six-fingered hand wrapped about my wrists, the other steadying me as it broke into a fast lope.

Donny could barely keep up.

Hischteeel's bony shoulder dug into my belly as it bounced along. I tried to work my hands free, but it was too strong.

"Emile, don't struggle with Hischteeel. It's trying to get us *out* of here," he said.

Flailing my body from side to side, I managed to shake myself loose, and tumbled head over heels to the ground flat on my back.

I came up with my Fairbairn knife in my right hand and my left hand on my belt. I thumbed away the plastic dome covering the ignition button of my jetpack.

"Come on, lizard," I said. My wiregun was lost somewhere behind us in the forest, but maybe a bit of juice could do the same thing. I'd throw the knife, and as the critter ducked, I'd hit the ignition button and fry the bastard as I took to the air.

I reversed my grip on the blade and pulled back my hand for the throw.

Donny leaped in front of me. "*No*, Captain. He's on our side." He turned back to the schrift and reached out a hand.

Hischteeel took a step toward me and knelt on its bony knees, its arms folded behind its back. It tilted its head up and back, presenting its throat for the cut of my blade.

"Please, please listen, Emile," Donny said. "It says: 'I will join your grouping, not attack it, brother-to-be'—that last isn't really close, Captain. You *have* to get a feel for this language. It's got *kkakjjer*—" He swallowed twice, hard. " 'We must hide, at least until dark. I know a place; accept me now, or kill me now.' "

I rested the slender point of the knife against its neck. Beneath the slick gray flesh, alien blood pulsed slowly. Once, twice, three times.

Maybe it was dangerous. But one of the first things they

teach you at the Contact Service Academy is that the universe is full of dangers; the second is that you can't kill all of it.

"*Shit*." I sheathed the knife. "Let's get the hell out of here."

I walked to the mouth of the cave and stepped out into the night, Hischteeel following me to take up a watchful position partway up a nearby tree.

Not that it could see very well in the dark; it had stumbled around the cave almost blindly. Its ancestors were night sleepers, apparently, not night hunters. Which would have made it a good idea for the three of us to try getting out of here in the dark, except that I didn't like the idea of climbing until we got some light.

I took another yellowjacket from my beltpouch, slipped it under my mask, and tongued it. It was bitter, of course. I wonder why they don't put some sort of sweet covering on them. Be too easy that way, I guess.

Easy or not, I needed the pill. Sleep was out for now, although with my wiregun gone, I was watching for the searchers on the plain below without a clear plan as to what I'd do if one of them found us.

Two jetpacks could get Donny and me out of here. But not far, not nearly far enough—and if there's a better way to announce your presence to someone nearby than by lighting off a jetpack, I'd like to know what it is.

The night was bright with the stars overhead, and threatening with the clouds rolling in from the west. And brighter and more threatening with the flickering of lamps on the plain below.

The searchers were moving away from us, though. Most of them.

I turned up the gain on my comset, and listened once again to the repeating message. " '. . . up the slope, at hex 390719—get your fucking map out of your pouch, asshole. If you can hear me, krauthead, I'll say again:

ignore the direction of this; I'm relaying via the comm laser through the message balloon.

"And for God's sake don't broadcast. I've got a hunch they're going to figure out soon enough that the apparent direction this is coming from is phony, but let's not give them a real direction too soon, eh?

"I can sort of crawl around inside here, but there's no way I'm going to be able to get out to the back to clear the engine. Two possibilities. If you get up here quick enough, maybe you can clear it. If not, before I—*engh*—shit, shit, how the hell did I ever—"

That sounded bad. With everything else I'd seen Norfeldt do, I'd never heard him complain like that, not about personal discomfort. He must have been in heavy pain, and not able to reach the rear of the cabin and either get into the autodoc or take the full medikit down from high on the wall to get at the neural blocks.

No, cancel that first—he couldn't allow himself to get into the autodoc; the autodoc might decide he was better off unconscious. The only major painkillers he'd have in his personal kit were the alkaloids, and if he used those, he might fall asleep.

I heard a gurgling. It seemed that the Dutchman was using a more primitive version of anesthesia. Fair enough, under the circumstances.

"Never mind that," the voice said, now sounding a bit stronger. "I know that you learned in school about how hard duplicating alien technology is, but I'm not going to take the chance that the locals went to a different school. Which is why I've rigged a deadman switch to the panic button. I *think* the clog in the rear engine will blow the ship to hell and gone, but that's not good enough, Emile. . . ."

I turned the sound down. There wasn't anything else to hear, and I had to work out what my next move was— what *our* next move was. I didn't have a lot of hope for my command surviving much longer, but I was going to do my damnedest.

The mission first, Serviceman. The mission first. Then the command.

The schrift dropped from the tree and stood in front of me, muttering something quietly in its own language.

Donny tapped me on the shoulder. "Hischteeel has to go do something."

"Do what?"

N'Damo shook his head. "It won't tell me."

"What do you mean it won't tell you?"

A ghost of a smile flickered across Donny's face. "I mean that when I ask it why, it says, 'I will not tell you.' "

Fucking helpful, Donny. Still, given our situation, I thought a little smartass showed a bit of spine.

"So?"

"So, it is asking your permission."

"Enough bullshit. Tell him to geek. Now."

A quick rasping conversation, then:

"I don't understand it, Emile. But he won't tell, and I can't read him when he's trying to keep a secret."

Well, if the lizard really wanted to go, there wasn't a damn thing I could do about it, not without my wiregun; Hischteeel had already proved that within a few moments of our first meeting. And since it was asking permission, I might as well grant it.

Of course, it could be going for help. Local help.

I shrugged. It didn't much matter. In for a penny, in for a pound; if Hischteeel's real intention was to betray us to the Artificers or another schtann, then we were already as good as dead.

No. Not quite as good. I held my Fairbairn knife in my hand, eyeing its gleaming blade, wondering if I had the guts to do the necessary. There was too much knowledge locked up in two heads. . . .

"Emile?"

"Wrong. Try again, Mister."

"Excuse me?"

I spun on him. "I said: 'No. Try again, Mister.' The

pilot and second-in-command of our Team is good old informal Emile. The commander of this ragtag party of two humans and one amphibian is Captain von du Mark, and you can put a *sir* after that. You catching my meaning, Lieutenant N'Damo?''

That caught him by surprise. ''Yes, sir,'' he managed to get out.

I was more surprised than he was—not at him, at me. Granted, Captain Patel had taught us in Command & the Nature of Authority that when you take command, the very first thing you have to do is make it clear that you *are* in command—if you don't, you're being unfair to your subordinates more than to yourself. Making it clear without making a jerk of yourself is considered to be high art, he'd said.

I wasn't surprised because I wasn't up to the high art—it was just that I hadn't known that any of what he'd taught me had taken.

''Tell him he can go,'' I said. ''But until he gets back, I don't want you more than two meters away from me. I'll entertain no questions.''

''Aye, Em—Captain. Sir.'' Donny turned to the schrift and answered in its own language. I guess that's the only thing I really envy about espers: the gift of tongues. The rest of it, the peeping into filthy little minds, that has to be like going through garbage, nose first.

Hischteeel vanished into the forest.

Gradually, the fan of my purifier had taken up a higher pitch; I opened the case and held both my breath and the HOLD button while I slipped out the micropore filter and slipped the spare into its slot.

I took out my Fairbairn knife and scraped at the bone-white ceramic surface of the dirty filter. Most of the real clogging was in the pores themselves, of course, but some of it was on the surface.

And, besides, it gave me an excuse to have the knife in my hands.

Some things were starting to become clear. Not good, mind, just clear.

First was the Dutchman and his situation. A blocked engine is like a hung bullet in a gun barrel, only more so: light the engine, and all you have is a rapidly expanding cloud of gas, slightly salted with fragments of metal and flesh.

Not good.

If the Dutchman couldn't clear the engine—and with a badly broken leg, he wasn't going to be able to—at least one of us had to get topside to clear it. Either that, or hope that Third Team would bring back our bones.

Of course, we could try to hold out in the shuttle.

No. Cancel that. Hischteeel was confident of the Artificers' abilities to make things; even though they hadn't changed over their power technology to combustion, they apparently had some pretty fine catalytic electricity generation going on. And that's tricky stuff.

I wasn't willing to bet that they couldn't duplicate far too much of the scout's equipment.

We hadn't seen many examples of advanced technology here, but that can be incredibly deceptive. Come to think of it, we'd only seen a very few examples of what the locals could do, and the more I thought about it, the less I liked the high green-to-brown ratio of their cultivated land. Agriculture is tricky.

So: the Dutchman was right. The scout had to either get topside, or get blown into very small pieces.

Which brought us back to problem two: the schrift.

I tucked the filter in my pouch, but I didn't put the knife away. "Donny?"

"Yes, sir?"

"How much of what you told me are you sure of?"

He eyed me levelly. "All of it."

Damn. I was hoping that most of what he'd gleaned from Hischteeel's mind was wrong. At least, I was hoping that it was low-reliability information, not hard intelligence.

Intelligence. That was the problem.

I'd never heard of even a *semi*-intelligent race of amphibians before, and a lot of the trouble came from the fact the schrift were amphibians, not saurian like the Sesss or vaguely mammalian like the poncharaire or onrians; they were legitimate amphibians.

The puzzle of Hischteeel's interest in the Contact Service, and the source of our problem, lay in an obvious fact: amphibians don't know who their parents or children are, and can't care. Females lay unfertilized eggs in the water; males come along and fertilize them by the zillions. Less personal than the kind of cathouses the lower-ranking Navy files patronize, although I wouldn't have thought it possible.

No vague idea of who your parents are means no family.

And the family is the basis of society: you can ask a mother cat teaching her kittens to clean themselves. If she won't answer, you can ask my father.

Without some way of transmitting cultural and intellectual information, a species might almost be better off not being sapient, specializing in something other than brains and adaptability; the main survival edge that intelligence gives us is learning to avoid being killed by our grandparents' mistakes. Family is necessary.

But the schrift didn't have families. Amphibians have no way of knowing who their children are. Or their parents.

Somewhere along the line, probably back when they had just come down from the trees or up out of the muck, they had evolved an alternative. As Hischteeel described it and N'Damo translated—and I knew I missed almost all the subtext; I made a mental note that if we ever got out of here, we'd have to make sure that all of Third learned the language—it sounded like a souped version of a guild system, but Hischteeel called the guilds *schtann*.

They were tight, empathic groupings based on professions—the schrift idea of professions. I'd worked out what the Teachers of Plants and Harvesters of Animals schtanns were, but . . .

"Donny—the Artificers with That Which Comes from the Ground. Are they potters, blacksmiths, or electronicists?"

His face went blank for a moment; he hadn't assimilated the language all that well, and translating was still a problem for him.

"A bit of all three, sir. I think, I think." He shook his head. "Not jewelers or large-structure builders, though; that's another schtann."

"That doesn't help me much." I had to get a hold on what was going on. The conflict and contact between the different schtanns was complex, and while I couldn't hope to get a good reading on the complexity at this stage of the Contact, I had to do the best I could.

Part of it looked like this:

Younglings were picked up and examined by members of the Childgrowers schtann shortly after they grew legs and came up on land. While the intelligence of the baby schrift was probably not as good as a dumb dog's, they could learn. Don't snicker; a three-month-old chimp's a *lot* brighter than you and I were at that age; the difference is where we plateau.

In return for not setting the children against the various other schtanns, the Childgrowers received food from the Farmers, and everything else they needed from the Artificers, Healers, Transporters, and so on. Naturally, they encouraged the best, the brightest youngsters to join the Childgrowers, but that still left a lot for the other schtanns. And when a youngster's instinctive and trained inclination to join a schtann ripened . . .

—specifically, when Hischteeel's instinct and inclination ripened, just as a Contact Service scout, a powerful esper aboard, was touching down—

. . . it had suddenly found itself in weak contact with Donny N'Damo's mind, and felt Donny's carefully ingrained loyalty to the Contact Service, and decided to join the Contact Service schtann, to which it immediately pledged its life, fortune, and sacred honor.

So it said.

"I've *got* to learn the language," I said. There's a lot of indications in a language as to the worldview of the user.

"Sir?"

"Language," I said. "There's got to be some hints in the language. "What's the word for stranger?"

"*Tsanav*," he said.

"Break it down for me. Any of the roots mean anything?"

He screwed his face up so tightly I thought he was going to break something. "Well, *av* is a radical suffix—means 'unknown,' or 'the answer is.' *Tsan* is . . . a lot like *ltsan*, which means enemy."

Figures. That's typical, all throughout sapient societies: stranger usually means enemy.

"Translate, quickly: my schtann."

"*Schtann*." He shrugged. "No difference, not even in reflection."

"Friend."

"*Kvaschtannassst*."

"I hear the word *schtann* in that. Any connection?"

"Well, *kvaschtannassst is* a schtann-mate."

"Any other word for friend?"

"There's *kdzheez*, but that means . . . a school chum? Close enough—but there's no word for just plain friend. Or if there is, Hischteeel doesn't know it."

It figured. "Translate: your schtann."

"*Klavashat't-tsan*."

"*Tsan* mean the same thing that it did a moment ago?"

"Yes, sir. The other part is like, like a collection of . . . objects. No. *Sharp* objects."

My schtann meant family; *your* family was a bunch of knives. Wonderful. Fucking wonderful.

One more step. "Allied schtann."

"*Avklavashat't-takshtsht-tsan*. Breaks down to *Klavashat't-tsan* in a weak container. But there's the *av* radical again."

And there it was:

Me and mine: human beings. No, not *Homo sapiens*: just people. Folks.

You, singular: unknown enemy.

You-in-general, plural: sharp knives.

You-my-allies, plural: sharp knives in cheap sheaths. What's unknown is when you're going to turn on me, or me on you.

"How many synonyms for 'treachery' can you come up with, Donny?"

"Well, there's—"

"Just count." There are human languages without a word for treachery; I was willing to bet that the schrift had several.

"Twenty . . . three."

That did it. A standard sort of strategy was out: maybe we could back a schtann, pay them off, show them how it was in their interests to protect Thousand Worlds interests, but all that would amount to would be loading a gun at our heads. Not with a worldview like that.

Damn. I didn't know *what* I'd recommend. Dropping right away seemed a bit premature, but what would work?

We could recommend that the Navy keep a battlecruiser or two in permanent orbit, but the Xeno War was started by the Navy's being too slow with a trigger. Almost better to drop a worldwrecker.

Almost, I said. We can't do that. One day, humanity will run into a race a lot more powerful than we are, and we have to be ready for that day. Having a bit of dirty linen in our closet is bad enough; having wiped out a sapient alien species without knowing for *damn* sure that it really represented a clear and present danger isn't the sort of precedent we'd want to set.

So. What was left? Maybe mess with their worldview by teaching them human languages?

Don't be silly—a whole *world?*

How about just one hostile schtann? No. Not when they already had twenty-odd words for treachery.

No; the schrift were going to be insular, and faithful to their own. Only their own.

I wasn't even sure I liked the idea of a Drop. This whole

schtann business sounded awfully powerful, awfully dangerous.

No treaty with the race, no treaty with a schtann, no wiping the whole species out, no Dropping them and leaving them be.

I needed another idea, but I didn't have one.

"Ehh-mhill," a rough voice whispered from behind me.

I spun; Hischteeel stood there, my wiregun held in its thick, alien hands. So it had betrayed us, after all. What was the reward for two hunted aliens?

Didn't matter. There was too much information in my head, and in Donny's; and his head held too much ability to communicate. I snatched at his harness and drew him toward me, holding him as a shield.

"Don't move, Lieutenant," I said, quietly, holding the blade against his neck. "I'm sorry, but—"

"We can't be taken alive," he said calmly. "I understand, sir. But—Hischteeel; *dshat vars*. English."

Hischteeel dropped the wiregun as if it was on fire; it backed away quickly.

"Nohh for," it hissed. "Fffoorr yoooo. Schtann. Conn. Servve. Schtann." It held out its hands, pleadingly. "Trrrussst keschun. *Trrrusst*." It backed away further.

I let go of Donny and stooped to pick up the wiregun. A quick glance showed me it still had ninety wires left.

Just to be on the safe side, I snicked the safety off and sent a single wire hissing into the soft dirt floor of the cave, well away from where we'd stashed the lifters.

"Ehmil—trusst Hischteeel. Blezee."

It knew from Donny what a wiregun could do, even if it hadn't seen the rabbit on the trail. And it could have taken the gun to one of the searchers, and turned us in.

But it hadn't. I looked at the triggerguard and at Hischteeel's finger; probably it couldn't even have fit its index finger inside.

It hadn't even tried.

Okay, Hischteeel, I thought, *I'll trust you. With my life.* "Yeah, trust, dammit."

I swear: the next thing I knew, this amphibian was hugging me.

Day broke like a bottle of dark wine dashed to bits on a cement floor.

Standing a few feet back from the opening of the cave, I was splattered by the dark sheets of rain clawing at the plain, while a small stream of dirty water worked its way between my boots and back into the cave.

Every few seconds, yet another bright finger of lightning would zigzag its way groundward. Even when the lightning was far off, I could always tell when the thunder would boom; it would start with a loud *rrrip*, just to warm up.

Off in the distance, the lamps of the searchers still flickered. I couldn't see them all that often, not through the downpour, but they were there.

Being a hunted animal isn't fun. I hadn't had the experience before, and I didn't like it much now. The schrift wouldn't stop for this; amphibians don't mind the rain. Mammals don't function all that well in it. Not well at all.

What do you think, Donny? I wanted to ask. Do we wait for the rain to clear, or do we go now?

But I didn't ask. Donny didn't have any information I didn't have, and I didn't need to have him doubt that I knew what I was doing.

I had enough of those kinds of doubts for the three of us. Hell, I had enough of those kinds of doubts to keep a regiment of St. Thomases happy in their cynicism.

I stood and let the rain beat down until I'd had enough. "Donny, Hischteeel—saddle up," I said. "We're moving out."

I'd been expecting N'Damo to have to translate for the benefit of the schrift, but Donny's instant language class seemed to be taking pretty well; the schrift nodded its massive head slowly, ponderously, as though the movement was strange to it.

"Esyess, Ehmill . . . saddloop. Hischteeel carreeeee keschun."

My belly was still sore from where it had bumped against the schrift's shoulder while it carried me. "No, thanks."

"Nohhthankssss keschun keschun."

"Means *no*," I turned to Donny. "No, I don't want it to carry me."

Donny listened as the schrift hissed a complicated refrain at him.

"No, it's asking about carrying the lifters." In confirmation, the schrift bent to demonstrate that it could carry the lifters easily in its broad hands.

"Negative. We leave them." There was no way we were going to be able to make the climb while carrying lifters.

Have them lift us, instead? Don't be silly. Four minutes of lift—max—wouldn't get Donny and me high enough, assuming that I could fly in the downpour. Forgetting that—trust or no trust—I wasn't going to leave Hischteeel behind.

It would have been nice to have lifters for the last few yards—by then, I hoped we'd be far enough away from the searchers that I'd be able to clear the engine and raise ship before any pursuit could arrive.

But the electronics . . . and the linings of the lifter's nozzles were not really something I wanted lying around loose. Not intact, that is.

"Wait for me in the rain, the two of you." I waited until they left, then set both controls to full blast, and rigged my lifter's igniter to time-delay for almost two seconds. I set a teetering deadfall over the ignite button and manually cracked the main valves on both, then carefully covered them over with a layer of soft dirt. With a bit of luck, none of the locals would spot them until we were airborne—and then I'd have kicked off a probe toward this cave.

But if something did poke around in the meantime, the slightest jar would start the fuel and oxy out of the tanks, and then light it a scant two seconds later. Which should take some steam out of the pursuit.

I stepped out into the rain after them.

Condition Blue, Dutchman, I thought. Attack expected. Then: *Fuck it: make it Condition Black.*

Condition Black: Attack initiated. *You stay the fuck out of my way, you slimy salamanders. Or you're all dead.*

I knew it was bullshit—I couldn't even take them one-on-one, and I'd run out of wires long before they ran out of schrift.

But it made me feel better, anyway.

The first few minutes were the easiest. We were pelted by raindrops only the size of grapes, barely moving at the speed of cannonballs. After less then a hundred meters, I knew it was impossible to make it while breathing through the filters—micropore filters weren't intended to filter out liters and liters of water—so I threw away my mask and invited Donny to do the same.

It wasn't going to matter. The rain was washing away any pollen in the air, and I was more worried about drowning in my mask than I was about getting an allergic reaction to the native histidines.

We climbed higher, into the thunder and lightning.

Every step became more difficult than the last for Donny. Even during the infrequent breaks I was forced to call, his chest heaved up and down like a stormy sea.

He wanted to stop, and when the lightning flashes illuminated his face, I could see him pleading with me to call a long rest, but we couldn't stop. Hischteeel did the best that it could and half-carried Donny during the rare level stretches, but when it came time to climb up rock faces, even its clawed toes couldn't get enough of a purchase on the slippery rocks to do more than support itself.

But at least we were unspotted, so far.

` It couldn't last forever, and it didn't. Less than a hundred meters short of where the Dutchman had landed the shuttle—and that's a hundred meters vertical, not horizontal—I was trying to figure out how to take the last rock face, when I heard an alien hiss from behind me, and spun to see a full-sized schrift ducking down behind a boulder.

"Move ahead, you two," I shouted over the thunder, slapping Donny on the shoulder and giving Hischteeel a push. The two of them ducked down behind a boulder, and I followed, drawing my wiregun out of the shoulder holster.

Ninety wires may sound like a lot, but on a full auto, the gun can fire that many in one point eight seconds; I set it for five-shot bursts and looked out from the boulder.

Downslope, at least three of the leathery beasts were making their way toward us, and climbing faster than I could have, even on my first wind. I sent a burst their way, and saw one clutch at its belly and fall a hundred meters while the others ducked for cover.

"Shit." I thumbed my transmitter on. "Okay, Donny," I said, hoping that he could hear through his bone-inducers over the crash of the thunder, "we're back on the air. Lock onto your freak, and lock your mike on."

"Yes. Sir."

I could hear him panting. "Turn the squelch up."

"Yes, sir."

I thumbed for the Dutchman's freak. "Major? Can you hear me?"

Take your pick; the recordings say that it was less than one second real time before the Dutchman answered me, but it was a million years Emile time.

"Yes."

"Coming in. But we've got trouble—Condition Blue. If you're not recording on all freaks, you'd better start now. And stand by the panic button."

"Who . . . the fuck do you think you are giving orders, Emmy?"

"Who do I think I am, shithead?" I forced a laugh. "I'm the senior officer not on the sick list, Mister Norfeldt. Now, you will say yes*sir*, then you will shut up and demonstrate some willing compliance with lawful orders, or I'll have you facing charges of insubordination, Dutchman, after I feed your fucking wooden shoes to you—

assuming I don't burn you down for mutiny in the face of the enemy. *You understand me, Mister?"*

He barely hesitated. "Understood."

I beckoned Hischteeel to me. I looked at its huge fingers, and at the wiregun's triggerguard, measuring them by eye. No, its finger wouldn't fit. And besides, even if Hischteeel could hold one, Donny was likely to be a better shot than an alien that had never held a pistol in its life.

"Translate, Donny. And listen up—" Thumbing the wiregun to single shots, I ducked out from behind the boulder and fired off a few quick ones, quickly answered by a pair of shots from the schrift below. I don't know what kind of slugthrowers they had, but one nicked a chip out of the boulder that missed my eye by a centimeter.

I ducked back, and slipped in a puddle, almost losing my balance. Sheets of rain pounded me, trying to slam me down. I forced myself back to my feet, in a half-crouch next to Donny.

"Listen up. We don't have much of a chance, and we've got zero chance if I can't get up to the shuttle and get the engine cleared, or at least get at the weapons locker.

"So I go, and you hold the fort. If you can." *If you survive long enough for me to get to the weapons, locker, Donny, I thought, I'll come back for you.* But I couldn't say that. It would have been a lie.

Telepaths are never to be armed; it's in the regulations.

I handed him the wiregun. He took it in his right hand and held it awkwardly; he'd never held one before.

There wasn't any choice. It was him or me, and I was the pilot. He was expendable, I wasn't.

"Do the best you can," I said. "In the meantime, I want you running a constant translation over your transmitter—words, phrases, anything from the local language."

"Yes, sir."

I swallowed. No, I couldn't take the chance: it had to be said. There was just too much knowledge in his head. "Donny, translate for me: Hischteeel, Donny is not to be taken alive. It would be very bad for the Contact Service schtann if that happens. Understood?''

Donny barely hesitated before hissing at the schrift.

Hischteeel nodded slowly. ''Yesss. Unnerstannn. Hischteeel keschun?''

I couldn't tell him; I couldn't. I owed it to the schrift, which thought of itself as my brother, as more than my brother.

But I couldn't tell him the truth. ''You are to be taken alive. And you are to tell the other schtanns, the sharp knives, nothing except your name and your schtann, that of the Contact Service. *Nothing* else. Do you understand me?''

Name, rank, and serial number, Hischteeel. That's all.

Donny hissed at it, then took a long look at me. He stood silent for a short moment, then nodded briskly. ''Yes, sir. Understood. By both of us.'' He actually smiled. ''Good luck, Emile. You'd better get going.''

The schrift forced a nod. It looked strange, unnatural for the creature to bend its head forward and back, but it nodded. ''Hischteeel unerstan.''

I'd often wondered what it felt like to send brave men out to die. It's strange: it was the worst thing I'd ever had to do, but mixed with the horror of what I was doing was burning pride that I'd been associated with Donald Kiri N'Damo, Lieutenant, TWCS.

And Hischteeel.

I turned the squelch on my transmitter down to zero, locked it on transmit, and stripped it off, dropping it to the ground. Transmitters are tough.

I slipped away into the storm. There was only a hundred-meter stretch to climb.

While the schrift killed my brothers, I scampered to safety.

Up on the ledge, the rain and wind whipped hard at my face as I hit the annunciator button, pounding on the hatch. ''Open it the fuck up, dammit!''

It snapped open; I stepped into sudden peace of the inner hatch and shouted at the Dutchman to open the inner door. This wasn't time for any kind of decontam protocol.

There was a trail of black, congealed blood on the steel floor. It hit me: the Dutchman had said he'd launched a balloon, and in order to do that he would have had to, at least, crawl to the door, pull the cord, and toss the package outside.

As the inner door slowly wheezed open, I squeezed into the cabin.

"How . . . how they hanging', Emmy?"

The Dutchman looked bad. Twenty-plus hours in the couch with a compound fracture of the knee hadn't left the fat man well off. A crude tourniquet was wrapped around his thigh; the leg was swollen and his khakis were caked with black blood below. But care for the leg could wait until we were topside.

His eyes started to roll up; I leaped over to the pilot's couch where he lay and quickly disabled his deadman switch. It was a neat idea: two springy contacts from the comm panel, held apart by the Dutchman's thumb. But we didn't need it, not anymore.

"It's going to be okay, Major," I said. "I'll get the engine clear." That was the first thing I'd checked: the engine. The jagged piece of steel was jammed in, but maybe I could pry it out.

"The . . . esper. And the lizard." He shook his head, trying to clear it. "They . . . didn't make it."

"I know."

"I . . . heard. I heard N'Damo die, heard the other lizards try to make Histeel talk."

"Hischteeel, Major. Lieutenant Hischteeel. 'All members of the Contact Service are officers,' Major. Look it up; you'll find the words on the first fucking page of *Contact Service Rules, Regulations, and Proprieties*, Major. So you say its name with respect: it was Lieutenant Hischteeel, TWCS."

The Dutchman's eyes widened. I didn't have time to

explain, and it wouldn't do any good for the Dutchman to suffer any longer, so I grabbed a hypo from the nearest medikit and gave him a full dose of morphine before I snatched up a crowbar and started for the hatch, reaching for the nearest wiregun.

I stopped myself. No. Better: tucking the crowbar under my arm, I took the Korriphila 10mm out of the weapons locker, slammed a clip into the butt, and pumped a round into the chamber before slipping a pair of extra clips into my pocket.

When I go, I'm going to be accompanied by the thunder of gunpowder, not the hissing of a wiregun.

The rain was worse than it had been. One eye on the ledge, I made my way to the rear of the shuttle.

The jagged piece of metal was wedged in tight, but it was jagged, and there was—barely—enough room to get the tip of the crowbar between the metal and the lining of the engine. I tried prying gently, not daring to risk chipping the lining, but nothing happened. It didn't give at all.

Even over the pounding of the storm, I could hear a scrabbling on the rocks below.

"Fuck it." I tucked the pistol in my belt, stripped off my E-suit gloves, and then wrapped my fingers around the crowbar and pulled, hard.

At first, nothing happened. I pulled harder, and then harder, until spots started to dance before my eyes and I thought I was going to black out.

Move, you sonofabitch. I pulled like I was Arthur, going for the Sword in the Stone.

The jagged metal squealed and popped out.

Wiping rainwater and sweat from my stinging eyes, I tossed the crowbar aside and drew the Korriphila, thumbing the safety off. Theoretically, I should have checked on damage to the nozzle lining, but there wasn't time. Besides, who cared? There wasn't another choice. As the old saying goes, if you're drowning and someone throws you an anchor, grab it.

I dropped to my belly and peered out over the ledge. Three schrift were working their way up, only a dozen or so meters below. I could have made it back into the shuttle, and maybe lifted before they reached the ledge, but that was only a maybe.

Besides, it only seemed right that Hischteeel and Donny get some sort of salute. I stood and gripped the Korriphila in both hands, and then pulled the trigger, sending them lead and flame until the gun clicked empty.

It only took a moment to reload. I kept firing until I was out of ammunition.

The Dutchman must have had the constitution of a horse; he was groggy but awake when I got back in the shuttle, slammed the doors behind me, and then buckled myself into his couch with one hand while I started the computer on the launch sequence with the other.

"Emile . . ."

"Shut up, Dutchman. Von du Mark's driving, and he's busy."

I'd done it before; it is possible to use charges intended to blow away stuck landing pods to bring the shuttle's nose up to horizontal, instead of firing up the belly jets. It saves fuel, and according to the computer, we had less than a klick-second to spare, unless—and I swear to God it said this—"you choose to wait for fifty-seven minutes and forty-three seconds for a better launch window for the upside stage."

Wait for fifty-seven minutes?

I swear I laughed as I punched the pods away and fired up the engines. The shuttle jerked itself to vertical.

Engines roaring a farewell to Donny, Akiva, and Hischteeel, the shuttle lifted into the storm; I barely remembered to fire off a probe to blow up the cave where I'd left the lifters.

Magic time?

No; I just flew the damn thing.

*   *   *

A few hours, a shower, a bit of work by the autodoc, and a liter of wine made a huge difference in how the Dutchman looked. As we left the dirtball behind us, he lolled back in his chair, still a bit groggy from the drugs. His broken knee was encased in a huge plaster cast, the tiny monitor the autodoc had left on it pulsing a constant green.

Norfeldt drank more wine. I would have told him to skip the alcohol, but what the hell, it was his life.

He nodded slowly from behind his balloon glass. "Play it again. Please." The question of who was in command wasn't really important, not at this point, and both of us were dealing with the question by ignoring it. That may not be regulation, but there are times when regulations just don't matter.

I scanned the audio record again, listening to Hischteeel's gentle words to Donny, Donny's brief cry, and the harsh voices of the other schrift.

"Hischteeel didn't tell them anything; I'll bet anything on that."

Norfeldt nodded. "We'll see what kind of translation they can hack together in New Berne—but so what if it didn't talk?"

I shook my head. "You're missing the point. Intelligent amphibians are dangerous, particularly if they're anything near as clever at duplicating what we can do as Hischteeel thought they'd be. It's a matter of either coming to terms with them, or being forced to commit genocide. Take your pick."

"But what kind of terms, Emmy? If they have that kind of worldview, we couldn't ever trust any of the schtanns, not if they're just waiting for an opening. It'd be like the West opening up Nippon—the Nipponese smiled and ducked their heads for a hundred years, and then bombed Pearl Harbor."

I drew another bulb of coffee from the dispenser and took a pull on it before answering. "You don't see it, do you?"

"No."

"Hischteeel was a test case. If . . . if a schrift could really maintain his devotion to the Contact Service, then perhaps we'll be able to actually set up a local schtann."

"To control the schrift." The Dutchman nodded approval. "Using them to protect us from their own kind."

"You can think of it that way, Major. Our future . . . schtannmates won't see the other schrift as their own kind; they'll see *us* as their own kind. I'm going to recommend that the Service send a Third Team back—a *heavily* reinforced Third Team—and set up a . . . recruiting station. And then the Contact Service schtann is going to recruit itself some local members." I took a long pull on the coffee, then tossed the bulb into the oubliette and punched for a beer.

I took a long pull of the beer, and when I was finished I punched for another. "We're not going to have a lot of trouble with the schrift members of the CS, not if they have the dedication of Hischteeel."

"There is that." The Dutchman nodded. "There is that."

I had to do it, Major. You haven't asked the real question: why leave Hischteeel behind, to be tortured and killed?

We can do it this way only *if the devotion of a schrift to this alien, Contact Service schtann can be as strong as the devotion of a schrift to a schtann of its own kind.*

And that was a question that had to be tested to destruction. There wasn't another way, I thought.

There wasn't another way.

I'd be telling myself that for a very long time: the rest of my life. No guarantees it'd be long; certain it would feel that way.

"Sounds good." The Dutchman drained his balloon glass and tossed it into the oubliette.

I glanced at the control panel; we were right on course for the Gate. Nothing to worry about; as long as the computer's working, a dog can navigate point-to-point in space.

I manually cut the boost to one-hundredth gee; the computer compensated by minutely turning the scout on its gyros. "Here, Major, let me give you a hand to your room; I'll take first watch." And second, and third . . . after all, if you're not going to sleep, you might as well make yourself useful, no?

"No. First things first." He worked his fingers together for a moment and came up with his Team Leader's ring, the one with the diamond on one side, the bezel on the other. "I've got a spare somewhere; I think you're going to need this."

I didn't move.

"C'mon." He held it out toward me. "Go ahead. Take it."

What was I going to say? *This is my reward for murdering two friends?*

I didn't say anything; the Dutchman said it for me.

"I was wrong, kid," he said. "I thought you didn't have the guts. I truly didn't. After Pon, after you let Ahktah live, I didn't think you could send a friend to his death." He placed the ring in the palm of my hand and closed my fingers around it. "But a Team Leader has to, Emile. That's not just part of the job, it's number one on the job description. You *know* that I would have left without you, and I wouldn't have spent a fucking second regretting it. You've got to do what's necessary; the universe doesn't forgive wrong-minded mercy."

Dazed, I eyed the cold metal.

The Dutchman rose gently from his couch, gripping my shoulder for a moment, then letting go. "But you know all that, don't you?"

"Major—"

"No. That was just a rhetorical question, Captain. If I didn't know the answer, I wouldn't ask it." He looked at me for a moment, then shrugged. "I only have one bit of advice for you. Emile, it doesn't get easier from here on in. Just the opposite. For the many nights when you'll hate yourself, when you'll absolutely despise yourself for sending friends out to die, I recommend wine, Captain von du Mark. Cheap wine, in great quantities."

The Dutchman shook his head slowly, his eyes focusing on something far, far away. "Sometimes, brother, it even helps."

Postlude

I let myself fall back on my bunk, pillowing my head in my hands.

Plenty of time to relax, and not much else to do: *Da Gama*'s skipper was going to seal the lower deck off just as soon as the greenie arrived. Yitzhak Aroni, Philippe Descalier, the greenie, and I would be on our own. It looked to be a good Team.

Descalier's psi rating was impressive, and this Yitzhak Aroni looked to be almost as tough as Akiva had been.

Not tougher; there isn't such thing.

Maybe it wasn't exactly fair to insist that Descalier and Aroni live up to the standards that Donny and Akiva had set, but the universe isn't fair. It's merciless, is what it is.

And I'm not all that merciful, myself.

The greenie was probably good; Jim Moriarty wouldn't have sent me the dregs of the Academy class. Good man, the Professor; a tour of teaching was probably just what he needed. I reminded myself to look him up, next time I was Earthside. When you're in the Contact Service, you tend to lose contact with people.

Not that that was important. The work was all that mattered. Soon we'd tumble out of *Da Gama*'s underbelly, and head for a new sky.

Where would that be? What sky would we see?

I didn't know, but a packet of sealed orders lay next to my bunk. General Snow had given me strict instructions to keep the orders sealed until after we were in our scout. Probably we had hit on a pretty hot assignment. Which was both good and bad . . . but sealed orders?

I chuckled and picked up the packet, snapping the seal open with my thumb.

And then I let the packet drop to my chest. No need to read the orders yet. I didn't much care where we were going; it's all the same to me. But disobeying orders is good for practice. After all, if you're good enough at what you do, you can get away with almost anything.

My name is Emile von du Mark.

And I'm not just good enough.

I'm the best there is.

My Team Leader's ring was tight around my finger. I pulled it off and spun it in my palm, the diamond set into the front and the shiner cut into the back of the band alternately catching and shattering the light of the overhead glow.

Damn right, Dutchman. One of these things does cost more than I would have thought.

I glanced down at the bottle of cheap wine that stood next to my bunk, and read the inscription on the label for the thousandth time.

Thought you might need this, you dumbass kraut, it said. *And good luck, Emmy. You'll sure as hell need that. —Lieutenant Colonel Alonzo Norfeldt (you can still call me sir).*

I shook my head as I slipped the ring back on. Wine doesn't help, Dutchman. It just dulls the pain. And only for a little while.

Donny, Hischteeel . . . I'm sorry.

There was a knock on the door. I sat up.

"Come," I said.

The door opened, and he stood there, all clean and well pressed, eager as hell to be off on his First Assignment.

Asshole.

"Well, Mister? Speak up—are you the hotshot Jim Moriarty sent me?"

"*Sir.* Second Lieutenant Daniel Oberon reporting to the Team Leader as per regulation—"

I cut him off with a thump of my hand against the bulkhead. When my ring hit the metal, it sounded like a pistol shot. "Listen, *Mister,* I don't want you quoting regulations at me. Ever. Listen—" I stopped. It was just too much. "Just get the fuck out of here and down to the Rec. *Move* it."

He shut the door behind him at a speed only a few klicks per hour short of light speed.

I had to do it. No question. There is no way that the greenie would have understood why his Team Leader tossed a packet of orders across the room, and then lay back on his bunk—

Laughing like a madman.

Author's Afterword

For those who, like me, are interested in such things, a few notes:

Emile and the Dutchman takes place in the same universe as *Ties of Blood and Silver*, although the action of *Emile* finishes several centuries before that of *Ties* opens.

Manuel Curdova is an ancestor of the Curdovas of *Ties of Blood and Silver*. The Emilita Curdova mentioned in this book is not the same one of *Ties*, however; by the time of *Ties*, Emile and Emilita have long been common given names among the Curdovas. The planet discovered in "Dutchman's Mirror" is indeed Oroga; the chiropterans Emile, the Dutchman, Bar-El, and N'Damo encountered are a limited-intelligence subspecies of t'Tant.

Emile von du Mark is a distant ancestor of Celia von du Mark, who appears in some of my Metzada Mercenary Corps stories; Akiva Bar-El, on the other hand, is only a collateral ancestor of Shimon Bar-El and Tetsuo Hanavi of the MMC stories.

JOEL ROSENBERG

ABOUT THE AUTHOR

Joel Rosenberg was born in Winnipeg, Manitoba, Canada, in 1954, and raised in eastern North Dakota and northern Connecticut. He attended the University of Connecticut, where he met and married Felicia Herman.

Joel's occupations, before settling down to writing full-time, have run the usual gamut, including driving a truck, caring for the institutionalized retarded, bookkeeping, gambling, motel desk-clerking, and a two-week stint of passing himself off as a head chef.

Joel's first sale, an op-ed piece favoring nuclear power, was published in *The New York Times*. His stories have appeared in *Isaac Asimov's Science Fiction Magazine*, *Perpetual Light*, *Amazing Science Fiction Stories*, and TSR's *The Dragon*.

Joel's hobbies include backgammon, poker, bridge, and several other sorts of gaming, as well as cooking; his broiled butterfly leg of lamb has to be tasted to be believed.

He now lives in New Haven, Connecticut, with his wife and the traditional two cats.

The Sleeping Dragon, *The Sword and the Chain*, and *The Silver Crown*, the first three novels in Joel's *Guardians of the Flame* series, are also available in Signet editions, as is his critically acclaimed science fiction novel *Ties of Blood and Silver*.